I0891594

THE GHOST

A LAKE SUPERIOR MYSTERY

R.T. LUND

LITTLE CREEK PRESS
MINERAL POINT, WISCONSIN

Copyright © 2024 by R.T. Lund

All rights reserved. No part of this publication may be reproduced, distributed, or transmitted in any form or by any means, including photocopying, recording, digital scanning, or other electronic or mechanical methods, without the prior written permission of the publisher, except in the case of brief quotations embodied in critical reviews and certain other noncommercial uses permitted by copyright law. For permission requests or other information, please send correspondence to the following address:

Little Creek Press
5341 Sunny Ridge Road
Mineral Point, WI 53565

ORDERING INFORMATION
Quantity sales. Special discounts are available on quantity purchases by corporations, associations, and others.
For details, contact info@littlecreekpress.com

Orders by US trade bookstores and wholesalers.
Please contact Little Creek Press or Ingram for details.

Printed in the United States of America

Cataloging-in-Publication Data
Name: Lund, R.T., author
Title: The Ghost / R.T. Lund
Description: Mineral Point, WI: Little Creek Press, 2024
Identifiers: LCCN: 2024923405 | ISBN: 978-1-955656-87-0
Subjects: FICTION / Thrillers / Romance
Mystery & Detective / General
Thrillers / Political

Book design by Little Creek Press

Revenge is an act of passion; vengeance of justice.
Injuries are revenged; crimes are avenged.

—SAMUEL JOHNSON

PART I

A PERFECT MATCH

PROLOGUE

A few minutes after midnight and, once again, Lincoln Barnes couldn't sleep. She sat up in bed and leaned to her left to turn on the lamp on her nightstand and grab the paperback she'd started earlier in the week. She hadn't been sleeping well since moving from the Twin Cities to Lake County four months ago to accept an offer from the Lake County Sheriff to be his only full-time detective. But the move was about much more than a job. It was about escaping the dysfunctional Minneapolis PD and a homicide investigation that had altered the course of multiple lives, including her own. Kate Patterson, the president of the city council, had been the victim, slaughtered while running in a park before dawn. Barnes's partner and mentor had lost a limb and nearly his life when a suspect had tried to run him over with his pickup. And then Barnes had shot the fleeing suspect, the only life she'd taken in her dozen years as a cop.

But none of that was the true reason for her move or the sleepless nights. The truth had everything to do with the judge, now a former judge, the enigmatic man she'd fallen for and followed to the shores of Lake Superior in spite of warning signs and misgivings about him and his past. And just when she'd decided to embark on a new life on the North Shore with Robin Gildemeister, she'd discovered disturbing evidence connecting him to the murder of Kate Patterson. She could have burned it, hidden it or used it to confront the judge and demand an explanation. Instead, she delivered it to her former boss at the MPD, causing Gildemeister to vanish and her to second-guess everything.

Barnes could hear thunder in the distance. She hoped a rainstorm was on the way. For whatever reason, she always fell asleep during a big storm.

ONE

It was Thursday, so Oscar made sure the kitchen was pristine before leaving a few minutes before midnight. His aging Jetta looked abandoned in the empty lot across Ninth Avenue. Though he'd shed a white polyester uniform in favor of cargo shorts and a T-shirt, he was already drenched in sweat after the short walk from the iconic Kitchi Gammi Club to his car. Folding his slender six-foot frame into the driver's seat, he started the engine, set the AC on max, and lifted his iPhone from a side pocket. He selected *the best of k. d. lang* from his Spotify playlist to accompany the seventy-minute drive to his mother's bungalow in Silver Bay.

Oscar had lived in Duluth most of his life and couldn't remember a hotter summer. His boyfriend, Jared, had a condo on Minnesota Point with an outdoor pool and a patio overlooking the harbor. That's where he wanted to go, but Jared was spending the next three days at a fundraising event for his boss, the DFL candidate for the Eighth District congressional seat, at a resort in Grand Rapids. No matter; Oscar had promised his mom he'd spend a few days at her place. It was still his legal residence, even though he lived at Jared's ninety percent of the time.

As he turned right from Superior Street onto London Road, the wind suddenly picked up, and a sideways rain started pattering against his windshield. A major storm was brewing.

Oscar hated the job at the Kitchi. Sous-chef. After two years of culinary arts school in the Cities and three years on the job, he was part dishwasher, part custodian, part fry cook, and part bartender but no part chef. His fifty-something boss was a control freak and a homophobe. But none of that would matter in a few weeks. That's when he'd be finalizing the lease on Oscar's Fish House, the restaurant he'd be opening in Canal Park. That's also when he'd be coming into a small fortune.

By the time he reached Two Harbors, a barrage of rain and pea-sized hail pelted the Jetta from the west, accompanied by random booms of thunder and flashes of lightning that lit up the sky over the lake, creating a surreal scene that reminded Oscar of an old black-and-white horror film he'd watched with Jared. He considered pulling into the Holiday station on the north end of town to wait out the storm, but it was already late, and he'd be home in thirty minutes.

Rapidly closing high beams in his rear-view mirror made him flinch. He was approaching the Stewart River bridge when an old pickup crossed into the lane of opposing traffic and started to pass him in the no-passing zone over the bridge.

"What the hell?" Oscar screamed when the oncoming headlights of a van, distorted by the rain, interfered with his view as the rumbling old truck struggled to overtake the Jetta and was certain to cause a head-on crash. The truck nosed ahead at the precise moment both vehicles cleared the bridge deck, while the driver of the van sat on his horn and steered to the shoulder to avoid a catastrophe.

Then, to Oscar's horror, the truck abruptly turned into the Jetta at a forty-five-degree angle, hitting the driver's side fender and pushing the smaller vehicle through the narrow, rain-slicked parking lot for Kelsey's Beach just east of the bridge. By the time Oscar comprehended what was happening, he had lost control of his car and his fate. There was no guard rail, no fencing, no barrier between the south end of the parking lot and a thirty-foot drop onto the rocky shore of Lake Superior.

Unfortunately for Oscar, the Jetta flipped over and smashed into the rocks roof first. His helpless torso was crushed in seconds like a grape in a winepress, and then a ten-foot wave combined with a massive riptide to suck the car's remnants into the blackness of the lake. Oscar had no chance. Amidst the fear, shock, pain, and anguish, he had one, final conscious thought:

"You fuck, Barton!"

TWO

“It’s done.”

“What do you mean?”

“Oscar Fawcett. He’s dead.”

“Dead? You were just supposed to scare him.”

“It was raining like son of bitch. Dumb fuck lost control of his car and ended up in lake.”

“You’re sure he’s dead.”

“I went back to bridge on foot an hour later. Cops everywhere. No car. No rescue boat. No one could have lived in that nasty lake.”

“Any witnesses?”

“No one saw me if that’s what you’re asking. No one ever does. Besides, no one up here knows me. I left piece-of-shit truck in park.

“I’ll be in touch.”

“I need cash.”

“I’ll be in touch.”

THREE

Lincoln Barnes had finally succumbed to a beckoning sleep. A paperback, *Harlem Shuffle*, was splayed across her chest, covering the mascot on her favorite college T-shirt. It took her at least five seconds to recognize the repeating Marimba ringtone. She lurched toward an antique nightstand to grab her iPhone, causing the book to fly off the bed and slide across the slick wooden floor moments before she heard the familiar voice of Deputy Ryan Hokanen in response to her groggy, "Hello?"

"Detective Barnes, it's Ryan. Sorry for the late call, but it looks like we might have a homicide down the shore just east of the Stewart River bridge. Sams is down on Kelsey Beach, and I'm sitting in the parking lot waiting for the Coast Guard to decide what to do."

"The Coast Guard? Why don't you fill me in while I splash cold water on my face," she said, nearly dressed before Hokanen replied.

"Dispatch got a call around one this morning from a guy named Schultz, Carl Schultz. He lives in Beaver Bay and works the early morning shift at the EPA lab on the Lester River in Duluth. Some kind of scientist. He was driving an EPA cargo van south on 61 between Beaver Bay and Two Harbors during the worst of the thunderstorm."

"I must have dozed off in the middle of that," Barnes interrupted and then gargled some awful-tasting mouthwash before lifting the keys to her Jeep off a hook in the entryway and heading outside. "Keep talking. I'm in my Jeep. Be there in ten."

"Schultz said the wind and heavy rain reduced visibility, but there was so little traffic it wasn't a big deal until he approached the Stewart River bridge and was nearly blinded by a pair of high beams in his lane, coming at him at a high rate of speed. He was forced to veer onto the narrow shoulder, avoiding a collision with the oncoming pickup truck by inches and then skidding and screeching to a stop to avoid slamming into the bridge abutment." Listening intently to Hokanen's account, Barnes was anticipating a violent road rage incident.

"Schultz said when he looked back to check on the truck, he couldn't believe what he saw. The truck had side-swiped a small sedan and was pushing it diagonally through the Kelsey Beach parking lot until the car disappeared over a cliff. The truck never stopped. It just got back on 61 and headed north."

"What did Schultz do then?" Barnes asked, trying to imagine the scene in her mind.

"He made a U-turn on the bridge, parked his van, and walked to the edge of the Kelsey lot to check on the car. It was still storming, and he claims all he could see were whitecaps on the lake and six- to eight-foot waves. No sign of a driver or vehicle. He returned to the van and called 911. Sams and I had been dealing with a minor domestic up on Highway 3, so I interviewed Schultz while he drove to work in Duluth, and then we headed to the scene. I told him we needed to get a statement, and he offered to come into the office when his shift ends later today. He was very cooperative."

"Sounds like it. What about a rescue boat?" Barnes knew Lake County had one, but she hadn't been around long enough to see it in action.

"We share a couple of divers with St. Louis County, but according to the Coast Guard conditions on the lake are too dangerous to send out one of our boats, especially because they say this is most likely a recovery effort, not a rescue."

"Have you notified the sheriff?" Barnes asked, remembering that Sheriff MacDonald was supposed to drive to the Twin Cities after work on Thursday. His brother was a teacher and coach in the Bay area, and MacDonald was going to meet him at a mutual friend's place in St.

Paul. He had purchased tickets to the Twins-Giants interleague games on Friday and Saturday night at Target Field.

"I debated whether or not to call him, but we all know how that ended. I left a message on his cell right before I called you. I hope he doesn't pick it up for a few hours."

Barnes arrived at the Kelsey Beach lot and parked next to the Lake County squad. She waved at Deputy Hokanen, who'd left the vehicle and appeared to be talking on his cell. She took a flashlight and binoculars from the center console, grabbed a baseball cap from the back seat, and zipped up her windbreaker before exiting the Jeep.

The rain was subsiding, but the wind had shifted from the northwest to northeast, and the temperature had plummeted from the eighties to the fifties. Barnes jogged over to Hokanen with her head down, stunned by the intensity of the blasts of cold air coming off the lake. She heard sirens on 61.

"Just spoke to the Coast Guard in Duluth," Hokanen shouted over the gale. "They've called off any recovery efforts on the lake until the winds die down. At least three hours, and by then we'll have daylight."

Looking past Hokanen at the lake below, Barnes saw no sign of a car, only a raging black sea with two-story waves exploding against the rocks.

Waving at a state patrol car and ambulance that had just entered the lot, Hokanen said, "I called in EMTs and any officers in the area before I knew what we were dealing with. We should give them an update and let them go."

Hokanen's cell started buzzing; it was Sams.

"What do you have, Michele?"

"Ryan, get down here and bring Barnes and the paramedics. The lake just spit out a body."

"You are shitting me. Any ID?"

"I haven't checked; I just dragged it about fifteen feet onto the beach. Grab some latex gloves out of the squad. Let's hope there's some ID because it's missing a head."

FOUR

Cooper Harding was one of several big-name, international law firms that had recently established a foothold in the Twin Cities by acquiring local talent and renting a few floors of formerly expensive office space in a downtown Minneapolis skyscraper, space rendered cheap and available because of the new world order created by the pandemic. No one could keep track of all the mergers, acquisitions, and lateral moves in the silk-stocking lawyer world with storied names like Briggs & Morgan, Lindquist & Vennum, and Leonard Street & Deinard disappearing from the legal landscape.

Jack Whitman, a burly, white-haired warrior with a photographic memory, was one of three senior partners in Cooper Harding's Minneapolis office. Whitman's former firm, Murphy, Brophy & Whitman, had been a boutique shop with only five lawyers and a small but enviable stable of clients, including Barton Industries, the holding company for a privately held conglomerate with fifteen affiliated companies and over eight billion in annual revenue.

Whitman's best friend and fraternity brother at Dartmouth College was Paul Barton Jr. Paul's father, the son of an iron ore miner from Eveleth, leveraged a fifty-thousand-dollar loan from the Small Business Administration to start a chain of convenience stores in the 1970s. By the time Paul Jr. graduated from Dartmouth in the late eighties, his father had thirty Kwik Stop stores in four states and had expanded the Barton empire by investing in a shale oil exploration operation in North Dakota and acquiring ten radio stations and twenty-two community newspapers in Iowa, Wisconsin, and Minnesota. When the elder Barton died in 2005, Paul Jr., known to friends and family as P. J., and his sister, Amanda, inherited everything, their mother having succumbed to kidney failure twenty years earlier. Amanda ran Barton Media. P. J. ran everything else. Armed with a master's in finance from Harvard and a certificate that signified he was a chartered financial analyst, P. J. believed he was an investment genius, and he spent much of his time trying to grow Barton Wealth Management, LLC, a registered investment adviser with ten private label mutual funds and a ravenous appetite for the high-tech sector and, more recently, cryptocurrencies.

To a degree, Whitman didn't care what P. J. did, so long as the family business continued to top the list of Cooper Harding's biggest clients in terms of annual billings. So when his new paralegal, a twenty-nine-year-old woman with a peerless combination of intelligence, beauty and poise, interrupted a serious discussion with a prospective client by striding into his office and handing him a note that simply read, "Mr. Barton needs you to call his cell NOW," Whitman politely excused himself and headed straight for the men's room. Making sure he was alone, he entered one of three stalls, locked the swinging door, and made the call on his iPhone.

"We need to meet, Jack. The Fawcett kid is dead."

"What? When and how did that happen?"

"I'm not sure, but by the time you get up here, I'll know more."

"But you had nothing to do with it, right P. J.? P. J.? Ah, shit."

FIVE

Four of the twelve licensed peace officers in the Lake County Sheriff's Department gathered in the large conference room in the Law Enforcement Center in Two Harbors about an hour after sunrise on the last Friday in August. Having left the Twin Cities shortly after listening to Deputy Hokanen's phone message, Lake County Sheriff Sam MacDonald had picked up donuts at Tobie's in Hinckley and a traveler of French roast at Dunn Bros. in Duluth on his way to the office, getting periodic updates from Detective Barnes about the unusual incident on Highway 61, also known as murder.

"Let's get started," MacDonald announced as he sat in a faded brown leather chair at the head of an oak conference table that was twice as old as the sheriff. Sams and Barnes sat on one side, Hokanen on the other.

Barnes looked around the room. This would be her first murder case, first major felony case, since joining the small department in May. A tall, athletic, thirty-something biracial woman with piercing brown eyes offset by an engaging smile that showcased two tiny dimples, she usually wore her short, black hair in tight curls, often, like this morning, covered by a baseball cap. Barnes had started out as a beat cop in an inner-city neighborhood of her native Chicago. Escaping a bad marriage to a fellow officer, she had migrated to Minnesota and advanced to the position of homicide detective on the Minneapolis police force.

"We've got a preliminary identification," she said, taking a healthy bite out of a maple glazed donut and washing it down with a sip of dark roast. "Oscar William Fawcett. Born December 20, 1994. Six feet tall and a hundred seventy pounds with an address in Silver Bay, a few credit cards, forty-five dollars in cash and an employee ID from the Kitchi Gammi Club in Duluth. We extracted that information from the soggy contents of Oscar's wallet. That was it. His phone wasn't in any of the pockets of his shorts."

"His body has been transported to Lake View Hospital until we get a more definitive identification," Sams added. She was a few years older than Barnes, a few inches shorter, and about twenty pounds heavier, yet she possessed a rare combination of physical agility and pure beauty even clad in a deputy's standard-issue tan polyester shirt and matching pants. Her mother, Clare, was full-blooded Ojibwe, raised on the reservation in Grand Portage, and her father, Delbert Sams, was a third-generation commercial fisherman from Grand Marais, where Sams spent her childhood before earning degrees in psychology and criminal justice from UMD and a master's in forensic psychology from the University of North Dakota. Early in her career, she reluctantly accepted jobs as a security guard and Brink's driver, experiencing blatant discrimination by multiple law enforcement agencies that delayed but didn't stop her unwavering drive to become a peace officer. She was working as a site guide at Split Rock Lighthouse three years ago when a casual conversation with Sam MacDonald led to a new career as a deputy. She lived up in Finland Township with her partner and normally worked out of the Fall Lake station on the outskirts of the Boundary Waters Canoe Area, though she enjoyed taking shifts out of Two Harbors and Silver Bay as a substitute for ill or vacationing deputies.

"I stopped at the hospital before coming here," said MacDonald. "The corpse is pretty gruesome. Anyone have a theory on how this young man was decapitated?" The sheriff's first wife had suffered a similar fate six years earlier, when her car slid under a semi on an icy road in McLean, Virginia, killing her and their six-year-old daughter instantly and precipitating MacDonald's move back to Two Harbors.

Barnes was quick to speculate. "The windshield of his car was likely shattered when it hit the rocks. He's unconscious or, more likely, already dead and not putting up much resistance. A combination of the car filling up with water and a riptide or strong undercurrent sucks him out of the gaping hole, and the jagged edge of the windshield severs his head from his body."

"That's probably as good a theory as any," said MacDonald not interested in dwelling on the subject.

"I have a feeling Mishipeshu had a hand in it," said Sams. Sheriff MacDonald grinned and waited for the inevitable.

"Mishipeshu?" Barnes asked, not having a clue but sensing bullshit.

"It's an Ojibwe water monster, also known as the Great Lynx, believed to be responsible for many unsolved disappearances in Gitchi Gumee," said Sams with a smug, satisfied grin. "She strangles her victims with her tail and then bites off their heads."

"Good to know," said Barnes with more than a hint of sarcasm.

"Any of you know this guy or his family?" asked the sheriff, choosing to ignore Sams's offbeat attempt at humor. No was the consensus response.

"I did a little research on the Fawcetts," said Barnes. "There are only two people with that name who live in Lake County—Oscar and his mother, Rebecca, the same Becky Fawcett who called this office twenty minutes ago to report that her son left work at midnight, never made it home, and doesn't answer his cell."

"Nice work, detective," said MacDonald, while Sams took a felt-tipped pen and wrote "showoff" on Barnes's legal pad. "We'll drive up to Silver Bay and deliver the terrible news to Ms. Fawcett after this meeting. Do we know anything more about the truck or the driver?"

"We put out a bulletin to the state patrol, park rangers, Cook and St. Louis County sheriffs and Duluth police, but there are hundreds of battered old pickups on the road," said Hokanen. "We don't have much of a description, but if the driver bought gas or stopped at a convenience store on 61, we might get a look at him. Or her."

"Okay," said MacDonald. "Maybe Becky Fawcett will know something about her son that will lead us to his killer because this doesn't seem like a road rage incident to me; it seems more like an execution."

MacDonald sat behind the wheel of a 2023 Chevy Tahoe, a metallic gray police pursuit vehicle recently purchased by Lake County to replace the 2015 Ford Explorer the sheriff had been driving since he was first elected. The cold front that had been the catalyst for last night's storms left a perfect summer morning in its wake. Barnes rode shotgun, reviewing brief notes she'd made about Rebecca Fawcett from the woman's sparse existence on social media.

"So, are you becoming acclimated to life on the North Shore?" MacDonald asked. "I'm sure the pace is slower than down in the Cities."

"It's plenty fast for me," said Barnes. "I thought I might get lonely, but Hallie and Michele have been great, and I get my kid fix from hanging with your little guy."

Besides being the Lake County Attorney and MacDonald's second wife, Hallie Bell was also the mother of two-year-old George MacDonald, the surprise and prize of their union and the namesake of George Redman, a former Bureau of Criminal Apprehension agent who'd been gunned down by Chilean mobsters in Duluth while assisting his good friend MacDonald on a triple homicide case.

"And the job so far?" MacDonald turned to face her for a moment.

"About what I'd imagined. I love the staff, and the investigation of the assaults and vandalism related to the copper mine protests has been a fascinating education on ecoterrorism, even though we haven't accomplished much. And now we've got the mystery of poor Oscar Fawcett."

MacDonald turned left off Highway 61 at Outer Drive and drove west to Penn Boulevard. A block south of Mariner Mountain Park, he turned right on Edison and there, two houses in on the left, was Becky Fawcett's place, a neat bungalow with fading ochre shakes and dark brown trim.

"Holy shit, sheriff, these properties are eerily identical. I've never been to this part of Silver Bay."

MacDonald laughed as he killed the engine. "This place is truly the stereotypical company town. I'll bet more than half the homes in Silver Bay are these two- or three-bedroom ramblers built in the 1950s and '60s to house families of the growing workforce at Reserve Mining's taconite plant. Now the operation is owned by Cleveland Cliffs, a big public company headquartered in Ohio. What was true seventy years ago is still true today. The town's economy is heavily dependent on the profitability of that sprawling iron pellet plant on 61."

Barnes and MacDonald exited the Tahoe and traversed a freshly cut lawn glistening with morning dew. The home was centered by a concrete porch with a row of arborvitaes on the right and a colorful assortment of petunias, geraniums and zinnias in a wooden planter under a picture window on the left.

"Even though the homes in this neighborhood all look similar, I assure you the residents are much more diverse," said MacDonald, letting Barnes take the lead up two narrow steps.

Before she could decide whether to ring the doorbell or knock, a compact, five-and-a-half-foot woman with straight, shoulder-length auburn hair and bloodshot blue eyes opened the inner storm door, looked up at the oversized, official-looking pair on the other side of the screen, and then exclaimed, "It's about Oscar, isn't it?"

"I'm afraid it is, Ms. Fawcett. I'm Detective Barnes and this is Sheriff MacDonald with the Lake County Sheriff's office. May we come in?"

"Of course," she sighed, opening the screen door and leading them past a small foyer into a modest but thoughtfully decorated living room anchored by a woodburning brick fireplace. A gold love seat facing the fireplace was flanked by a leather swivel recliner and two square armchairs separated by an oval antique table.

"Please sit wherever," she said in a kind of daze and then lifted her cell phone from a side pocket. "I need to text my manager that I'll be late this morning." She was wearing navy medical scrubs, a V-neck, short-sleeve top with matching pants, and white canvas sneakers.

Barnes sat on the love seat, hoping Becky would join her, while MacDonald stood by one of the overstuffed armchairs, waiting for their distraught host to sit. When she did, next to Barnes but not too close, she folded her hands in her lap and, head down, began to weep.

"I know he's dead; otherwise, you would have called," she sobbed, not looking up, "but please tell me my beautiful boy didn't suffer."

Barnes wrapped an arm around Becky's narrow back and gently patted her shoulder while giving MacDonald the nod to begin the unfortunate tale with an inescapably ghastly ending.

The sheriff had enough empathy and experience with these kinds of meetings to engage the family member in conversation before delivering the worst news.

"Can I ask, Ms. Fawcett, when was the last time you talked to Oscar?"

Becky sat up and turned toward MacDonald, placing her hands on her knees to steady herself. "He called me just before midnight to tell me he'd finished closing the kitchen at the club and would be home between 1:30 and 2:00, depending on the weather. I told him it was already storming up here, so he needed to be careful. The last thing I said was, 'Love you, son.'"

"I'm sure he knew that, Ms. Fawcett," said the sheriff, who paused a moment to let Becky regain her composure. "Based on another driver's account of what happened, it appears that during the worst of the storm Oscar's car was literally run off the road and into the lake by a pickup truck near the Stewart River bridge. As of this morning, we haven't located his car, but his body washed up on Kelsey Beach within an hour after the accident."

"But it wasn't an accident, was it?" Becky stated as much as asked, suddenly animated.

"We don't think so," said Barnes. "And though it's little consolation, given what we know so far, it's likely he died instantly."

Becky's demeanor completed its transformation. She leaned toward MacDonald with a piercing stare and spoke in a loud, confident voice. "I know who killed my son," she declared. "He may not have been driving the truck, but he planned and financed the whole operation. I'd bet my life on it."

Barnes shot MacDonald a WTF look, her eyes as big as silver dollars. She turned to face Oscar's mom on the love seat and got right to the point. "Who is it, Becky?"

"His name is Paul Barton. He used to be one of my patients. He also used to be my fiancé."

The name didn't mean anything to Barnes, but MacDonald was familiar with Barton Industries and P. J. Barton, its flamboyant chairman and chief executive officer.

"Didn't he nearly die a few years ago?" the sheriff asked, knowing Becky would elaborate.

"Like his mother, Paul suffered from polycystic kidney disease. When I met him in 2018, I was the senior nurse in the dialysis unit at the Duluth Clinic, and he was a frequent dialysis patient in desperate search of a living donor. He has a rare blood type, and his treating doctors at the Mayo Clinic in Rochester told him that his chances of a successful transplant and a long life would increase dramatically if he could find a living donor with a healthy kidney and one who matched his blood type.

"He's a handsome, very charming man, about ten years older than me, though he didn't look it even when he was sick. I'd lived in Duluth all my life but had never heard of him. He was so friendly, and I was lonely and flattered by the attention. My husband, Oscar's father, died about twelve years ago. He was an engineer for Cirrus, the company in Duluth that makes small jets. He was also a pilot who loved to restore and fly old Cessnas and Piper Cubs, until the night he crashed into a fence just short of the runway at the Sky Harbor Airport."

"That must have been awful for both you and your son," said Barnes, wondering where Becky Fawcett was headed with this story.

"It took me at least five years to move on after Jeff's death. And that was emotionally. Oscar and I never really recovered financially. All he left us was a sixty-thousand-dollar life insurance policy and a pile of bills for half-built airplanes.

"Losing his father as a teenager was devastating for my son. We both believed Paul Barton was our savior. We both got sucked in. He asked me out after his second visit to the dialysis unit. It was the most exciting time of my life. He took me to the best restaurants, to galleries and museums and out on his boat, or I should say yacht, on Lake Superior. He has a house overlooking Northland Country Club in Duluth and an incredible log home near Gooseberry Park on Lake Superior, not to mention places in Naples and Monterey. Over the course of a few months, we became lovers, and I moved into his place on Lake Superior. But throughout this time, he was dying, and I was both his girlfriend and his nurse. He was consumed with finding a living donor, and I was determined to help him. The biggest mistake I made was during our very first conversation at the clinic. He told me he wanted to find a younger donor with his rare blood type. I said that the type wasn't that rare; that both my deceased husband and son had it. At that time, I never imagined that Oscar would end up being Barton's donor."

"Didn't he have any kids or siblings with the same blood type?" asked Barnes.

"He'd never been married. He inherited his condition from his mother, who died in her early forties, so he was reluctant to have children. His sister is married and has a couple of kids, but no one in that family is a match. He told me once that when he was in grad school out East a woman he'd dated a few times got pregnant, but that his father paid her to have an abortion more than thirty years ago.

"I was such a fool. I fell into his trap. After we'd dated for about a month, he told me he wanted us to be together always, but he was so far down the deceased donor allocation list he didn't think that could happen. That's when I broached the subject with Oscar. Knowing how much he loved me, I never should have done that. Of course, he said he'd give up one of his kidneys. But I didn't tell Paul right away. A few weeks later we took his private jet to Naples, and after an incredible dinner at Ocean Prime, he showed me a three-carat diamond ring and asked me to marry him. That's when I told him about Oscar's offer."

"How long ago did this happen?" MacDonald asked, intrigued by Becky's story.

"We were engaged in late April of 2019. I quit my job in May and moved into Paul's house in Duluth. The surgery was scheduled for July 2, and our wedding in Napa Valley for the last weekend in September. The surgery was a success. I was so proud of Oscar's bravery and selflessness. At first Paul was elated, saying that meeting me was the best thing that ever happened to him and how thankful he was to have another chance at life. He wanted to convalesce at his log cottage on the lake in Beaver Bay. But after I took him home, everything changed. At breakfast that first morning he told me the wedding was off; that I needed to move out. He'd let me stay at his house in Duluth for up to two months, so I'd have time to find my own place.

"I was shocked and furious at the same time. And then, before I could even pack a bag, she shows up in a red convertible filled with luggage." Becky bent over and covered her face with her hands. "It's so painful to relive this on the day my boy died," she cried, convulsing with every word.

"You don't need to continue if it's too hard," MacDonald said, while Barnes gently stroked her back.

"No, I need to get this out now," she said, accepting a tissue from Barnes to wipe her face. "Melanie Patton, the thirty-something head of marketing for his companies, had been Paul's whore during the whole time he was wining, dining, and defrauding me to get Oscar's kidney. She was waiting in the wings, prepping to become the trophy wife of a billionaire. But only if he survived. He actually called her from the hospital to tell her what a huge success the operation was and to invite her to spend the rest of the summer on the lake with him. And get this—she knew all about his scheme to get the kidney. She knew he had broken off our engagement that morning, and she had the audacity to approach me in her black pumps and low-cut blouse, with her fake tits sticking in my face, and say 'Hi, I'm Melanie, nice to meet you.'"

"You are kidding me," Barnes said incredulously. "What did you say?"

"I said, 'fuck off' and hurried past her with my head down so she couldn't see that I was crying. I tossed an overnight bag in the back seat of my Honda and drove off."

"That's an incredible story and a horrible story," the sheriff commiserated. "But I assume that wasn't the last of your dealings with Paul Barton."

"You're right. After the shock wore off, Oscar and I visited with a lawyer who was a friend of Oscar's long-time boyfriend, Jared Cheslak. I didn't know it back in 2019, but Paul had been a big supporter of the MAGA movement. Jared and Oscar were the polar opposites of that. Our lawyer had been a prosecutor with the U.S. Attorney's Office in Minneapolis during the Obama years. She moved up here and joined a Duluth firm after the 2016 election. Her name is Jane Monson. She threatened to sue Barton under at least ten different theories—fraud, breach of contract, theft of a kidney by swindle, and a litany of other things I can't recall. She told us the legal theories would be tough to prove; that you can't force someone to marry you, but Barton was afraid of the bad publicity that would come with a lawsuit about a guy who jilted his fiancé after taking her son's kidney. Through his lawyer, a guy named Whitman who reminded me of a bulldog, Barton offered to invest five million dollars in Oscar's restaurant venture, but only if both he and my son were alive four years after the big transplant, on September 1 of this year. Oscar thought that was fair, so we took the deal." She paused for a few moments to think about what to say to conclude her story, then continued.

"I have no doubt that that self-centered prick is responsible for my son's death."

"Given those facts, I think Paul Barton is definitely a person of interest," said Barnes. "He had a significant financial motive and, with his money and connections, could have hired a professional assassin either directly or, more likely, indirectly. We'll definitely want to interview him."

"Oscar didn't have an enemy in this world," Becky said with conviction, "so if Barton didn't do it, I don't know who did."

"Is this agreement or arrangement in writing, and, if so, do you have a copy we could see?" asked the sheriff.

Becky sprang from the couch, grabbed a manila folder from a file cabinet in the kitchen and handed it to MacDonald. "Here's my file on Barton," she said. "There's not much to it, but the settlement agreement is in there. I still have the engagement ring. I was going to make it into a necklace for Oscar, but now I guess I'll sell it." Tears trickled down Becky's cheeks, ruining her makeup. She returned to her seat next to Barnes.

"Oscar wanted to be cremated," she said, "but can I see him and touch him one last time before he's gone for good?"

Barnes shot the sheriff a look that clearly put the onus on him to tell Becky the awful truth. Of course, they wanted to spare her, but better to hear it today from them than in a news story next week or, even worse, the discovery of Oscar's rotting head by a diver or fisherman next year.

"Ms. Fawcett, it's your choice, but I think it would be best if you don't see Oscar in his current state," the sheriff explained. "I'm very sorry to tell you that his body washed ashore but his head is missing. We think the windshield of his car was smashed and its jagged edges may have decapitated him when rushing water ejected him into the lake."

"Oh, no! Oh, please no!" Becky cried out. "My poor, poor Oscar. I'm telling you, sheriff, if you don't arrest and convict the man who destroyed our lives, I swear I'll rip my son's kidney out of his body and kill him with my bare hands!"

SIX

After devouring a shrimp salad sandwich washed down by an Arnie Palmer at the Links Grill, Paul Barton hit balls on the range for twenty minutes, starting with his gap wedge and hitting a shot or two with each club in his bag. He finished by launching a half-dozen drives with a new PXG Gen5 Driver the club pro promised would improve his crooked tee shots.

As he drove a gas cart from the range to the first tee of Northland Country Club, he spied his lawyer's vintage 1970 Jaguar E-type convertible entering the parking lot. It was 12:25 and, as usual, Whitman arrived at the course five minutes before their tee time. He would order a Maker's Mark Manhattan on his way to the tee and start playing without so much as a practice swing. By the time Barton completed his stretching routine, his playing partner and two teenage forecaddies had arrived.

"Playing the back tees today, Mr. Barton?" asked one of the caddies.

"He shouldn't be," teased his lawyer, "but as usual we'll be playing the blacks today boys."

"Screw you, Jack. I'm down to a nine playing the blacks three times a week. Christ, I shot a 75 at Superior National on Thursday."

Ignoring Barton's whining, Whitman finished his drink and tossed the plastic cup into a trash receptacle near the tee. Then he lifted an ancient Titleist driver from his bag, removed the head cover and took an easy practice swing while surveying the first fairway of his favorite course. Reaching into a front pocket of his expensive Galvin golf slacks, he pulled out a three-inch tee attached to a new Pro VI and deftly stuck the combination into the ground between the tee markers, about four hundred twenty yards from the pin. His pre-shot routine hadn't changed since he was a junior golfer at Interlachen Country Club, still his home course. Standing as straight and still as a statue a few yards behind the tee, he picked out a target with his eyes and in a matter of a seconds took a slightly closed, shoulder-width stance with the ball directly in front of his left heel and unleashed a compact yet powerful swing that catapulted the tiny white sphere into a cloudless blue sky. Neither Whitman nor his playing partner was surprised to observe a prodigious golf shot, drawing slightly and landing in the center of the fairway nearly three hundred yards from the tee.

"Nice shot, counselor," Barton conceded as he slipped the head cover off his new driver and approached the tee.

"Hey, what have we here?" asked Whitman, scrutinizing the shiny, high-tech mallet. "Not another new driver."

"It's just what the swing doctor ordered," said Barton. "Donny, the assistant pro here, recommended it to cure my hook."

Whitman didn't comment; he simply smiled and shook his head while Barton went through his two-minute pre-shot routine, reviewing five crucial swing thoughts before finally taking the club back a tad too far on the inside and then lashing furiously at the defenseless white ball, resulting in a low, screaming duck-hook that ended up on a steep side-hill in the deepest rough on the course only about a hundred sixty yards from the tee.

"Fucking cocksucker! God, I hate this game sometimes," Barton lamented as he slammed the driver back in his bag, sat in the cart next to Whitman, and drove down the first fairway.

"Relax, P. J. You didn't summon me up here on a Friday afternoon just to beat your sorry ass in golf, though I don't think I've ever turned down a chance to play Northland. Tell me what you know about Oscar Fawcett. I called the Lake County Sheriff's office on my way up here and was told there was a fatal accident on 61 northeast of Two Harbors last night, but no details would be released until later today."

"Becky called me just before I contacted your office this morning. She was hysterical, Jack. Absolutely, fucking hysterical. Asked me how much money was enough. What was five million to someone like me? She claimed my 'henchman' ran Oscar's little car into the lake last night and that his dead body was recovered without a head. Her beautiful boy had been decapitated, and she was going to take back his kidney and cut out my heart."

"Decapitated? Oh, my," sighed Whitman, shaking his head. "But you had absolutely nothing to do with it, right?"

Approaching one of the forecaddies who was pointing at the top third of a golf ball buried in deep rough, Barton stopped the cart and hopped out without answering Whitman.

"Distance?" he asked.

"Two hundred to the front of the green; two ten to the pin," said the caddy.

Taking a hybrid four iron from his bag, Barton had to take an awkward stance on the sidehill and manufacture a slashing half-swing to have any chance of getting the ball on the green. His club exploded into the turf about two inches behind the ball but with enough force to propel it out of the rough. Barely airborne, the muddied ball sliced across the fairway and landed in a bunker about thirty yards short of the green.

As soon as Barton had exited the cart to hit his second, Whitman grabbed his wedge and putter and walked down to his ProVI basking in the middle of the fairway less than a hundred ten yards from the pin. His exquisitely struck approach shot landed five yards beyond the pin and spun back, leaving him with a three-foot birdie putt.

Upset with his game, Barton didn't utter another word until both had putted out and returned to the cart. Grabbing a pencil with his rather stubby fingers, he ruefully scribbled a seven next to his name on the scorecard and a three for Whitman.

"A birdie for you and a triple for me. A great start for the home team," Barton said sarcastically. "Okay, Jack, I'll confess. I didn't want to pay that money-grubbing cocksucker the five million, and if there'd been an easy way to renege on the deal without damaging our businesses, I would have been all over it. But murder? I hope you know me better than that after all these years."

"Five million was a bargain, P. J. Even if their legal theories were shaky, the publicity would have cost Barton Industries a multiple of five million, and you know it. Becky hates your guts and can still cause trouble. I just don't understand who would have had any reason to hurt Oscar. He was a nice, harmless kid."

"Maybe a jealous former lover or a creditor," mused Barton.

"That agreement was a good compromise, Paul. I suggest you offer to pay the five million to Becky to avoid a PR nightmare and to be done with this once and for all."

"No fucking way."

"You manipulated her to get her son's kidney and then discarded her."

"Don't push your luck or our relationship, Jack. I said no fucking way."

SEVEN

Sheriff MacDonald drove Detective Barnes to the Law Enforcement Center after their emotional and revealing conversation with Becky Fawcett and headed home to get some sleep after a very long night. He felt comfortable letting Barnes take the lead on the investigation of Oscar Fawcett's murder, and he knew she wouldn't heed his advice to go home and get some rest.

Though Becky Fawcett's harsh indictment of Paul Barton was both disturbing and understandable, it was difficult for MacDonald to believe that Barton would risk his substantial fortune and business empire by getting involved in a murder-for-hire scheme, especially when he had to know that Oscar's mother would vilify him publicly with her personal story of betrayal and deceit. But, as the sheriff well knew, some men were delusional, believing they were special; that any act that advanced their interests, burnished their brand or padded their bank account wasn't subject to the rules and social mores that applied to mere mortals. If a former U.S. president believed that, why wouldn't the CEO of a huge conglomerate? In any event, Barnes would set up a meeting with Barton, and, though she didn't need him to accompany her, he knew he would. At this stage of his career, not much piqued his curiosity, but this case did.

Driving up the winding gravel road that led to the split-log cabin he shared with Hallie and young George, he couldn't help but marvel at the beauty of the late morning sun streaming through the red-and-white pine forest that enveloped the secluded, ten-acre piece of heaven he'd purchased six years earlier when he'd quit his job with the Secret Service and moved back to Lake County. Buying and refurbishing the dilapidated 1920s gangster hideout cost him his entire federal retirement account, not to mention all the nights and weekends of sweat equity, but the finished product was well worth it.

He parked the Tahoe in the detached garage he'd added that included a full bathroom and a dovetail wood-fired sauna. Perched over two hundred feet above the lake on a sliver of private land between Split Rock and Tettegouche state parks, the property provided unique and breathtaking views of the area, views and vantage points that no doubt attracted gangsters and bootleggers back in the Prohibition era. From the screened-in porch or the backyard fire pit, MacDonald could see Palisade Head, the marina at Silver Bay harbor, and the big lake as far as the eye could see.

The sheriff had called Hallie from the Cities shortly after he'd made the decision to return to Lake County to deal with the Fawcett murder, so he knew she was working all day and had dropped George off at a day care in Castle Danger. He'd left a raspberry white chocolate scone and a cup of gourmet coffee on her desk at the courthouse before seven and received a triple heart emoji text in return. He also knew that someone would be very excited to see him when he unlocked the back door and entered the laundry room.

"Okay, Fred, I love you too," he said, slowly but firmly pushing the ninety-pound German Shepherd/Husky mix down after enduring the dog's routine greeting—two massive paws on his shoulder and as many slobbering licks on his face as MacDonald would allow. He kicked off his shoes in the entryway, plugged his phone into a charger on the kitchen counter and walked through the great room to his favorite napping place, the screened-in back porch.

Stretching out as much as his six-foot-four frame could on the cushions of a wicker sofa, he positioned his favorite throw pillow under his head and, for at least a few hours, his troubles drifted into the evanescence.

As she walked up the steps to the Law Enforcement Center, Detective Barnes nearly collided with Deputy Michele Sams, who'd busted through the middle set of doors in a hurry to go somewhere.

"Heading home?" asked Barnes. It was after 11:00. Sams and Hokanen should have finished their shift at 8:00. Sams looked startled to see her colleague but quickly recovered.

"I should be," said Sams, "but Craig needs some help up at Fall Lake, so I'm heading up there instead."

"What's up?" asked Barnes. Craig Darrow and Sams had been together for about a year. Originally from Waterville, Maine, Darrow had earned degrees in forest resources and wildlife management from the University of Maine and then pursued a career as a park ranger, first in Vermont and then in northeastern Minnesota. His current assignment as a senior park ranger in the Superior National Forest was with the Kawishiwi Ranger District headquartered in Ely. A small, wiry man in his late thirties, Darrow had intense blue eyes and a broad, engaging smile enhanced by oversize white teeth. The coarse black beard that covered two-thirds of his face highlighted his other features and gave him the appearance of a lumberjack. He'd met Sams while each of them was snowshoeing alone near Four Mile Lake. The mutual attraction was immediate. After cheeseburgers and beers at the Trestle Inn and a weekend at Darrow's place in Finland Township, they'd been a couple.

"It's a strange situation and might be nothing," said Sams, downplaying the issue but wanting Barnes's company. "I know you're busy with the murder investigation, but if you've got time to tag along, I'll fill you in."

"I was going to make some calls to set up an interview, but I can do that from the car, so let's go."

Sams and Barnes's friendship had evolved during the five months Barnes had been a Lake County detective. Without adequate time to train, they'd entered and finished Grandma's Half Marathon in late June fueled by trash talk, power bars and a lot of laughs. Needing someone other than her boss to unload some of the personal and professional baggage that had led to her move north, Barnes quickly developed a kinship with her Native American colleague.

Barnes climbed into the passenger seat of Sams's well-used silver

F-150, while Sams lifted two cans of Diet Coke out of a cooler in the back seat and gently tossed one to her friend.

"Is this trip official police business or a personal adventure?" Barnes asked, appreciating the cold soda and thinking she'd probably need the caffeine or some very stimulating conversation to stay awake during the ninety-minute drive to Fall Lake.

"It's a fluid situation," said Sams, "but I'm taking my ride because Ryan took the squad up to Gooseberry to check on a battered old pickup that appears to be abandoned and might be the one involved in last night's run-off."

"That would certainly save me some work. What about Craig?"

"He was on call last night. At about three this morning, a group of tenderfoots in tents near the Fall Lake campground got spooked by a prowling animal that allegedly attacked a black lab before someone scared it away by banging on metal pots. The campers described it as a mountain lion or cougar and asked that someone from the DNR or Forest Service check it out. No one took a photo with a phone, so it could have been a wolf, a coyote or even a big raccoon, or maybe it was a cougar. At any rate, Craig drove over there and searched the area, but, big surprise, he never saw anything but a few skinny coyotes and a gray fox. At about 5:00 a.m., shortly before daybreak, all the campers had returned to their tents and RVs, and he decided to drive to the district office in Ely rather than return home for a few hours. Before leaving, he went into the entry station to use the restroom and jot some notes on his iPad. The sound of a revving engine moving through the campground from the forest startled him. What he observed out the station window surprised him even more. A late model Land Rover with tinted windows had to be doing seventy on a stretch of road through the campground with a twenty mile per hour limit.

"Craig always, and I mean always, carries these powerful little binoculars in one of his pockets. I think they're Bushnells. Anyway, he ran out the door to get a license plate off the Land Rover and got lucky when the driver hesitated before turning left at the campground exit. He tried to call me so we could run the plates, but that's when Ryan and I were transporting Oscar's corpse to the morgue. I ran the plates an hour ago—the owner is Tri-Metals Minnesota, LLC."

"The mining company with mineral leases under Birch Lake and into the BWCA?" Barnes asked.

"Wow, for a city bitch you learn fast." Sams had a foul mouth, but Barnes was used to much worse.

"I've had no choice with all the protests and rallies up there, but I assume the speeding Land Rover is long gone, so why are we speeding up County 2?"

"About an hour ago the head of the Duluth field office of the FBI called Craig with a confidential inquiry. She said the CEO of Tri-Metals Minnesota had been kidnapped from his room at the Grand Ely Lodge between midnight and five o'clock this morning, when he had asked for a wake-up call. According to Craig, the feds are not involving local law enforcement yet because of some threats made by the kidnappers. They called him because of his knowledge of the remote areas in Superior National and the BWCA."

"Do we know who they are or what they want?" Barnes had never been involved in a kidnapping investigation. A rush of adrenaline mixed with the caffeine in her bloodstream. She'd gone from drowsy to hyper-alert in fifteen minutes.

"Apparently, they called the FBI on a burner phone and demanded that Tri-Metals agree to cancel all of their mineral leases in northern Minnesota and essentially leave the state or their CEO would never be found."

"Who would do that?" Barnes asked.

"Definitely not the Chippewa or Anishinaabe, and I can't imagine any of the reputable environmental groups would be so stupid. Think about it. Even if the company did agree to give up their leases, the kidnappers couldn't enforce the deal without implicating themselves in a felony."

"So, if the feds are handling this, why are we getting involved?"

"Craig told them about the Tri-Metals' Land Rover driving through the parking lot at Fall Lake and his suspicion that there's a connection between the SUV and the kidnapping.

"The feds told him not to play detective, to sit tight in Ely until their team got there with a helicopter. They were supposed to get further instructions from the kidnappers within an hour."

"I take it Craig didn't like that answer," said Barnes.

"He told them to get fucked in a nice way; that they should call him when they're on the way. He asked me to pick him up at the district office so we could enjoy a picnic lunch at the Fall Lake campground. That's why I'm exceeding the speed limit by a notch or two," Sams said with an impish grin. Like her, Darrow had an independent streak and wasn't afraid to ignore protocol to do what he thought was right. She hoped he'd be okay with her inviting Detective Barnes. But, most of all, she wondered what Sheriff MacDonald would think of this little adventure.

Trying to take in the fast-moving scenery, Barnes started to feel sick to her stomach as Birch Lake came into view and her phone buzzed in a cupholder on the center console.

"Ryan, why aren't you home in bed?"

"For the same reason you're answering your phone after one ring."

"You mean you're a passenger in a speeding, weaving pickup driven by Deputy Sams, and you're about to throw up?"

"Really? Where are you?"

"On a secret mission. We'll fill you in when we get back to the office. What's up?"

"I think I've found the truck that ran Oscar Fawcett off the road."

"Tell me about it."

"I drove up to Gooseberry this morning to check the parking areas for suspicious vehicles. In the south lot near the lake, I spotted a black Silverado with fresh dents and scratches on the front passenger side quarter panel and splotches of white paint that may have come from the missing Jetta."

"What about the plates?"

"They'd been removed, and the interior was completely cleaned out, no manuals, no receipts, no pop cans, not even a used wad of chewing gum."

"So, I doubt we'll get any usable prints, then," mused Barnes. "Was it hot-wired?"

"No doubt about that. But the perp did make a mistake. A used car dealer in West Duluth reported a 2011 black Silverado had been stolen from his lot between ten and midnight last night. They don't have CCTV or any other video surveillance, but the Minnesota Power substation across the street has several pole-mounted cameras used to monitor activity near their fenced parking lot. The cameras got a few shots of a man breaking into a truck and driving away about a minute later. The guy was wearing black jeans and a black T-shirt. He's a bit over six feet tall with arm and chest muscles that were bulging out of his shirt. He has a neck and shoulders like Herschel Walker."

"How did you have time to gather all this information?" asked Barnes, clearly impressed.

"I saw the match to the abandoned truck on the Duluth PD overnight activity report and called the dealer. He'd already done all the legwork and texted me the surveillance."

"Great work, Ryan. I've got an interview with Paul Barton tomorrow morning. We can compare notes after that. You need to get some rest."

"Right. You two be careful, whatever it is you're doing."

Sams briefly crossed into St. Louis County before entering the gateway to a vast and beautiful wilderness, also known as Ely, Minnesota, a town of some three thousand permanent residents in the heart of the Vermilion Iron Range about fifteen miles south of the Canadian border. Home to canoe outfitters, fishing guides, public steam baths, and unique attractions like the International Wolf and North American Bear Centers, the town also served as the northern Minnesota headquarters for Tri-Metals, whose annual meeting was held yesterday at the Grand Ely Lodge on Shagawa Lake.

Sams turned right onto State Highway 169 in the middle of town and drove about a mile to the parking lot of the Kawishiwi Ranger District office. She turned off the engine and looked apprehensively at Barnes while grabbing the door handle.

"Wait here," she said. "I'll be back in a minute."

"He doesn't know we're coming, does he?" Barnes asked, sensing uncertainty in Sams's voice and wondering why she hadn't called or texted Craig before their arrival.

"Let's just say there might have been a misunderstanding," she admitted, exiting the truck and slamming the door.

Barnes's phone started vibrating before Sams made it to the double doors at the entrance to the station. It was MacDonald.

"I thought you'd be in dreamland by now," she said, though she wasn't surprised he was calling.

"I think I slept for an hour before Fred tried to sit on my head to get my attention," he said. "It's turning out to be a busy Friday. I just got a call from an old Air Force buddy who's now with the FBI's domestic terrorism unit in D.C. Apparently, the CEO of Tri-Metals Minnesota was abducted at gunpoint from his room at the Grand Ely Lodge a few hours after the Oscar Fawcett incident. The kidnappers must have persuaded him to open the door because there were no signs of a forced entry, and a camera in the parking lot captured him in nothing but gym shorts and a polo shirt walking between two large homo sapiens wearing dark suits and masks and carrying automatic weapons. They were smart enough to park offsite to avoid any photos or video of their vehicle. They used a burner phone to call the FBI in Duluth. They claim to represent a coalition of native peoples and environmentalists who aren't asking for money—they want the company to formally abandon all mineral leases in the state and to pledge not to mine copper, nickel or other non-ferrous metals for the next hundred years."

"They'll never do that, will they?" Barnes asked skeptically, debating whether to tell the sheriff she already knew about the kidnapping and was about a mile from Grand Ely Lodge with Sams and her boyfriend.

"Of course not. Instead, they'll work with the feds to rescue or recover him quickly while keeping his disappearance a secret for as long as they can. I think the whole thing is very, very strange. By the way, I hope you're at home and not still at the office."

"I'm actually in Ely." Barnes knew MacDonald would find out about their little escapade sooner rather than later, so she told him everything and held her breath.

"So, do you consider yourselves on duty?" MacDonald wasn't mad, just concerned. After all, the purpose of his call was to inform his chief detective of the kidnapping.

"Honestly, sir, I came to support Deputy Sams. She was concerned that Ranger Darrow might need backup in Fall Lake, but say the word and we'll head back to Two Harbors."

"I have a lot of respect for Craig Darrow. He and Sams are better trackers in these forests than anyone from the FBI, but I'm surprised he doesn't want to wait for direction from the feds."

Barnes hadn't seen Sams and Darrow emerge from the station office. When she looked up from her phone, they were about ten feet from the truck engaged in an animated conversation.

"Here's Craig now," she said, "I'm going to put you on speaker, and we can all get on the same page."

As soon as Sams opened the driver's side door, Barnes held up her phone and announced that the sheriff was on the line.

"He knows about the kidnapping."

Sams shot Barnes a WTF look, but Darrow was the first to speak.

"Hi Sheriff. Craig Darrow here. Tri-Metals is discussing its options with the FBI. The feds have sent a team to Ely, but as far as I know they haven't heard back from the kidnappers. I told them what I observed up in Fall Lake this morning and they're clearly skeptical about any connection between the Range Rover and the abduction. They advised me to wait for their team, which is what I intended to do until your deputies showed up. I'm suspicious of this whole kidnapping story, sheriff. As you know, I'm familiar with the local native populations and the major environmentalist and conservation groups. This doesn't sound like any of them. I have a theory, and, if I'm right, the CEO of Tri-Metals is sitting in an abandoned camper cabin in dense woods about a mile south of Fall Lake."

Darrow was the opposite of a bullshitter, so MacDonald was inclined to give his theory some credence.

"What about the FBI?" asked MacDonald. "Are they expecting you to wait for them before you venture up to this cabin?"

"Deputy Sams has convinced me that we can check out the cabin and be back to the station before the feds get here," said Darrow, absorbing a jab in the shoulder from Sams without flinching. "Fall Lake is in your county sheriff; what do you think?"

"If your hunch is correct, the sooner you get up there, the better. I remember back in the early nineties one of the big banks in the Twin Cities brought in a hired gun from California as their CEO. This guy was short in stature but had a tough demeanor and ruthlessly cut costs. He fired about twenty percent of the employees and decimated perks and benefits for the remaining staff. A good friend of mine was an intern there until this guy, Jack was his name, ended the intern program. The employees hated his guts, but the stockholders loved him. He was allegedly abducted at gunpoint in a downtown parking lot one night and driven to a rest area off the interstate. He claimed the kidnappers tied him up, wrapped him in a rug and dumped him in the woods near River Falls, where he claimed to have freed himself and walked to the local county sheriff's office. The kidnappers were never apprehended or even identified, and no ransom was ever paid. At the time, some people thought old Jack staged the whole thing as a PR stunt to garner sympathy and improve his image. I wouldn't be surprised if the Chilean owners of Tri-Metals haven't conjured up a similar stunt, so I approve of your plan to check out the area near the old cabin. But, if there's anyone up there guarding the place, do not engage. Contact the FBI and me immediately and return to your vehicle. Are you okay with that, Ranger Darrow?"

"Yes, sir."

"Barnes and Sams—be smart and safe." He clicked off before they could answer.

EIGHT

“Where are you? I thought you were coming to the Cities today.”

“I picked up a side job from foreign contact I met in Crimea. You don’t want to know.”

“A side job? Can I assume this contact paid you a large sum for executing this job?”

“Again, you don’t want to know. They knew I’d be here this summer, so their need for my special services and my availability intersected nicely.”

“When will you be back, then?”

“Not until after the main event. Then I’m going home, not to Minneapolis.”

“That’s fine, but please don’t fuck it up.”

“It’s the main reason I’m here. Of course, will be perfect. A big payday for all of us.”

“Let’s hope so. Keep me posted. If you get caught, we’re screwed.”

NINE

The rustic log cabin had been closed and boarded up by the Park Service in 2019. It was about a half mile south of the campground and only accessible via a dirt path through a densely wooded section of the Superior National Forest. Unlike most of the camper cabins, the Fall Lake unit had no running water or electricity, which is why it had rarely been used by campers during the decade before it was closed.

Sams parked her truck near the campsite closest to the forest path. The sun was high in a cloudless, early afternoon sky with hardly a breeze and an air temperature approaching eighty. The only campers visible were canoeing out on the lake. At Ranger Darrow's suggestion, Barnes and Sams applied sunscreen and bug repellent to exposed body parts and then followed him through a vacant campsite and down a well-worn path lined with birch, pine and aspen. They had a plan for approaching the old cabin and a contingency plan for retreating.

Barnes sensed they were gradually gaining elevation until they reached a clearing. She could see the small cabin about fifty yards ahead directly behind a mammoth blue spruce that could provide cover if they needed it. Darrow lifted his right arm in a stop gesture and turned to face the two women.

"The boards have been removed from the door and front windows, so someone has been in there," he said. "And the ground between here and the door has recently been trampled with some heavy objects as well."

"If any of the kidnappers are with a hostage in there, it would be odd for no one to be in a lookout position," said Barnes, unzipping a small backpack and removing a pair of miniature binoculars.

"Way to be prepared," said Sams, wishing she'd remembered to grab hers from the glove compartment of the truck. Darrow had already taken his out of a fanny pack and was focusing on the front of the cabin and the woods on either side of it.

"I don't see any sign of life or activity," he said.

"Is there a side or back entrance?" asked Barnes.

"No," Darrow replied, "but there is a large window on the west side from which you can see the whole cabin."

Feeling responsible to take charge, especially since Darrow wasn't armed, Barnes gave instructions to carry out their plans.

"I'll swing below the trees and peek into that side window. Michele, you belly out to the left and get down by the front porch but out of sight of the door. Craig, you stay right here. I'll signal the number of people I see inside with my fingers. If there's no one or just the victim, I'll meet Michele on the porch, and we'll go in. Otherwise, we'll all meet back here and call for backup."

"Got it," said Sams.

"Okay," Darrow agreed reluctantly. "But be careful."

Both women crouched down to reduce the visibility of their tall frames and headed in opposite directions. Barnes tried to avoid the sightlines of the door and windows as she navigated her way through the thicket and approached the back of the cabin, a log wall without openings. Dropping to her knees, she crawled along the ground near the cabin's foundation until she was directly below the main window, utilizing well-developed calves to elevate her torso so her eyes were flush with the bottom right corner of the screen. At first, she couldn't accept what her eyes clearly observed. Briefly closing them to refresh the processor in her brain, she scanned the interior of the one-room cabin until she was certain of its contents. Then she reached for the sky with her right index finger and motioned to Darrow to come to the cabin while sprinting to the porch and calling out to Sams.

"Looks like the victim's alone and down!" she yelled, removing her Glock from a side holster as a precaution and waiting for Sams before entering the cabin.

"Jesus F. Christ!" Sams cried, as Barnes knelt next to a gray-haired man sprawled on the floor, face down in a pool of blood still oozing from a gash in his neck. His eyes and mouth agape, reflecting a combination of shock and horror, reminded Barnes of an image she couldn't erase from her mind—the face of the murdered president of the Minneapolis City Council.

He was wearing a blue Duke University T-shirt, black running shorts and fancy Hoka sneakers without socks, and his left ankle was manacled and attached by a steel chain to a huge iron ball that looked like it weighed a couple hundred pounds. He was lying between a Coleman cooler and a canvas-backed folding chair. The only other furniture in the room was a portable card table on top of which were two open cans of Diet Coke, a plastic sandwich wrapper, and a package of fried cinnamon rolls with a few missing.

"Oh, no," said Ranger Darrow coming to a dead stop after rushing into the cabin. The screen door swung shut behind him with a bang.

"He's dead," said Barnes, turning to face her colleagues, "but the wound looks fresh; the blood hasn't even started to coagulate. I don't think this happened more than a few hours ago. And whoever did this was strong and a professional killer." She moved aside, giving Sams and Darrow an unobstructed view and worried she was going to throw up. "This guy's nearly decapitated."

"Looks like no one thought he'd be here for very long," said Darrow. "A cooler, a folding chair, and a card table. Your average ice fishing house is better stocked than this place. If you two want to do what you need to do in here, I'll go outside, walk the perimeter, and call the FBI."

"For an outdoorsy kind of guy, he's got a weak stomach," Sams said after Darrow was gone. She removed a pair of latex gloves from her backpack and checked the pockets of the victim's shorts for evidence to confirm his ID. A black leather wallet yielded credit cards, eighty dollars in cash and one Minnesota driver's license for Lawrence Brian Osgood, date of birth 12/08/1967, six feet tall, a hundred eighty-five pounds, residing on Pleasant Lake Drive in North Oaks, Minnesota.

Larry Osgood, a native of Hibbing, Minnesota, had worked in the mining industry since graduating from the Colorado School for Mines in the early 1990s with a degree in metallurgical engineering. A more gifted communicator than many of his peers, Larry moved from engineering to management at Cleveland Cliffs before he turned thirty-five. When he was hired by a Chilean international mining concern to lead Tri-Metals in 2018, he was a regional chief operating officer for US Steel. The Chileans had paid Larry millions to secure all state and federal approvals needed to begin copper and nickel mining operations in northeastern Minnesota, one of the most fertile geological sites for such activity on earth.

Divorced with no kids, Larry was, on paper at least, the perfect candidate for the job. Unfortunately, what seemed like a slam-dunk in 2019 had devolved into mission impossible, as the company's most valuable mineral leases had been terminated by the feds, and lawsuits and protests by various environmental groups were multiplying. Some would argue that none of this had been Larry's fault. The political winds had shifted in 2020. His owners needed to *Make America Great Again*, but the prospects of that happening were slim, so the Santiago brain trust had devised an alternative strategy.

Even though Barnes and Sams knew the FBI had primary jurisdiction and might want to process the scene, they created their own inventory and took photos of Osgood and the cabin's sparse contents. There was a thermos of coffee under the card table and bottles of water, wrapped cold sandwiches, fruit and cans of Diet Coke and Diet Mountain Dew in the cooler.

"It's odd, don't you think, that the kidnappers would bring a copy of today's *Wall Street Journal* as well as the *Star Tribune* for Osgood to read?" asked Barnes. "You think your typical environmental terrorists would do that?"

"I think the choice of beverages is also weird, but who knows who had responsibility for refreshments and reading material?" Sams mused. "Maybe they wanted to portray themselves as humane, humane terrorists."

"Or maybe they knew him."

Darrow returned, holding his phone and out of breath. "I just heard from the FBI. They're in Ely and on their way here with the BCA and someone from the coroner's office. Apparently, Tri-Metals' parent company told the Minneapolis agent-in-charge they were willing to meet remotely or in-person to negotiate a resolution. The kidnappers responded to that offer with Osgood's location. The feds weren't surprised when I reported what we found. They requested that we let them notify Osgood's family and the media."

"That's fine," replied Barnes. "Even preferable if you ask me, but we should let Mac know what's going on up here."

"Right," said Darrow. "I think I might have discovered something significant out there. Because of the wet ground, it's easy to identify areas that were trampled by whoever brought Osgood up here. But what really caught my eye is someone, most likely a large man, recently came through the clearing and into this cabin from the south end of the property, not from the campground. There are prints from a size thirteen to fifteen work boot going in both directions, but, more important, there are scattered drops of blood starting at the bottom stair of the porch and following the boot prints south into the forest. I'm betting someone parked near the Spot Lake Trail and navigated some dense woods to get up here."

"So, it's possible that the killer isn't even connected to the kidnappers, right?" asked Sams.

"Possible, but highly unlikely," said Barnes. "I don't believe there's anything random about this. Whoever hiked several miles through the thicket knew the identity of the prisoner in this cabin and was probably carrying out somebody's assassination order."

"I agree," said Darrow.

"After we tell the feds what we know, Michele and I need to get back to Two Harbors," said Barnes, starting to feel the effects of being on duty for fifteen hours.

"They'll probably want me to accompany a small detail to search for evidence between here and Spot Lake, so I'll catch a ride back to Ely with the FBI," said Darrow.

Before either of the women could respond, they heard voices and a barking dog in the clearing on the north side of the cabin.

"They're here," said Darrow.

"Big fuckin' deal," said Sams, stuffing her gear back in her backpack. She clearly had never forgiven the FBI for rejecting her application for employment without even a phone call.

"I hear you, Michele," said Barnes. "Let's make this quick and be on our way. I'm going to bet if the feds lead this investigation, we'll never really know who carved up this poor, rich, dead son of a bitch."

TEN

Jack Whitman had arranged to meet her at The Boat Club, the nautical-themed restaurant on the lower level of Fitger's Inn in Duluth. He didn't see her in the bar or dining room, but, glancing out a picture window, he spied her long limbs and silky black hair at a high-top table on the outdoor patio overlooking the lake.

"How was golf?" she asked, while Whitman tried to get comfortable on a chair with a round vinyl seat that was too small for his expansive haunches.

"I've never had a bad round at Northland," he said. "It's unique and challenging and my favorite course in the state. I shot a 76, and P. J. shot a 91, but carded an 82, with his typical number of mulligans and miscounted flubs." She flashed a knowing smile.

"His office called wanting to confirm that you're available for an interview with the Lake County Sheriff tomorrow morning at 9:30," she said, sipping a tall Tanqueray and tonic. Her name was Donna Morgan. She'd been Whitman's combination legal assistant and paralegal for four months and his mistress for three. Flaunting her figure and Coppertone tan in a blue spaghetti strap denim sun dress, Donna was sure that golf was the furthest thing from her boss's mind right now.

"I figured they'd want to talk to him sooner rather than later," he said. "I assume you said I'd be there."

"Of course," she said, caressing his inner thigh with a skilled bare foot and giving him her full attention with her sapphire green eyes. "Do you think he had anything to do with Oscar Fawcett's murder?"

Whitman ordered a Maker's Mark Manhattan and a couple of appetizers before answering. "Under normal circumstances, I'd say not a chance. He's a calculating bastard, and he has way too much to lose. On the other hand, I remember how incredibly pissed he was when Oscar and his mom wouldn't accept a three-million-dollar settlement offer and kept pressing for five. He felt it was extortion. It comes from being an entitled prick. For Christ's sake, Donna, the kid gave him a new lease on life simply because he loved his mom and thought they'd all be family. The only person who committed a crime back then was P. J., and the crime was fraud. Not to mention extreme cruelty, and even though he's been my friend and client for over thirty years, I don't condone how he's handled things. But if he did hire someone to kill that boy, he's crossed a line, a point of no return as far as I'm concerned."

A male server brought Whitman's drink, a second gin and tonic for Donna, and a platter of crab and artichoke dip with grilled pita bread. Whitman often drank too much during his rendezvous with Donna, not because he wanted to party, but because the alcohol helped to suppress feelings of guilt.

Whitman and his wife, Nancy, a successful Twin Cities realtor, had been married thirty-four years and shared two adult children, three grandchildren and hundreds of happy memories. Whitman still loved Nancy and their life together; before Donna he'd never strayed, but over the past few years, he and his wife had started to grow apart, partly because of their busy work lives, and partly because, with their kids grown and out of the house, Nancy seemed to have lost interest in their relationship, and certainly in any intimacy with Jack. Perhaps that had contributed to Whitman's interest in Donna. There was something about her he found irresistible, and it was much more than her beauty, sensuality and sexy body. She was intelligent, perceptive and witty, and . . . dangerous.

"You look tired," she said, leaning in and stroking the side of his face with the back of her hand. "Why don't we order some dinner to go? I've reserved a room upstairs in the hotel in my name."

Donna preferred to be on top, which was fine with Whitman. After consuming a ten-ounce peppercorn filet with a Caesar salad and a bottle of 2018 Lamborn Cabernet, Whitman knew there wasn't enough fuel in the tank to satisfy her, but he gave it the old college try just the same. He accepted the reality that a few of her full-throated moans and affirming sighs were manufactured for his ego rather than the natural consequence of unbridled pleasure. His best attribute as a lover was a long, strong and indefatigable tongue, something all multitasking lawyers should have.

It was nearly midnight when Donna languidly dismounted and laid her head on Whitman's broad, hairy chest, their naked limbs intertwined, while a whirring fan above a four-poster king bed cooled their overheated bodies. Whitman felt himself falling into a dream state, but Donna wasn't ready to let him go.

"Do you think Barton and Melanie will ever have children?" she asked.

"Not a chance in hell," Whitman said confidently, though he wasn't fully awake.

"Why not? She can't be forty."

"Because she's even more driven for wealth and power than P. J. She wants to succeed him as CEO of Barton Industries. Kids would just get in the way."

"What about Barton? He's never wanted kids?"

"When he was younger, maybe. But once his sister had a few, he preferred to be the fun uncle without any parental responsibilities. I also think an unfortunate experience in graduate school scarred him for life when it comes to relationships and kids."

"What experience?" Donna asked while gently stroking the gray hairs on Whitman's chest.

"I thought I told you about the Russian girl he impregnated when he was living in Cambridge."

"What? You never told me about that."

"Really? Do I have to mention this is highly confidential?"

"Of course not," said Donna, as her hand deftly migrated from Whitman's chest to his cock. Now he was fully awake or at least partially aroused.

"I was in law school at Cornell when P. J. was a graduate student at

Harvard. He never made the trip to Ithaca, but I would drive down to Cambridge at least one weekend a month to hit the bars, attend a Celtics or Red Sox game or just hang out at his spacious two-bedroom condo, which beat the hell out of my tiny efficiency. When he was in his last semester, he met a woman at a sports bar in Cambridge. She worked there as a server but claimed she was a model at the Boston Agency. She was born in St. Petersburg and spoke with a sexy Russian accent. I only met her once, but once was enough to see she was an incredibly beautiful young woman. P. J. was totally smitten. It all happened fast, and I've never completely understood how it ended."

"Ended?" Donna asked, inching closer to Whitman.

"Turns out, Elena Krasikova was a twenty-year-old foreign student at Boston University who worked part-time as a receptionist at the Boston Agency. This was right around the time the Soviet premier, Gorbachev, was increasing individual freedoms using terms like *glasnost* to signal to the world that Russia was moving from totalitarianism to a political democracy. Without question, it was easier for Russian citizens to move in and out of the country at that time. The Soviet bloc was literally disintegrating." Donna stared into Whitman's eyes with a level of interest and concentration that surprised him. He was a human encyclopedia, and, as usual, she had to endure being bored out of her mind before he finally got to the point.

"Elena spent a handful of nights at P. J.'s apartment over the course of those few months and, of course, became pregnant. When she said she wanted to keep the baby, he got scared and told his father. Then the shit hit the fan. A week later P. J. was back in Duluth. He completed the last month of graduate school from home, and the senior Barton paid Elena a hundred thousand dollars to get an abortion and never contact P. J. again."

"Did she sign some sort of agreement?" Donna asked.

"The elder Barton disliked lawyers even more than his son. He was concerned about P. J.'s future and reputation, so he figured the fewer people who knew about it the better. He typed a one-page letter agreement and presented it to Elena along with that big check. She probably would have signed anything to get the money. Apparently, she hated and feared her family back in Russia and never wanted to go back. In any event, before he died, Paul Senior gave me a copy. I scanned it into P. J.'s confidential estate planning file. Basically, it says if she ever contacts P. J. or any member of his family, she forfeits the money. It's probably not enforceable."

"And the abortion?"

"That was also part of the agreement. There's a report in the file from a private investigator who followed Elena to a clinic in Newton on the day she was scheduled to have the procedure. His report simply states she entered the clinic at 9:00 in the morning and left at 11:30. I guess that's all we'll ever know about that. The strangest thing . . . P. J. has never said another word about her to me over all these years."

"Do you know what happened to her?"

"I'm curious, but to be honest, I hadn't thought about her for nearly twenty years. As I said, Senior gave me the original letter agreement a few months before he died. Then, about five years ago, when P. J. was desperate to find a suitable match for a new kidney, I thought about her again, wondering whether the child she didn't have all those years ago could have been the perfect match that saved P. J.'s life. So, in answer to your question, I have no idea what's become of Elena."

"What a story," Donna said softly while stroking Whitman's cheek with the back of her hand as he began to snore. Thanks to Donna, he was spent in every way imaginable. She sat up and reached for her purse on the nightstand. In it were two noise-canceling earbuds and a bottle of Xanax, the key ingredients to a decent night's sleep next to her boss.

So, he had no idea what had become of Elena Krasikova. She had an idea. In fact, she knew better than just about anyone.

ELEVEN

By the time Barnes returned to her rented cottage in Castle Danger, storm clouds were invading from the west, blocking out the sun and transforming the hue of the agitated lake from royal blue to titanium gray. She and Sams had grabbed a burger and a beer at Black Woods Grill in Two Harbors after filing an electronic report recounting their gruesome discovery near Fall Lake and their interaction with a team of qualified but condescending assholes, also known as the FBI. Whether you were a cop in Cook County, Illinois, or Cook County, Minnesota, the feds made you feel like a second-class citizen. And no one knew that better than Sam MacDonald.

When Barnes had checked in with him shortly before the feds arrived, his instructions had been clear.

"They'll want to take the lead on this, and we'll gladly let them. Give them everything you've got and offer to support their efforts. We've already got one murder to solve, and I'm guessing they'll need our help sooner rather than later on this one."

Barnes changed into sweats and sneakers, grabbed a stemless wine glass from a kitchen cupboard and filled it with a chilled Rombauer chardonnay, one of her favorites, even if a bit pricey.

She opened a sliding glass door that connected the main living area to a back porch overlooking the lake. The porch was barely big enough to accommodate two antique cane rockers separated by a cast iron patio table. Setting her wine glass and Bose Bluetooth micro speaker on the table, Barnes settled into one of the rockers and selected a jazz piano station on the Pandora app on her phone. She gazed out at the vast, ever-changing lake and contemplated how recent events had changed her life and might influence her future while the Ahmad Jamal Trio played *Poinciana*.

The man she knew as Robin Gildemeister but still referred to as "the judge," the man she'd followed to the North Shore despite a mountain of misgivings, had abandoned his new law office in Two Harbors and his renovated cottage on the lake and had vanished. He disappeared the day after she'd delivered his incriminating diary to Lieutenant Sherm Moe, her old boss at the MPD. The contents of the diary were proof that the former judge had murdered the president of the Minneapolis City Council or proof that he was deeply disturbed, or maybe both. His only response to her note and voicemail message on that fateful day was a cryptic text:

I need to leave until this is resolved. Hope you can forgive me.

According to Warren Lindquist, her mentor, former partner at the MPD, and recovering amputee, the former judge was now one of a trio of "persons of interest" in Kate Patterson's violent murder. Without some corroborating evidence, the diary confession was not enough to get a conviction. Although Moe claimed he wanted to question Gildemeister, he still believed Major Andrew Slayton, the man who'd maimed Warren with his truck and the only person Barnes had ever killed in the line of duty, had executed Patterson to impress Natalie Brinkman, his billionaire girlfriend with a major axe to grind against the city council president. Warren didn't buy it; Barnes wasn't sure.

The third member of the trio was even more surprising—former Minneapolis Mayor Marcus Sampson. Sampson had resigned after Warren had exposed his failure to report millions in campaign loans from a company controlled by Natalie Brinkman's family. Warren claimed someone in the mayor's family, perhaps his spouse, had leaked damaging evidence about Sampson's whereabouts on the night of the murder. It was especially damaging because both Sampson and his young wife had consistently maintained he'd been home all night.

But the Patterson case wasn't Barnes's problem anymore. It had been months since the murder and the disappearance of Robin Gildemeister, and Barnes was beginning to wonder whether anyone really cared about solving the case that nearly killed her partner and ended her career as a Minneapolis cop.

The distinctive roar of a classic cigarette boat, a rare sight on Lake Superior, captured her attention. She was clueless when it came to watercraft. In fact, other than kayaking with the judge, the only experience Barnes had had on a boat was taking the ferry to Madeline Island for a weekend getaway in late July with Sams and Hallie Bell, her new best friends. They'd rented a three-bedroom, craftsman-style cabin near Amnicon Point. A sandy beach was only a handful of steps from the four-season porch, where the three women spent most of their time, conversing, reading, drinking wine and admiring the big lake from an incredible island view.

Persuaded by Sams to dive off the dock, Barnes had been surprised by the sandy bottom and cool but swimmable waters near the south shore, especially compared to the rocky floor and frigid waters of the North Shore. But not nearly as surprised as she'd been on the ride from their rental back to the ferry on Sunday morning.

"That's him!" she'd cried out from the back seat of Sams's F-150 as it headed west on South Shore Drive.

"Who?" asked Bell from the front passenger seat, turning her head to see what or who had caught Barnes's attention.

"It's Robin Gildemeister on a fucking bike. Quick, make a U-turn Michele."

They'd spent the better part of that Sunday morning looking for the judge, from Amnicon Point to Big Bay State Park and on every inch of roadway on the island. But there would be no other sightings of the judge, and Barnes couldn't get the image of a tanned, shirtless Robin Gildemeister on a fat-tire bicycle out of her mind.

It hadn't helped matters when, a week after she'd returned from the Madeline trip, Sheriff MacDonald had given her a large manila envelope he'd received from the Lake County real estate recorder's office. Inside were a recorded quitclaim deed transferring legal title to Gildemeister's cottage on Lake Superior to Lincoln Barnes together with two keys and a handwritten note from the judge asking MacDonald to deliver the contents to Barnes "if she decides to take the job."

"The recorder's office is a bit behind in filing documents," MacDonald had explained with a chuckle when he'd given her the keys and the deed. "Are you going to move in?"

She'd been living in the perfect rental for five months courtesy of the sheriff. The owner of Gooseberry Lakeside Lodge and Cabins in Castle Danger was his cousin, a cousin who owed MacDonald a huge favor related to an incident at his daughter's apartment involving her boyfriend, a knife and a lot of cocaine. The owner had rented Cabin 5 to Barnes for six months at $1,200 per month, even though the current market rate was $400 a night.

"I'll think about it," she'd said. "Or maybe I'll just sell the place and pocket the cash."

Barnes reminisced about her time with the judge at his cottage as she finished her glass of chardonnay, grabbed her speaker and opened the slider to get inside before the evening mosquitos attacked. She couldn't decide whether those memories were now bitter or sweet. Perhaps she'd have to visit her new property on the lake to refresh her recollection.

TWELVE

“I remember you, Sheriff,” Paul Barton said with a smirk, as he sat in his customary leather high-back at the head of the bourbon cherry, boat-shaped conference table that adorned Barton Industries’ boardroom on the top floor of the Maurices Building. Though most of the organization’s senior employees were located in the Twin Cities and Chicago, P. J. kept the holding company’s headquarters in Duluth for personal reasons.

The other attendees at the Saturday morning gathering were Barton’s wife, Melanie Patton Barton, his lawyer, Jack Whitman, Lake County Sheriff Sam MacDonald, and Detective Lincoln Barnes. Whitman had facilitated brief introductions and indicated the sheriff’s office had requested the meeting to discuss Barton’s relationship with the late Oscar Fawcett.

“I was a sophomore in high school at Duluth East, watching our football team play the Two Harbors Agates from my usual vantage point at the end of the bench, and you were the stud senior quarterback for Two Harbors. You threw a couple of long touchdown passes and returned a kickoff for a touchdown in the second half. Of course, we still won 35-31. In fact, I don’t think we ever lost a game to the mighty Agates in any sport during my four years at East.”

“You have a much better memory than I do,” MacDonald said.

"Which is good because I'd like you to tell us everything you know about Oscar Fawcett, a young man who was killed less than thirty-six hours ago and a man to whom you would have paid five million dollars had he lived two more weeks." The sheriff was not in a good mood, and that made Barnes smile on the inside because there was something about this group she didn't like.

Melanie Barton, who'd retained the surname Patton professionally, had recently been promoted to executive vice president of Barton Industries. She was twenty years younger than P. J., and, though she had fake tits and the lean body of a swimsuit model, she was no bimbo, with an MBA from the Kellogg School and a résumé of successful business projects that rivaled anyone under forty. She wore a conservative navy business suit with a silky white blouse that softened the pained look on her face as she challenged MacDonald in support of her man.

"That doesn't prove anything, Sheriff. And besides, Paul was in bed with me during the storm on Thursday night."

"I don't think anyone believes that Mr. Barton was driving the truck that ran Oscar Fawcett off the road and into the lake," said Barnes, "except maybe Oscar's mother, Rebecca."

"That bitch is crazy," said Barton. "Of course, I didn't want to pay her deadbeat kid all that money. His restaurant would have hemorrhaged cash for a few years and ended up in bankruptcy. But the more important fact is I had absolutely nothing to do with his murder, and I don't know how you can be so sure that his accident was murder."

"With all due respect, Sheriff and Detective Barnes, I'm not sure why we're even meeting today," said Whitman, feeling like he needed to act like a criminal defense lawyer even though he knew more about the Morse code than the Minnesota criminal code. He was the only one in the room in a suit and tie, and the only one with a hangover. "What evidence do you have connecting my client to any of this other than a settlement agreement that was executed more than three years ago?"

MacDonald abandoned any attempt to hide his feelings of disgust. Ignoring Whitman's question, he turned to the head of the table and stared right through Paul Barton. "That crazy bitch was your nurse, live-in girlfriend and fiancé when you were dying and desperate for a kidney, and now that deadbeat kid's organ is keeping you alive. You're an asshole, Barton, and you'd better hope there's no evidence linking you to this unfortunate crime because if there's anything out there, Detective Barnes and I will find it."

Barnes had never seen the sheriff so angry. Before a stunned Barton could react, she poured a little gasoline on the fire.

"Regardless of your involvement in Oscar's murder, do you intend to compensate his mother with a portion of that five million?"

"That's really none of your business," said Barton, his ruddy complexion even redder than usual. "You've got a lot of nerve, Sheriff, making accusations and threats against me on the day we've chosen to celebrate fifty years in business. I had feelings for Becky Fawcett back then and never asked her to persuade Oscar to donate his kidney, but when she and Oscar sued me, defamed me, and basically extorted more like ten million dollars when you add in all the lawyers' fees and public relations expenses, any feelings I had for them turned to resentment and bitterness."

MacDonald gave Barnes a nod, and she slid her iPad into a nylon case as they both stood and exited the boardroom without saying another word.

No one said a word during the elevator ride or the walk from the lobby to MacDonald's Tahoe parked on Superior Street a block from the main entrance to the Maurices Building. The forecast called for a rare ninety-degree day in Duluth. A few minutes before ten in the morning it was already in the eighties.

"Is it too early for a beer?" MacDonald asked as he fastened his seat belt and started the engine. "Barton is such an arrogant prick; I needed to get out of there before I did something that would have made me feel good but cost me my job."

"It might be a little early for beer," Detective Barnes agreed, "but it was the perfect time to drink the Starbuck's Italian roast that Barton was serving."

"Should we go back for our coffee? I have to admit I was eyeing the cinnamon scones and caramel rolls too."

"I know you think it's doubtful Barton was involved in Oscar's murder, but you made him think otherwise just in case. I totally get that. But I don't understand why you didn't tell him about the incident at the morgue this morning with Becky Fawcett. Don't you think she might try to take justice into her own hands?"

Against MacDonald's advice, Becky had insisted on seeing Oscar's headless corpse at Lakeview Hospital, and, when she did, she went berserk, screaming incoherently and promising she would deliver a headless, dickless Paul Barton Jr. to the very same morgue before the end of the weekend.

"Didn't I tell you about my conversation with Barton's lawyer?" asked MacDonald, turning left from London Road into the Dunn Bros. Coffee drive-thru lane.

"No, you told me you called Becky and assured her we'd be interviewing Barton this weekend as part of our investigation."

"I did call Becky, but I also called Jack Whitman and told him he might want to get his client out of town for a while for his own safety. He acknowledged the wisdom of that advice but reminded me who is client is."

"Who or what?"

"I'm getting an egg and cheese biscuit with a large Ethiopian. What can I get you? I'm buying."

"In that case, add some turkey sausage to the biscuit and two shots of espresso to the coffee."

"What an asshole. Coming here on the day of our big celebration and practically accusing me of killing Rebecca's idiot son." Barton scowled. He hadn't moved from his seat at the head of the boardroom table, but, in an effort to improve his mood, Melanie had retrieved a bottle of Jefferson's Reserve Kentucky bourbon and three glasses from the bar in his office and filled each with a generous pour of brown liquor, no ice needed.

"He may be an asshole, P. J., but he's just doing his job," said Whitman, taking a healthy swig of the expensive bourbon. "You have to admit there are at least five million reasons that make you a suspect, not to mention the fact that Becky Fawcett is on the warpath."

"I doubt that mousy little bitch is capable of doing much damage," said Patton, "but I was impressed with MacDonald's sidekick, Detective Barnes right? She must be six feet tall with eyes like a Cooper's hawk and the legs of a model who doubles as a distance runner." Both men took too long to digest that description, so Barton changed the subject.

"I need to get out on the lake one more time while the weather's so glorious, but we'll head to Monterey for a few weeks tomorrow night. Maybe I can kick your ass at Pebble next week, Whitman."

"As much as I'd like to let you try, I'm closing on the acquisition of a small media company in Madison for your sister next week, and then Nancy and I are heading to Italy to celebrate our thirty-fifth right after Labor Day." The trip had been planned two years ago, but Whitman knew Nancy was trying to cancel it and get a refund because of a recent foot injury while playing tennis. He also knew that wasn't the real reason.

"Italy? That can't be your idea," said Barton, finishing his glass of bourbon. "Sorry to break up the party, but I need some alone time in my office to finish my speech for the gala tonight. Mel, can you call Jimmy and ask him to have the Vision ready for a nine o'clock take-off tomorrow night?" The Vision was a Cirrus FJ33-5A seven-passenger jet that Barton Industries had purchased for its CEO. Barton had a pilot's license but never flew the small jet without a professional copilot.

"Only if we take Tabitha," Melanie said. Tabitha was a tiny white Bichon Frisé that Melanie took everywhere.

"I hate that fuckin' little whiny excuse for a dog and you know it," Barton said with exaggerated disgust. Melanie didn't say a word, but her big blue eyes narrowed into caustic slits that quickly had the desired effect.

"Of course we'll take the little prick," Barton conceded as he got up to leave the room. "See you tonight, Jack. Drinks in the locker room at six." And with that he was gone.

Before Whitman could gather his things and leave, Melanie pounced.

"Hey Jack, I can't recall your RSVP. Will you be bringing Nancy or Donna to the party tonight?"

"Very funny, Melanie. How did you find out?" Whitman knew better than to deny the relationship; better to find out how much damage had been done.

"I could say it's the bulge in your pants every time she's in the room, but I think that might just be a permanent condition. The truth is the concierge at Fitger's is both very observant and a good friend. Need I say more?"

"Does P. J. know?"

"He doesn't have a clue, and I don't have a good reason to tell him."

"Thanks," said Whitman. "I owe you."

"Yes you do, counselor. Yes you do."

THIRTEEN

It was a rare Saturday morning when both Sams and Darrow were home and in bed at eight o'clock. Darrow hadn't made it back from a frustrating afternoon with the FBI until well past midnight, and, after working a double shift on Friday and consuming half a bottle of Patron Extra Anejo while waiting for her partner's return, Sams had gone to bed and lost consciousness at about 11:00. She didn't even stir when he crawled in next to her at 2:00.

Sams rolled out of bed to calm a pounding headache with three Advil washed down with a cocktail of Fresca and orange juice. Darrow followed her into the bathroom to take a piss and neutralize the bile in his mouth with half a bottle of Listerine. Wearing nothing but bear print boxers, he crawled back into bed and spooned around the naked form of his favorite Native person.

"What the fuck, Darrow? No call? No text? When's the last time you hunted a murderer? I'll tell you the answer—Never. I was so worried I had to drink myself to sleep."

"I'm really sorry about that, Sammy, but by the time I had decent cell service, it was after one, and I didn't want to wake you." Darrow started caressing Sams's taut midsection and slowly moved south from there.

"If that ever happens again, and I hope it won't, call no matter how late it is, okay?"

"Promise." Darrow wasn't physically afraid of Sams, though she could probably whip his ass in a fight, but his deep affection for her was coupled with a healthy dose of respect. He knew she'd want a full accounting of his evening.

"The feds brought dogs and drones and a copter to the party and didn't find squat. Whoever murdered Larry Osgood is a professional killer. We started out together—three FBI agents, two dogs and me. As I explained to you and Barnes, it was easy to follow the splatters of blood and boot prints to an entry point in the forest. There's no question that this guy intentionally created this trail and then continued with the same pattern for the first fifty or sixty yards into the woods. At that point, all signs of a hulking man running through the dense brush disappeared. The feds and their entourage forged ahead, assuming the perp caught himself thrashing and suddenly became careful. They fanned out in a southerly direction, thinking the killer parked somewhere on the closed service road two miles away. When I suggested that he could have led us into the dense forest and then backtracked to the campground parking lot, they basically told me to fuck myself; that I was giving a violent killer on the run too much credit.

"'Good luck then,' I told them. 'I'm going to check out my theory and then head back to Ely.'"

"I'm sure they loved that," said Sams, reaching back to check her partner's overall readiness.

"The AIC just shrugged and told me to report back if I found anything. I'm not sure whether he remembered that I didn't have my truck and was relying on them to take me back to the office.

"I took the most indirect route back to the entry station, avoiding campsites, and looking for anything suspicious. Fifty yards or so from the station, I see a stocky man dressed in black emerge from the front door and get into an older, silver Mercedes sedan with those distinctive North Dakota plates. He looked around right before getting into the car, so I did get a glimpse of his face. Our eyes met for a few brief seconds, and he had this awful look on his face, like he couldn't believe anyone would ever get a good look at his ugly puss.

"Unfortunately, I can't make out the plate number and don't have time to grab my binoculars, but I call the AIC and tell him I think this might be our man. I know he's skeptical when he tells me to enlist local law enforcement to assist. As you know, local law enforcement up there consists of the Ely police and the St. Louis and Lake County sheriff's offices. I know the Ely police won't give a shit unless the car is within the city limits. I also know it's unlikely there's a sheriff's squad within twenty miles, so I call the Ely dispatch and request a BOLO for a late-eighties silver Mercedes 300D likely driving south on U.S. 169. I ask that they contact me or the FBI for further instructions.

"Then I waited in the station until midnight for the feds to return. They were in a foul mood having discovered absolutely nothing."

"And what did your BOLO produce?"

"Absolutely nothing."

Darrow started massaging Sams's upper back and shoulders and before he could say anything she had maneuvered her body into a position that communicated the time for talking was over.

FOURTEEN

"Did you finish that other job?

"Yeah. It was an easy way to make a few hundred grand."

"I don't want to know, though I have an idea. Are you ready for Sunday?

"Of course. I'll be staying near Duluth with an old friend until Sunday morning."

"What's your exit strategy after baiting the trap?"

"I'll find a place to hide until I know there will be payday. Then go north to Canada before going home."

"You'll need a new burner for our next communication."

"You make me laugh. Who has the experience in these matters, me or you?"

"The world is constantly changing, and if you don't adapt, especially with new technology, you'll be scraped off the pavement like roadkill, no matter what you've done in the past."

"Roadkill. I'm more like wood tick. You can smash me with a sledgehammer or an anvil and I'll just keep moving until I satisfy my lust for blood, or in my current state, money."

"What about vengeance?"

"No longer high on my list. You be in charge of that today."

"With pleasure."

FIFTEEN

Mickey Kaye was exhausted. Most people he knew took weekends off; Mickey never did. He'd just finished a double shift as an emergency medical technician for Samaritan Hospital in Troy, New York. He and his partner had responded to two heart attacks in Troy, a drug overdose in Schenectady, a car/motorcycle accident on I-90 in Albany and, near the end of the second shift, the aftermath of a violent confrontation between three teenagers, a business owner and two uniforms outside the '76 Diner in Latham.

After a night of reckless experimentation with fentanyl-laced heroin, cocaine and cheap tequila, the teens sought out comfort food at the 24/7 diner. When they bolted without paying a hundred-dollar tab, the owner, an obese, fifty-something Chicano wearing Air Jordans and wielding a baseball bat, called the cops and chased them on foot for two blocks, where they all arrived at the getaway car, a rusting Mercury Montego. The feisty owner may have used an expletive or two when demanding payment for their meals, but he didn't make any disparaging comments or slurs about their race (two of the three were African American), so it didn't seem fair that one of the two black teens grabbed a loaded handgun from inside the Montego and shot him multiple times in the face and torso just as a Latham PD squad arrived on the scene.

The young man with the gun pointed it in the direction of the cop car, but only for an instant, after which his chest literally exploded from catching two 127-grain, high-tech hollow point rounds from a Glock 19, fired well before he could even pick out a target in the squad. The other two boys thought about running until the shots were fired. Then they quickly complied, kneeling on the pavement and raising their arms above their heads. Perhaps they'd had prior experience with the drill.

Incredibly, Mickey and his partner, with help from the medical staff at Samaritan, saved both men, though the teen would die a month later and the manager would be severely disabled. Kaye had never seen so much blood, at least not since he found his own mother in a pool of it on her kitchen floor on Christmas Eve of 2019.

After showering and changing into jeans and a T-shirt at the hospital, Kaye drove his black 2010 Toyota Tacoma to his one-bedroom condo in a renovated warehouse on State Street in Albany, where Roger, his five-year-old golden lab, would be anxiously awaiting his dinner and a long predawn walk. This would be their last weekend in upstate New York for a long time, maybe forever. His last day at Samaritan would be Monday, when he'd also close on the sale of his condo. He'd pack up his stuff in the Tacoma and a rented trailer that night and make the twelve-hundred-mile trek to Minnesota, where he'd rented an apartment and would start a new job with the St. Paul Fire Department. He couldn't wait to leave, though he understood that the nightmare he'd endured over the past four years would haunt him wherever he went.

SIXTEEN

After dropping Barnes off at her rental, Sheriff MacDonald remembered that Hallie had told him she needed to spend most of Saturday at the office, meaning young George was spending the afternoon with his favorite babysitter, and he should head to the government center and offer to take his wife to a late lunch. Whether karma, ESP or simply a coincidence, he got a text message within thirty seconds of turning south on 61 to return to Two Harbors:

Hey, Sheriff, I just ordered a couple of salads and a pizza from Do North. Are you able to pick them up and meet me for a late lunch in my office?

H

MacDonald smiled and replied:

Perfect. See you soon.

Mac

Fifteen minutes later, he passed by the empty cubes and unoccupied offices that comprised the Office of the Lake County Attorney on a gorgeous Saturday in August. Carrying a pizza box, two salads and two Diet Cokes, he was startled when a closed office door suddenly opened, and his favorite mongrel accosted him, knocking the Diet Cokes off the top of the pizza box and onto the floor. Oddly, the dog was more interested in licking his master's face than sniffing the contents of the pizza box.

"Holy shit, Fred, I didn't know it was take your dog to work day."

"Hey, he misses you. You've hardly been home this week," said Hallie Bell, lifting the plastic bottles of Diet Coke off the floor and setting them on her desk to settle.

They sat at the small round conference table in Bell's office, Fred content to sprawl out between them under the table. Bell was wearing her favorite T-shirt, a souvenir from their honeymoon in the Riviera Maya a few years earlier, and gym shorts, whereas the sheriff looked uncomfortable in his polyester uniform.

"I'm so hungry the stale crap in the vending machine was starting to look good," Bell said, handing MacDonald a paper napkin and choosing a wedge of the sausage and mushroom pie. "All I've had all day is a cup of coffee and a granola bar."

The sheriff didn't mention the egg sandwich he'd devoured an hour earlier. Instead, he flipped open the Styrofoam box marked "Caesar" and speared a ripe tomato with a plastic fork.

"How'd the meeting with Paul Barton go?" asked Bell.

"About as worthless as I'd anticipated. He may be a first-class dick, but, unlike Becky Fawcett, Lincoln and I don't think he had anything to do with her son's murder. He's far too egotistical and narcissistic to risk a billion-dollar empire to avoid paying out five million, as distasteful as paying Oscar seemed to him. But we had to do the interview, to satisfy Becky if for no other reason."

"Any other leads in the case?"

"Ryan has tracked the origin of a stolen pickup truck abandoned in Gooseberry that likely ran Fawcett off the road. If we can identify the person who stole it from a used car dealer in Duluth, we'll know a lot more than we do now. Lincoln will follow that thread and also have a conversation with Oscar's boyfriend to inquire about anyone else who might have had a grudge or benefited from his death."

"The whole thing seems so strange, Mac. It reminds me of a classic Mafia assassination. Murder made to look like an accident, but not very well."

"Speaking of strange," MacDonald replied, "the kidnapping and murder of the Tri-Metals CEO up at Fall Lake makes no sense to me. None of the environmental groups or local tribes I'm familiar with would do this. They're all too smart."

"It's the main reason I'm still here on a Saturday," said Bell. "What did Lincoln have to say about the scene at that old cabin?"

"Not much. The feds commandeered the investigation. Osgood never had a chance. He was chained to the floor. She said the killer was a professional—strong and adept at wielding a knife or machete. Nearly decapitated the poor bastard. Apparently, he did leave some shoeprints and a trail of blood near the cabin, but that was probably intentional."

"Really? I got a call this morning from an assistant U.S. attorney from Minneapolis. He claims the FBI is at a dead end on the case. They believe the killer is a skilled Ojibwe hunter and tracker hired by the tribe to send a message to the copper mining companies. They've asked the BIA, St. Louis County and us for assistance."

"What an absolute crock of shit, Hallie. They're nothing but condescending, ignorant, bigoted city slickers. An Ojibwe hunter and tracker? Maybe it was Tonto or Mingo. On our way back from Duluth, Lincoln and I got a call from Michele and Craig Darrow. Craig knows the woods and terrain up at Fall Lake as well as anyone. He volunteered to help the feds gather evidence and search for the killer. But when he suggested that they were heading on a wild goose chase through the forest; that the killer had staged a misdirection ploy, they laughed at him and spent an unproductive afternoon in the thicket with blackflies, poison ivy, and thistle. Meanwhile, Craig nearly caught up with the man he thinks is the killer."

"Any description?" asked Bell.

"The same one Craig gave the agent-in-charge. A stocky male dressed in black and picked up by a silver Mercedes with North Dakota plates. Craig said the AIC pretty much ignored his report, not wanting to admit they'd wasted a day in the woods. Besides, what does a park ranger know about tracking a dangerous suspect? We don't have the resources to conduct two complex murder investigations at once, but I have an old friend who's still the executive assistant director for the criminal investigative division in D.C. Maybe she can finesse placing someone in charge of this case who has some relevant experience."

Bell had been married to MacDonald for three years and had known him for about five, but she still wasn't sure whether her attraction to him was based more on professional admiration or animal lust. He was also the kindest human being she'd ever met, and that played a part in the equation as well.

"I'll leave that to you and stay out of it for now," she said. "I need to spend another hour preparing for the county board meeting next week. You want to take the rest of this pizza home?"

"I'll take the pizza and pick up George. Maybe I'll take him and Fred for a walk and then clean the grill to make some tuna steaks for a late dinner."

"That sounds too good to be true, Sheriff. Let's hope for a quiet Saturday night in Lake County."

"I guarantee it," he said. "By the way, Lincoln has decided to move into the Gildemeister cottage next week."

"Good for her," said Bell. "Do you think he's gone for good?"

"Probably not, but I don't think he killed Kate Patterson, and you do."

"We'll just have to agree to disagree on that one."

SEVENTEEN

"I thought you liked staying at Fitger's Inn," Nancy Whitman said to her husband while applying her makeup and picking out just the right jewelry for Barton Industries' fifty-year anniversary gala at the historic Kitchi Gammi Club. They'd met at Edina Country Club in the late 1980s. Whitman was a recent college graduate at the time, playing in a member/guest event with a college buddy and his father, a longtime member.

Nancy Greene had been the top singles player on one of Edina High School's many state championship tennis teams and was home for the summer after her junior year at Gustavus Adolphus College, where she'd played varsity tennis and majored in business communications. She interned at a marketing firm in Minneapolis during the week and worked as a server at the club on weekends. Whitman asked her out before he ordered lunch, and four years later they were married. Though Jack was a successful business lawyer, Nancy was the top revenue-producing residential realtor in the Twin Cities office of a national broker, specializing in high-end homes on Lake Minnetonka and in tony suburbs like Edina, Wayzata and Orono.

Jack had always been attracted to Nancy's athleticism and drive. Playing softball as well as tennis in school, she'd pushed herself to become a twelve-handicap golfer even though the pace of the game annoyed her. But she'd persevered so she could enjoy the game with Jack and be competitive at club events. With the blonde hair, blue eyes and petite, turned-up nose often characteristic of women with a Scandinavian heritage, Nancy was pretty in a Gretchen Carlson kind of way, but barely five feet tall with sturdy limbs and small breasts. Despite a disciplined, low-fat diet and rigorous exercise regimen, she'd been losing the battle against post-menopausal weight gain for a couple of years. Nevertheless, she was, and always would be, considerably more attractive than her spouse. She'd found him ruggedly handsome, a lovable teddy bear, when they were younger, but had been disappointed with the trajectory of their relationship in recent years. Jack was consumed with work and golf, and their social life revolved around his clients. Unbeknownst to him, she had her own active social life. She'd never imagined she'd have competition for his affection from another woman, especially a young, attractive one. It's not that she was jealous; she just didn't want to be embarrassed by someone taking advantage of his fragile male ego and dormant libido.

"We always stay there," Jack replied. "I've heard so many good things about Pier B that I thought we should try it. I love the views of the harbor and bridge from here. Plus, we can keep our distance from all the company people staying at Fitger's." And, he didn't have to worry about anyone at Pier B remembering him from his recent rendezvous with Donna.

"Fitger's has those specialty shops and restaurants, and I love Va Bene," Nancy said as she walked out of the bathroom and sat on the edge of their king bed in her gold-sequined midi dress, while Jack stared at his wide, sunburned nose and ruddy complexion and fumbled with the fancy cravat that accompanied his black tuxedo. "The hotel is way more romantic than this place, but I guess that doesn't mean much to you these days."

"What kind of talk is that?" asked Jack, sitting next to his wife on the bed and curling his left arm around her back to draw her close. "This is a big celebration with one of our best clients and closest friends. Let's have some fun together, okay?" He kissed her softly on the cheek.

"Okay," she said, grasping his right hand with her left. She tried to remember the last time they made love but couldn't. Fortunately, she had other outlets to take care of her needs.

As they walked out of the hotel holding hands, she turned to him and asked, "Will Donna be coming to the party tonight?"

Several of the rank-and-file employees at the Kitchi Gammi Club were incensed that the club's general manager, a skinny, dyspeptic fifty-year-old fellow, gallingly obsequious around members and an inflexible tyrant around staff, didn't cancel or at least postpone the Barton gala on Saturday in light of the death of their friend and sous-chef, Oscar, less than forty-eight hours earlier. In fact, a few of the servers and a bartender assigned to the celebration simply didn't show up. That could be a problem if most of the expected two hundred guests appeared.

The invitees included senior executives and spouses or significant others from more than a dozen Barton Industries operating companies, an assortment of loyal customers from the investment and media operations, and a handful of company vendors and advisers, including Whitman's law firm, which received five invitations.

The schedule called for cocktails and heavy appetizers at 5:30 on the veranda, a plated dinner at 7:00 in the main dining room, a brief program at 8:30, and dancing to *Belladiva* from 9:00 until midnight in the ballroom.

The air was thick with moisture, portending late-night storms, on another unseasonably hot August evening in Duluth, as a crowd of mostly rich, mostly middle-aged people, sweating through their best formal wear, drank Tanqueray and tonics and expensive chardonnay, munched on antipasto skewers, beef spiedini and whitefish and waffle bites, and enjoyed the bluegrass sounds of Trampled by Turtles, the favorite band of P. J.'s sister, Amanda, who didn't hesitate to agree to pay the group eighty thousand dollars for forty-five minutes of music without consulting her brother.

The mood of the partygoers was ebullient, if not inebriated, by the time a combination of club and Barton staff moved everyone into the dining room at about half-past seven. Most of the guests didn't remember much about the rest of the evening because of the incident.

The family was seated on only one side of the head table, so they could see all of the invitees who'd been assigned spots at long tables perpendicular to royalty row. The head table consisted of two power couples: P. J. Barton and Melanie Patton Barton and Amanda Barton and her husband, Billy Slocum, a celebrity personal injury lawyer in the vein of Saul Goodman, but without a sense of humor or an ounce of humility. Amanda's two adult daughters and their spouses completed the family row.

Guests had chosen their entrees weeks earlier from an online menu that included a bacon-wrapped filet with garlic mashed potatoes and asparagus, broiled barramundi with creamed peas, carrots, and chili threads, and green curry eggplant over rice for the vegetarians. All of the tables had been preset with salads, dinner rolls, water, coffee, and bottles of chardonnay and cabernet sauvignon. After a brief greeting from Amanda (P. J. had prepared a ten-minute speech to accompany dessert and a video highlighting the organization's growth and accomplishments), servers began delivering dinner on silver trays with six to eight plates carried confidently overhead to their assigned tables.

Melanie was a frequent patron of the club, familiar with most of the wait staff. Although the woman about to set a tray on a stand next to the head table looked familiar to her, it wasn't because she was a club employee. The platinum blonde hair didn't fit the plain, middle-aged face that Melanie recognized.

Like most of the guests and staff, Melanie gasped when a young woman in heels and a black cocktail dress sprinted up an aisle leading to the head table and tackled the platinum blonde server to the floor, causing the SIG Sauer handgun in her right hand to discharge a round prematurely and hit Billy Slocum in the right leg, shattering his tibia.

Before the server could react, Barton's director of security was on top of her, straddling her torso with his knees. He snatched the gun and handed it to the off-duty Duluth cop he'd hired at the request of Jack Whitman. Then he zip-tied the server's wrists behind her back while the cop called for reinforcements. She strained to look up at the head table, where everyone had stood to watch the spectacle, and started shrieking in desperation:

"No! Oh, God, no! Paul Barton killed my boy after stealing his kidney and none of you rich fuckers care! Nobody cares!"

When the security director assisted the distraught server to her feet, a blonde wig remained on the floor.

Now Melanie knew who she was. "It's Becky Fawcett!" she cried, grabbing P. J.'s bicep like her team had just scored a touchdown. "Who's the other woman, the one who might have saved your life?" Melanie knew who she was, but wasn't sure if P. J. did.

The other woman was Donna Morgan. She lingered on the floor, rubbing a kneecap that hurt like a toothache, though she thought it was only a bruise. The off-duty cop, an overweight, twice-divorced lech named Bob, shoved the SIG Sauer between his belt and backside and offered her a hand. She accepted reluctantly, not wanting to draw more attention to herself, but was disgusted when his eyes didn't move from her cleavage while helping her up.

"That's Jack's new assistant. Donna, I think that's her name," said P. J., though he knew perfectly well that it was.

"Pretty attractive young woman," Melanie commented, as three uniformed officers from the DPD arrived and whisked a sobbing Becky Fawcett away while a couple of EMTs attended to Billy Slocum. The well-known ambulance chaser stared at the stream of blood running down his leg and shouted a string of expletives that was quite original and almost humorous before he passed out and was taken to St. Luke's via stretcher and then ambulance. Apparently, Amanda wasn't too worried about her spouse; she patted the top of his head and whispered something in his ear while the EMTs secured him on the stretcher, then she returned to her seat, guzzled a full glass of chardonnay, and started eating her salad.

"Does Nancy know about Donna?" asked Melanie, seemingly more interested in Whitman's new paralegal and the impact on his marriage than in the commotion stirred up by Becky's failed attempt to kill her spouse.

"I'm sure she does, but why don't you ask her?" P. J. said dismissively, visibly upset but not about Donna. "That crazy bitch almost ruined everything. I need to calm things down a bit before guests start leaving." He walked over to the dais near the head table and flipped on a wireless microphone on the lectern.

"Good evening, everyone. For those of you who don't know me, I'm Paul Barton, chairman and CEO of Barton Industries. I'll echo the sentiments of my sister, Amanda, thanking each of you for your connections and contributions to our companies and our family. I'll withhold most of my remarks until after dinner, but I want to apologize for all the commotion and for the histrionics of a person who, as the staff here at the club well knows, has suffered the tragic loss of a child. Unfortunately, she is under the misconception that my family is somehow responsible for his death, and I assure you that nothing could be further from the truth. I have had no contact with the young man for over three years. Further, tonight I am offering one million dollars for evidence that leads to the arrest and conviction of the person or persons responsible for the murder of Oscar Fawcett. Now, please everyone, refreshen your drinks and enjoy your dinner. I'll be back with happier news while you're enjoying dessert."

When P. J. returned to his seat at the head table, Melanie slapped his knee with an open hand.

"Nice save, big man," she said. "Way to confront the issues head-on. A million dollars. By my calculation, even if you have to pay it, you'll gain a ton of goodwill and still save four million."

"Precisely," he replied.

"I think your little speech might have tweaked my horny gene."

"Just hold that thought."

While P. J. Barton was giving his speech, a Duluth police sergeant was interviewing Donna in the club's library. She'd declined his offer to have an EMT examine the abrasions on her knee and forearm. They sat facing each other on upholstered armchairs, an antique mahogany coffee table between them.

"I'm curious," said the sergeant, "what did you see from across the room that made you jump out of your seat and tackle that woman?"

Not wanting to disclose that she recognized Becky Fawcett, especially with the blonde wig, Donna did what she did best—she lied.

"I was sitting with a group from our law firm. I took a sip of water at the exact time she walked by our table. By happenstance, I looked up and saw part of the handle of a pistol sticking out of the side pocket of her apron. It looked so out of place that I kept watching her. After she set her tray down, she reached back for the gun; that's when I sprang from my seat and tackled her. It was all surreal, like I was in the middle of a dream."

Her story didn't quite add up from the sergeant's perspective, dream or no dream. He wondered how she could have covered the thirty feet between her table and Becky Fawcett after Fawcett had grabbed the pistol but before she'd been able to shoot.

"Do you know Rebecca Fawcett?" he asked.

Donna chose her words carefully. "I'm a paralegal at Cooper Harding in the Cities. We represent Barton Industries and Paul Barton, personally. That's how I got invited to this party. My boss is Jack Whitman, Mr. Barton's personal lawyer. I've only been with the firm for six months, but Mr. Whitman told me about Paul Barton's relationship with Becky Fawcett and the kidney transplant after her son was killed."

"Did you recognize her before you tackled her?"

"No sir."

The sergeant was vaguely familiar with the Paul Barton kidney transplant story. He recalled the headlines several years earlier about a woman suing business mogul Barton for reneging on a marriage proposal after receiving her son's kidney. And then yesterday the DPD captain had briefed everyone on the status of the Oscar Fawcett murder and his mother's claim that Barton had orchestrated the killing to avoid paying a multi-million-dollar settlement.

"Do you think Paul Barton was involved in any way in the murder of Oscar Fawcett?" He couldn't help himself.

"I have no idea, sergeant."

"How long will you be in Duluth?"

"Just until tomorrow morning."

"Okay, that's all for now. I'll need your contact information, Ms. Morgan; we may need to talk again. You're sure you don't need medical attention?"

"I'm sure, officer."

Earlier in the evening Jack Whitman had regretted giving Donna one of the firm's five invitations to the Barton gala. Originally, all five had been distributed to the three partners and two associates who handled most of the Barton legal work. Each one included a "guest" invite as well, which worked out perfectly for the table of ten set aside for Cooper Harding. But when one of the associates had to decline after being hospitalized with a difficult pregnancy, Donna literally begged Whitman to take her place. Not surprisingly, he was finding it more and more difficult not to give her whatever she wanted.

Like everyone else, Whitman had been shocked when Donna leaped out of her seat and tackled Fawcett. But he was relieved and grateful moments later when he realized that she'd probably saved the life of his best client. By the time she returned to the Cooper Harding table with a double vodka martini in hand, most of the guests had finished their main course and were sampling a variety of decadent desserts. Jack asked if a doctor had checked her out after the tumble.

"I'm fine," was Donna's reply, giving him a demure glance that said more. She poked at her salad and decided she wasn't hungry. The Grey Goose martini tasted good. At least a few of her tablemates wanted to ask how she'd recognized Becky Fawcett, but only one had the temerity to do it.

"How'd you know, Donna?" asked Nancy Whitman, who was already sure she didn't like her spouse's new paralegal, glorified secretary, or whatever she was, in spite of her recent heroics. "How'd you know that woman was P. J.'s old girlfriend?"

"I didn't," she lied. "I saw a gun handle sticking out of her apron pocket when she walked by our table. I didn't know who she was, but I kept an eye on that gun, and when she grabbed it, I moved as fast as I could."

"Are you some kind of undercover cop?" Nancy asked.

"No, but I've been exposed to more than my share of violence in my thirty years, so I'm definitely tougher and probably more vigilant than most women I know." Nancy Whitman was curious about Donna's past, but decided to ask Jack for details in private. One of the other senior partners' wives, a woman in her late seventies, broached a subject that was also on Nancy's mind.

"You may be tough, Miss Morgan, but you're also a smart and beautiful woman. Where's your date tonight?" Donna almost spit up her cocktail but quickly recovered.

"I think most of you know that I'm a last-minute replacement at this table. I would have asked my boyfriend, but he had a prior family commitment in Chicago." Lying came too easy to Donna.

EIGHTEEN

Neither Lincoln Barnes nor Michele Sams was scheduled to work on Sunday. Both were usually up before dawn on general principle, so when Barnes texted Sams at 6:15 to ask whether she wanted to help her move into the judge's cottage on the lake, she replied within thirty seconds.

WTF! You're really doing it?? Where and when should we meet?

Barnes packed most of her earthly belongings into her old but reliable Jeep Wrangler, paid the outstanding balance for her rental at Gooseberry Cottages and drove south on 61 to her favorite coffee shop in Two Harbors. She ordered two blueberry coconut scones, a green tea latte for Sams and an Ethiopian reserve for herself at Cedar Coffee Company. When she returned to her SUV with the goodies, Craig Darrow was turning into Cedar's tree-lined lot near the entrance to a dense woods. Sams hopped out of the passenger side of Darrow's pickup with a backpack, while Darrow gave Barnes a quick wave and sped off in the direction of Duluth.

"Looks like someone's in a hurry this morning," Barnes observed, handing Sams her tea before sliding into the driver's seat of the Jeep. Light rain began to fall, but the forecast called for clearing skies by noon and another hot, humid day on the North Shore.

"He's been summoned to Duluth for a meeting with the regional director of the Park Service and a bunch of big shots from the FBI and Homeland Security. Seems a call from our boss to an old friend in D.C. led to somebody connecting some dots at Homeland. I guess the guy Craig spotted up at Fall Lake might be a foreign spy or assassin."

"Holy shit," said Barnes. "You mean someone might have hired this guy to kill Larry Osgood? I stopped at Mac's place to get the keys to the cottage. He had big news but nothing about Craig or the Osgood case."

"That's a yummy scone," Sams tried to say with a mouthful of food. "I doubt Mac knows what his call has triggered. Craig got a message from the regional director at five this morning. I'm not sure why he couldn't tell them what he saw over the phone; it's already in his daily report. I guess the connection to North Dakota is also meaningful. Craig agrees with Mac that the Chileans might have hired a professional killer with no ties to the States to assassinate their own guy, so they could blame it on ecoterrorists and my people."

"What's so shocking about that is the average citizen doesn't have a clue about all the crimes and other evil deeds these powerful multinational companies commit behind the scenes to accomplish their objectives. I wish we could get involved in the Osgood case."

"Don't think that's going to happen now, girlfriend. What was the other big news from our sheriff?"

"Sad news, in my opinion," said Barnes. "Barton Industries had a big celebration last night at the old private club in Duluth, the Kitchi Gammi. Becky Fawcett, probably frustrated because we haven't arrested Paul Barton, disguised herself with a blonde wig and convinced someone to hire her as a server for the party. Given the staffing difficulties at restaurants these days, that's no surprise. Anyway, one of the guests either recognized her or saw the handgun in her apron pocket and tackled her just before the gun discharged. Instead of hitting Barton, she wounded his brother-in-law in the leg. She's been arrested and will face charges ranging from assault to attempted murder. Mac feels terrible about it. He reminded me that Oscar had been the sous-chef at the Kitchi, so I'm sure that bit of irony also pissed her off."

"You're a lot closer to that situation than I am, but I can relate to Becky Fawcett's frustration. Unfortunately, she crossed a line when she pulled the gun."

"You're right. The guy she thought was the man of her dreams turned out to be a nightmare, a narcissistic fraud if you ask me. If she'd succeeded in killing him, I think she gladly would have served the time. She hates him so much she'll never believe anyone else was responsible for her son's murder."

"Any ideas on that front?"

"No, though I'm not as convinced as Mac that Barton wasn't involved. One other tidbit from the boss. Becky made a phone call last night to her lawyer, who advised her not to say a word to anyone until he got to the courthouse today. That's not unusual, but the lawyer's name is Charlie Fallon."

"Not the federal judge whose wife was murdered up here a few years ago by his former law partner."

"Yes," said Barnes, "that Charlie Fallon. I remember reading about it and being shocked when a Ramsey County jury acquitted him after he beat the guy to death with a golf club. According to Mac, he moved to Grand Marais after the acquittal and opened a bike and ski shop with his best friend, some guy who left the priesthood in St. Paul in protest of the celibacy requirement. Mac said Fallon was a great judge who takes on a handful of cases a year on a reduced fee or *pro bono* basis."

"Okay," said Sams, "but you said Becky called him. How did she know he was taking cases?"

"Because he's sleeping with her."

Turning right at a familiar driveway on Highway 61 about twelve miles north of Two Harbors in the unincorporated village of Castle Danger, Lincoln Barnes felt more than a little anxious. It had been months since she'd spent two of the best weeks of her life at this place with a man she'd desperately wanted to trust because she was physically, intellectually and emotionally infatuated with him. Her decision to drive back to the Cities and deliver the incriminating diary to her former boss at the Minneapolis PD had not been easy. The easy play would have been to burn the stupid thing and pretend it never existed, but she couldn't do that, and she'd been second-guessing herself ever since.

One of the reasons she'd decided to accept the judge's "gift," at least temporarily, was to look for clues within the cottage that might help her decide once and for all whether the man she still loved was a sociopathic killer or a decent human being who'd endured a lifetime of anguish over his obsessive love of a woman who was not Lincoln Barnes. But to what end, then, were his final, disturbing entries in the diary and his failed attempt to destroy it?

"Earth to Lincoln," said Sams. "You're a million miles away. Thinking about the Fawcett case? Larry Osgood?" Barnes had driven down the tree-lined gravel driveway and stopped in the parking area between the detached two-car garage and workshop and the split-log cabin overlooking the lake. She'd been staring at the garage in a semi-catatonic state.

"The Mercedes."

"What?"

"Robin's Mercedes is in the garage. I can see it through the window. I was sure he'd taken it. How did he get to Madeline Island? Oh, well. Let's have a look around."

They exited the Jeep and walked about thirty feet to a narrow set of steps leading to a small porch that had recently been rebuilt with native cedar planks and black iron railings. Barnes slid the key into the slot on the cylinder lock in what might have been the cottage's original oak front door and gestured Sams to enter first.

"Oh, Lincoln. This place is perfect," gushed Sams, admiring new Sub-Zero appliances and granite countertops in the kitchen and then moving to the two-story great room with a vaulted ceiling, stone fireplace and a wall of windows facing the big lake.

"Perfect is not always perfect, if you know what I mean, but this place is pretty special. I'll give you the five-minute tour before we get my stuff. That'll make about ten total. There are two bedrooms and a shared bathroom down the hall and a master bedroom with a walk-in closet and full bath up there," she said, pointing to the second floor loft.

The two women walked through the cottage, one wide-eyed, the other wary and curious. Someone had thoroughly cleaned the place, maybe the judge, but probably not. When they got to the master bedroom, Barnes spotted a ring of keys, one to the garage and two for the Mercedes, sitting on a folded piece of notebook paper on a nightstand next to the bed. She slid the keys into the back pocket of her running shorts and read the note.

I'm very happy if it's Lincoln who's reading this. Please enjoy your new home and make use of the old car. Again, I'm so sorry for everything, but circumstances force me to stay away indefinitely. You are responsible for replacing the anger and despair in my life with hope, at least for now. Robin

"What does it say?" asked Sams.

"Just that I can use the car," Barnes said, deciding that the rest was for her eyes only. "How about a five-miler after we move my stuff in? We can drive to Split Rock and take the Gitchi trail back here now that we have an extra vehicle. We can shower here, and I'll buy a late lunch at Grand Superior when we're done." Sams was one of the few women Barnes knew in the area who could keep up with her sub-seven-minute mile running pace, and both women loved an endorphin high whenever they could get it.

"Sounds great. Luckily, I'm wearing the right shoes. Maybe we'll get an update from Craig before we're done."

"Or he could meet us for lunch and share all the bureaucratic details."

NINETEEN

“Why don’t you answer your fucking phone? I’ve called you ten times since last night. Something almost interfered with our plan.”

“Needed to take care of some business with former associate. I’ve picked up car I can use for the next few days. Found better plates, though. Minnesota. Are we good to go?”

“As far as I know. Let me know when you’ve finished the work in Silver Bay.”

“My contacts in Canada can’t meet me until at least Tuesday.”

“Will that be a problem?”

“What do you think?”

“Right.”

TWENTY

"It's Woody, Mac. Sorry to bother you on a Sunday, but I wanted to get back to you on the Larry Osgood matter." Woody was Woodrow Bartholomew Wilson, former Secret Service, now a deputy director at Homeland.

"No worries, buddy. Hallie and I just got back from a walk in Tettegouche with little George and Fred. George is napping and Hallie just got in the shower, so your timing is perfect."

"This may be a dead end, but I've given the FBI the same information I'm sharing with you now. Back in 1992, about a year after the collapse of the Soviet Union, a few senior officers in the KGB, which by then had been dissolved and replaced by the Russian FSB, decided the new regime didn't have a place for them. Most landed somewhere in Europe or the Middle East, but one in particular came to the U.S. and somehow managed to abscond with about twenty million dollars of Russian oligarch money. As you know, this is years before the Yeltsin handoff to Putin, so no one in the Gorbachev government did anything about it, though rumors persisted that his theft and defection irritated a young lieutenant colonel named Vladimir Putin, who was living in St. Petersburg and moving up the ranks of the new government. Anyway, this defector had grown up on a farm near Leningrad and was divorced without any kids. He bought a huge sugar beet farm in the

Red River Valley near Fargo, North Dakota, married a local woman, had two daughters, and changed his name from Ivan Andropov to Evan Andresen. Initially, he was on the radar of both the FBI and CIA, simply because of his background, but over time he blended into the community without any provable connections to the Russian government or any other suspicious activity." Wilson paused to catch his breath.

"Until now?" asked MacDonald.

"Perhaps. His wife called local authorities in Fargo yesterday morning indicating he'd gotten a phone call on Friday that scared him. He said he needed to meet someone in Minnesota; that he'd be back later that night. But she said he was clearly upset. Nothing like that had ever happened during their twenty-five years together. And he never came home."

"So, you think he picked up Osgood's killer at the Fall Lake campground?"

"Based on Barrow's description of the car and the North Dakota plates, yes, but there's more. This morning an Itasca County sheriff's deputy responded to a call from a janitor at a rest stop off U.S. 169 near Grand Rapids. He was cleaning the restroom and discovered a severed head in a waste container. The coroner's office took photos and ultimately Mrs. Andresen tentatively identified the head as belonging to her husband, but you can imagine what kind of emotional state she's in right now."

"And no more information on the mystery man in black this Russian defector may have picked up?"

"They were hoping the park ranger, Barrow, could shed some light on that; otherwise, we've got nothing."

MacDonald shared the Oscar Fawcett story with Wilson, only because it occurred at the same time as the Larry Osgood abduction and involved another severed head.

"I thought you moved back to Minnesota to get away from all the craziness, Mac."

"I'm afraid those of us in law enforcement are always moving toward chaos, not away from it."

"No doubt, my friend. Anyway, thanks for the heads-up on the Osgood case. Let's keep in touch until we capture this guy."

"Of course. Though I have a feeling that he's a kill or be killed kind of suspect."

"You're probably right about that too."

TWENTY-ONE

Though he desperately wanted to leave Minnesota until the furor died down over Oscar Fawcett's murder, P. J. Barton couldn't leave the North Shore on a gorgeous summer day without taking *All Mine*, his sixty-foot yacht, for an afternoon cruise on the big lake. The boat was an extravagant, million-dollar gift to himself after the successful kidney transplant. The Azimut 60S Cruiser with inboard diesel engines and a fiberglass hull had all the electronic and radar bells and whistles known to the modern yacht enthusiast and was the most impressive vessel at the Silver Bay Marina. Barton paid the marina staff generously to stock the fridge and bar with an assortment of delicacies and adult beverages so he and Melanie could enjoy a carefree afternoon on the lake. He liked to head northeast and sometimes docked on the eastern side of Isle Royale to explore and then enjoy a cocktail or two at the Rock Harbor Lodge.

On this Sunday afternoon, he was content to cruise fifteen to twenty miles from the marina. They dined on shrimp cocktail, Caesar salads with grilled salmon and a tray of fruit and cheeses. Melanie drank Tanqueray and tonic and a Hess chardonnay, while Barton started with a glass of Schramsberg sparkling wine and then shifted to his favorite bourbon, Jeffersons Reserve very small batch, neat. After a few of those, he let the cruiser drift atop the rolling waves while he tried to convince

Melanie to get naked in one of the boat's three staterooms.

"Does life get any better than this?" he asked his wife rhetorically as they gazed up at a clear blue sky through the yacht's open sunroof after taking care of business.

After reading his son *Hop on Pop* and tucking him in for the night, Sheriff MacDonald hoped to have a late dinner with his spouse and finally get a decent night's sleep. But when the number that displayed on his buzzing cell phone was the deputy in charge of the county's search and rescue team, such hopes were quickly dashed.

"Hi Shawn, what's up?"

"Hello, Sheriff. We have an unusual situation out on the lake, and I'm not sure whether and how we want to get involved."

"Okay, what do you know?"

"You're familiar with Paul Barton of Barton Industries, right?"

"Yes."

"He keeps a huge pleasure craft at Silver Bay; some would call it a yacht. He and his wife took it out for a cruise this afternoon. She radioed an SOS to the Coast Guard station in Duluth about thirty minutes ago, indicating their position about sixteen miles east of the Silver Bay marina, and that they're dead in the water, out of gas."

"What? I've seen that monster. I can't believe they'd go out for an afternoon on the lake and not have full tanks and maybe even an emergency reserve."

"She said someone must have messed with the fuel lines. And that's not all. She claims they've been poisoned; she's vomiting and feels faint, and she thinks her husband might be dead."

"Has anyone else been aboard their boat?" MacDonald asked, trying hard to make sense of the situation.

"I can't be sure, Sheriff. I got a call from the chief at the Duluth Coast Guard station. They have a rescue boat on a training mission near Two Harbors, so they're on their way to Barton's yacht, but because of the potential crime scene, they're asking whether we want to make it a joint operation."

"Let's grab an EMT from your rescue crew or the Silver Bay PD. You can operate the boat, and, if she's available, Detective Barnes and I will meet you at the marina in fifteen to thirty minutes. I assume our friends with the Coast Guard have the ability to repair or replace a fuel line or two, so a tow shouldn't be necessary."

"That's what they said, Sheriff. See you when you get here."

MacDonald called Barnes. She picked up on the first ring.

"Hi, Sheriff. Is this about the Larry Osgood case?" Barnes had just returned to the judge's cottage, her new home, from dinner with Sams. Craig Barrow had joined them after his meeting with the feds. He had news about the Osgood case.

"No, but we should talk about that too." He explained the SOS from Barton's yacht, and they agreed to meet at the marina.

MacDonald apprised Hallie of his evening plans on his way out the door. She was disappointed but not surprised, flipping him an apple and reevaluating her own plans for dinner.

TWENTY-TWO

"The lake seems a bit rough," said Detective Barnes, feeling the blackened walleye she'd eaten for lunch rumbling uncomfortably in her gut. It was 7:50 in the evening when Barnes, Sheriff MacDonald, an EMT borrowed from the Silver Bay PD, and Deputy Shawn Soltau left the Silver Bay Marina in Lake County's twenty-foot Sea Ray search and rescue watercraft equipped with a 200 hp Mercury Verado outboard. Everyone had a life vest; Barnes and the EMT were wearing theirs.

"The radar and weather data show scattered thunderstorms out of the west that should get here in about ninety minutes," said Soltau. "Nothing awful, but with wind gusts up to thirty knots, there are small craft warnings on the lake."

"And we're a small craft, right?" Barnes asked.

"Yes we are, detective."

"Do we have decent video equipment on board, Shawn?" MacDonald asked, ignoring the weather talk.

"Yes, Sheriff. I'll get out the video cam, check the battery and give it to Lincoln. Trying to preserve evidence out on this lake can be tricky."

"Right. Depending on what we find, I may want to videotape everything and everyone on Barton's boat. Lincoln, I called my contact at the BCA to alert them we might need some help with a new investigation. The feds are all over the Osgood case, but if there's foul play related to Barton, we could have more than we can handle."

"Understood," said Barnes, wishing the county had a bigger boat. "So, you heard about the severed head discovered in Grand Rapids?"

"Appears there's a professional killer in the area," MacDonald replied. "Someone who wants to make a statement either as a scare tactic or maybe to show off. Let's hope that's not the case."

"Isn't it possible he'll simply disappear now that his mission's been accomplished?" asked Barnes, not at all convinced by her words.

"I'd believe that if Osgood were his only victim, but this other hit, a former KGB operative who changed his name and led a quiet life in North Dakota—it only makes sense if the killer is settling a score from decades ago. If that's the case, where is he from and what else will he do?"

"Two ships visible on the starboard, Sheriff," said Soltau. He flashed the boat's high beams and sounded his horn to let the Coast Guard know he'd be tethering to the other side of Barton's yacht. He cut the engine, and he and MacDonald tied their boat to Barton's larger vessel while one of the Coast Guard's crew members helped MacDonald and Barnes onto the yacht.

"Welcome aboard, Sheriff," said a short, stocky fellow wearing a blue ball cap and orange life vest over a gray Coast Guard uniform. "I'm chief boarding team officer Jensen. We've got two team members on board this boat and two back on our rescue vessel. Let's sit up at the table in the galley, and I'll fill you in on what we've discovered."

MacDonald and Barnes sat across from Jensen while Soltau and the EMT stood outside near the bow.

"There were two civilians on board when we arrived, one female unconscious and possibly comatose and one male in cardiac arrest and flatlining. My medic worked on him with a defibrillator for ten minutes but there was no response. We think both have been poisoned but don't know either the substance or the method. Your folks can examine him, but we've concluded he's a fatality. She needs more sophisticated medical attention stat to determine the potential toxins and if there's an antidote. We've been communicating with the trauma center at St. Luke's and administered an IV with fluids at their request. We found identification on both. Paul J. Barton and Melanie Patton Barton. Follow me down to the stateroom and you can have a look yourselves."

MacDonald was impressed with Jensen. "Thanks, Officer Jensen. Shawn, why don't you take a look at the fuel lines while we go with Officer Jensen?"

"We've already got that situation pretty well in hand, sheriff," said Jensen, turning back to the group that was following him down the stairs to the stateroom, where Melanie Patton was lying on a bench, an IV in her arm. "There are multiple fissures in the two lines close to where they attach to the Volvo diesel engines, so they leak fuel continuously under the boat but feed the engines fuel for an hour or two. It's clearly sabotage by someone who knew what he was doing."

Barnes carried a small iPad for notes and a Sony Handycam video recorder, which she'd already clicked on, recording Jensen's summary and the luxurious upper deck of Barton's yacht. She sensed the wind was picking up as the yacht started to rock from side to side in the water.

Barnes couldn't help but notice that Melanie was a beautiful woman even in repose. Wearing a white coverup over a blue-and-white-striped bikini, she appeared to have a slight grimace on her lips, as if suspended in a nightmare, which perhaps she was. Barnes captured the look on the video cam and tried to piece together in her mind how the afternoon on this boat had regressed from pleasure to pain to potential oblivion.

P. J. Barton was also in repose, a permanent one, flat on his back in an adjacent stateroom. He was shirtless, and his bare chest showed evidence of both hand compressions and a defibrillator, though his skin had already started turning gray. His swimming trunks were navy but covered with tiny gold and silver sharks.

There were several bottles of booze open and fully or partially consumed in the galley and on side tables near the bed as well as plates of food throughout the cabin. There was also a pervasive stench in the bowels of the yacht, a combination of vomit, death and rotting food as well as the effect of warm, humid air on all three.

The EMT checked out Barton for about thirty seconds then turned to MacDonald and simply shook his head. Barnes finished taping every surface and cranny on the yacht, including the small utility and engine compartment and made a list on her iPad of all open containers of food and beverage. She also noted that the boat had its own drinking water supply, a freshwater storage tank and filter, that might have been contaminated.

After assessing the scene for about five minutes, MacDonald asked Jensen about the fastest way to get Melanie Patton to St. Luke's Hospital.

"I talked to both the Guard and St. Luke's about bringing a helicopter out here to airlift her. While that would be the fastest means, the approaching storm with high winds makes it too dangerous. I think we should transport both Barton's body and Ms. Patton to the marina in Silver Bay on our boat, and then have an ambulance take both of them to St. Luke's, one to the ER and the other to the morgue. My engineer can get this vessel operational and drive it to the marina if you want to stay close by in the county's boat in case there's a problem."

"Good thinking," said MacDonald. "We'll return Barton's boat to its slip in Silver Bay and cordon it off for processing as a crime scene. I'll arrange to have a Lake County Emergency vehicle meet you at the marina. You can let St. Luke's know you're on your way."

"Thanks, Sheriff. We should get moving before the storm hits us full force."

The boat ride back to the marina was an indoctrination for Lincoln Barnes. The air temperature dropped twenty degrees, and a thirty-mile-an-hour westerly headwind made it almost impossible to plane the relatively small county rescue boat. A cold, driving rain was pelting her in the face, and lightning bolts appeared to be diving into the lake on either side of their boat. But none of that bothered the battle-tested detective from Chicago enough to complain. It was the nonstop bouncing over the whitecaps that pushed her over the edge.

"I should have stayed on Barton's luxury liner," she yelled so MacDonald could hear her over the cacophony created by the weather and the boat. "It feels like the hull on this thing is going to explode."

"I promise you it won't," MacDonald assured her. He thought changing the subject might be a good idea. "How was your first day at the new place?"

"Interesting. It's one of my favorite places for a variety of reasons. It's just difficult to be there when the true owner is AWOL."

"Wait minute. I thought you were the true owner."

"Right. Did you know he left his Mercedes in the garage with the keys in it? Do you think he took an Uber to Madeline Island?"

"You're sure he's on Madeline Island?"

"As sure as I am about anything to do with the man."

"You know he had access to a boat that had the range to get him there."

"I did not know that, Sheriff. He never talked about any boat other than his kayak and a couple of canoes."

"His father had a thirty-foot Chris-Craft that I believe sat in what is now your garage for many years. He may have sold it, or he may have made it seaworthy and piloted it to an island getaway."

Now Barnes recalled the sheriff telling her a story about that boat that involved the drowning of the judge's mother and a long prison sentence for his father. "Okay, now I remember why he never talked about that boat."

"Speaking of boats," said MacDonald, "I'd like to hear your ideas about who had motive, opportunity and the skill set to board Barton's yacht, sabotage the fuel tanks and plant some kind of poisonous substance. It's too noisy on this boat to have that discussion, and it'll be too late when we get to the marina. I think we can safely eliminate Becky Fawcett as a suspect, since she won't be arraigned until tomorrow. I'll ask Shawn to work with the marina to make sure the entire yacht is covered with caution tape and designated a crime scene not to be entered without our permission."

"Sounds good. Unless Melanie Patton regains consciousness or something shows up on the marina's CCTV or surveillance video, we won't know much without an autopsy and an analysis of everything they might have consumed or been exposed to on that boat. Or possibly even before they boarded."

MacDonald was concerned about the state of affairs, mostly criminal affairs, in his beloved county. More often than not, he could make sense of the players and motivations involved in crimes committed in Lake County. But there was something highly unusual about the recent sequence of three and potentially four murders occurring in a place that could go years without any. He had a feeling that all three (Fawcett, Osgood and Barton) were connected in some way. He was grateful he had Lincoln Barnes to help him make that connection even if the main reason she'd taken the job was to be with a man who was deeply flawed and might never return.

TWENTY-THREE

“What can you tell me?”

“Job is done. Not sure if woman is dead. I can’t get close enough to marina, even with binoculars. They’re transporting both in van.”

”Good. It doesn’t really matter whether she’s dead or not, but better if dead. You swapped out cars, I hope.”

“Of course. I picked up nice Japanese truck in park.”

“We shouldn’t communicate again until you’re home. Are you leaving for Canada tomorrow?”

“I haven’t been paid for side job. No credit to my account. It’s a problem. I need to put pressure on local office in St. Paul.”

“That would not be smart. Making any kind of appearance in the Twin Cities would be a huge mistake and could jeopardize everything.”

“Don’t push me. I know what I’m doing. You know this plan is nothing without me. I am concerned that someone saw my face on Friday. No one sees my face. I may have to take care of that too. I need to be in Ottawa by the fourth of the month, and then I’ll be home by the eighth. You said first payment should come in six months.”

“I said six months to a year. This is family by the way.”

“If no payment, family means nothing. I won’t contact you until Ottawa.”

“Fine.”

TWENTY-FOUR

Jack Whitman recognized the number on his smartphone but was surprised that Amanda Barton would be calling him at 9:30 on a Monday morning, or even calling him at all. She'd never liked sharing counsel with her brother.

"He's dead, Jack. P. J. is dead." Amanda sounded more like she was reporting the weather than her brother's demise.

"What? How? Did they crash the Cirrus?" Whitman was stunned, but he knew Barton had been scheduled to fly out of Duluth in his private plane on Sunday night, and those mini jets were slick but not the most reliable.

"I had a twenty-minute call with the Lake County Sheriff, some guy named MacDonald, and a doctor from St. Luke's Hospital up in Duluth. They said he was out on his boat on Lake Superior yesterday, and they think someone poisoned him and Melanie. Put the poison in their food or air circulator before they even got on the boat and also fucked with the engines, so the boat stalled out miles from shore. They're still investigating and running tests to determine what the poison was and who's responsible. They said when the Coast Guard boarded the boat, P. J. was already gone."

Unlike her brother, Amanda couldn't wait to move away from northern Minnesota. She and Billy had a sprawling mansion with a pool and putting green on Lake Minnetonka in posh Wayzata, and, when the cold weather hit, more expensive getaways in Jupiter, Florida, and Mauna Lani on the Big Island of Hawai'i. She didn't hunt, fish or participate in any winter sports and thought the North Shore was a cold, rocky wasteland inhabited by rednecks with pickup trucks and environmental zealots. She preferred private clubs, Ivy League schools and Republicans not named Trump.

"What about Melanie? Is she dead too?" Whitman knew Amanda wasn't fond of Melanie for a variety of reasons.

"No. Not yet, anyway. She's in a coma, but her vital signs are stable. What happens now, Jack? I need to know."

"What do you mean, Amanda?" He thought he knew what she meant, but it was premature and ultra-crass to ask about P. J.'s estate, even for her.

"If she survives, does Melanie get Jack's sixty percent ownership in Barton Industries?"

"I'm truly sorry for your loss, Amanda. You know he was much more than a client to me. Shouldn't we be spending our time trying to figure out who did this? They may have had some kind of a vendetta or grudge against the company. You and the rest of the family might not be safe."

"Cut the crap, Jack. My brother may have had enemies, but I doubt any of them cares about Barton Industries or me and my family. He hasn't been involved that much in any business but the investment advisory firm for years, but that finagling bitch Melanie has her hands in just about everything. He would never discuss succession planning, even before the transplant when he only had months to live. You know all the answers, and you know I'll know them eventually, so unless you want me to find other counsel for everything that's in my power to move, you'll tell me everything you know now."

Jack did know the answers, but he was more interested in what happened on that boat. Becky Fawcett wouldn't be released from jail until at least later this morning, and she didn't have the capability or connections to pull off such a clandestine and technical mission. But what if Oscar's boyfriend, the congressional aide and former naval officer, were involved? He'd have to follow up on that thought.

"There's not much to know or to worry about, Amanda. Despite my bugging him for years to create an estate plan, a family foundation, and a succession plan, and his concurrence that he needed to do it, he never did any of it, except for one thing."

"And what is that?"

"He has no Will, but he had us prepare an antenuptial agreement before he married Melanie. She wasn't happy about it, and she and her lawyer negotiated a bit, but the final result was fair. You'll be happy to know that at P. J.'s insistence the agreement does not give her any part of Barton Industries."

"That's great. What does she get?"

"She gets a cash payment, the yacht, ironically, one vehicle of her choice, and the house in California. Like you, she's not a fan of northern Minnesota, especially in the winter."

"How much cash, Jack?"

"The cash payment increases with each four years of marriage. If he dies before they've been married four years, she gets twenty-five million. The amount increases by fifteen million on the fourth anniversary, the eighth anniversary and so on. They haven't reached four years, so twenty-five is the number. She could try to contest and take her statutory share of his estate, but that would be foolish since she negotiated the prenup with counsel, and she's no fool."

"She'll need the money because next week she'll be unemployed."

Whitman didn't think that was a good idea for a number of reasons, but thought better of arguing about it at this point. He and his firm might be on the chopping block soon enough.

"You said he doesn't have a Will," said Amanda, now getting to the heart of it. "What does that mean in this situation?"

"It means he died intestate. He has no children and no living parents, so his next of kin will inherit everything. Since you're his only sibling, it means you will own one hundred percent of Barton Industries plus an airplane, four homes, five vehicles and, well, you know most of the rest of what he has. North of five hundred million with very little debt, and that doesn't include the shares in Barton Industries."

"How soon can we start the proceeding to get everything transferred to me, and how long will it take?"

"P. J. was a legal resident of Lake County on the North Shore when he died, so we can file a petition to administer his estate a hundred twenty hours after his death, so no earlier than Thursday or Friday of this week. It's a huge, multi-state estate, subject to federal and other estate taxes but, for the most part, any creditors or other claimants will have about four months to file claims with the Court. Best case scenario, we will be able to close the estate in about fifteen months, but that's assuming no major hiccups."

"File it as soon as you can. Because I'm the only heir, I assume I can take complete control of Barton Industries immediately."

"I don't see why not. The prenup precludes Melanie from being the administrator or executor of the estate, so you're next in line to be the personal representative, giving you full control of P. J.'s stock."

"Let's pursue that, then. Jack, I know you must think I'm a total bitch, but ever since I was a little girl, I've been living in the shadow of my big, swaggering dick of a brother, and, you have to admit, he's not been the easiest person to work with."

"Oh, I know that as well as anybody," Whitman agreed. "But he was also a pretty smart guy who grew the family businesses and kept everything together during the pandemic. How is Billy doing, by the way?"

Dead silence. Amanda ended the call. Apparently she got what she needed. Billy must be doing fine.

Though he figured she'd be in the office by now, Whitman hadn't seen or heard from Donna since the tainted celebration on Saturday night, after which an inebriated Nancy had confronted him about their relationship. He'd conceded that Donna was a dynamic, attractive young woman, but vehemently denied that he had anything but a professional working relationship with her. He'd gone overboard in complimenting Nancy's outfit and showering her with the kind of attentive, verbal foreplay that she used to have difficulty resisting. But, instead of initiating a love-making session, she'd patted him on the head like a good dog and then turned her back to him and started snoring. He definitely needed to be more careful in the future or to break it off with Donna. He needed to be more careful.

He debated whether to call Donna, send her an email or get off his ass and visit her cubicle with the news of Paul Barton's death. He called her office phone.

"Good morning, boss. Quite the event on Saturday night."

Whitman was buoyed by the cheery tone in Donna's voice.

"How are you feeling today? Still sore from your heroics?" he asked.

"My right knee is bruised, and I have a hairline fracture on my wrist, but otherwise I'm fine. I canceled my hotel room Saturday night and drove home. I have to say I got some negative vibes from your wife that night and didn't feel like running into her on Sunday morning. Besides, I got tired of answering all the insipid questions about my motives. I was just trying to do the right thing, for god's sake."

"I'm so sorry, Donna. I think everything's okay with Nancy for now. We can talk in private about that later. But something shocking has happened that will make the local and even national news this morning and have a direct impact on you and me and this firm."

"What is it?" asked Donna.

"Paul Barton's been murdered. Apparently poisoned on his boat. Melanie's been poisoned as well. She's hanging on but in a coma for now."

"Oh, my god, Jack! That's awful! How did it happen? Do they know who's responsible?"

"I don't have much information at this point. It happened on his yacht on Lake Superior. That's all I know. But for us today, it means we need to start a probate proceeding up in Lake County. I think you already know there's no Will, so if you could prepare a memorandum addressed to me that summarizes Melanie's rights under her antenuptial agreement, both if she survives and if she dies, and then prepare a separate memo from me to Amanda Barton, outlining the steps we need to take to file a petition for formal administration of Paul Barton's estate. Amanda will be the petitioner, and I'll get you a summary of Barton's probate and non-probate assets for the petition."

"When do you want to file?" asked Donna.

"Let's shoot for Friday, so we can get a hearing date and publish notice within the next month."

"Where's the body?" asked Donna, more interested in learning the gory details of Barton's demise than in preparing memos for his sister.

"In the morgue at St. Luke's in Duluth. There'll be an extensive autopsy to determine the cause of death and the nature of the substance or substances that killed him."

"Must have been something powerful to kill him that fast," Donna observed. "I'll get to work on those memos this afternoon."

"How about lunch later at the Capital Grille?" Whitman knew it was a bad idea. He was a well-known lawyer in Minneapolis, a well-known *married* lawyer, yet he and Donna had been frequenting downtown eating and drinking establishments popular with professional elites. He knew Nancy was suspicious, but what about other lawyers and staff members at his firm? What about other professionals who might be friends with his wife? Yes, it was a bad idea to take Donna to expensive restaurants three or four days a week, but he was completely smitten. He simply couldn't resist her. After all, at some point when Donna fell for a younger man or simply lost interest, it would be over. But not yet. Not today. Not while he was grieving his best client and friend.

"I'm sorry, Jack. I have a physical therapy appointment at TRIA at 11:30. Thanks for the offer though." Donna did have an appointment, but a week ago she would have rescheduled to have lunch with her boss.

"Of course. I've got the Ramsey Foundation board meeting at 2:00. Maybe we can touch base later this afternoon." Whitman remembered the first time he'd made love to Donna on the leather couch in his office after a late afternoon meeting that turned into a celebration with clients who'd just sold their waste hauling and recycling business for four million dollars. The celebration in a Cooper Harding conference room started with a bottle of expensive champagne and ended with flaming shots of Patron. The clients left to have a steak dinner at Manny's. He and Donna took the Patron to his office. His recollection was that Donna had initiated the physical intimacy, and that he had resisted her advances for at least ten seconds. Maybe now she was making him pay.

"I'll be here," she said.

TWENTY-FIVE

The Duluth field office of the FBI, located in the bowels of the historic granite federal building, provided a variety of investigative and administrative services for the agency but was rarely the situs of a strategy session related to the investigation of a crime that might have national and even international significance.

On this Tuesday morning in late August, Lake County Sheriff Sam MacDonald, his chief detective Lincoln Barnes, the special agent in charge of the Minneapolis field office, and Edward Higgins, M.D., chief pathologist for Mid-States Medical Examiners, the private company that performed autopsies for many of the smaller counties in Minnesota, sat on gray vinyl chairs around one side of an oval laminate conference table. Participating virtually via Microsoft Teams on a sixty-five-inch screen in the fed's main conference room were deputy directors from the FBI and CIA and MacDonald's buddy from Homeland Security, Woodrow Wilson.

Though Higgins' team had not completed the autopsy and toxicology tests on Paul Barton, Higgins had contacted MacDonald after consulting with Melanie Patton's treating physicians and toxicologists at St. Luke's Hospital, where Patton was still in a coma. When MacDonald relayed the substance of Higgins' call to Wilson and the FBI, Wilson's boss not only directed him to call this meeting but also gave specific instructions to keep a tight lid on any information that might alarm the public.

"Thanks for attending on short notice," said Wilson, sitting at his desk at DHS headquarters in Washington, D.C. "I have asked Dr. Higgins to give us an update on the progress he's made in determining the cause and manner of Paul Barton's death and, maybe more important, the likely substance that poisoned Mr. Barton and his wife. Dr. Higgins, I'll turn it over to you."

Even at sixty, Higgins was an imposing figure. His shaved head that resembled a pumpkin in size and shape sat almost directly on rounded shoulders and a six-and-a-half foot frame. With slate blue eyes, a broad, prominent nose and an authoritative baritone voice, he resembled an extra-large version of Kojak. Higgins had been an army medic during Desert Storm, having financed his college education by joining the ROTC. He'd concluded with the help of his medical school adviser that his demeanor, keen intellect, and quirky sense of humor were best suited for dealing with the dead.

"Good morning," Higgins said, opening a leather folio where he'd organized typed notes and test results. "Mr. Barton died a fairly quick but painful and likely pretty horrible death. As of now, my office together with the toxicologists at St. Luke's and a couple of toxicologists and biochemists I consulted at Bethesda Naval, believe both Barton and his spouse are victims of cholinergic toxicity as a result of acute Novichok poisoning. Some of you agency people can provide more background on the use of this stuff over the past thirty years by the Russian government, but suffice it to say that the name Novichok represents a group of nerve agents created by the former Soviet Union during the Cold War to be the most lethal chemical weapons known to man. They are organophosphorus compounds designed to be both incurable and undetectable.

"Fortunately for Melanie Barton, one of the toxicologists on call at St. Luke's, Dr. Nguyen, wrote a major doctoral paper on Novichok and its documented use by Russia against Charles Rowley and Dawn Sturgess, two British nationals, in 2018, and against Alexei Navalny, one of Putin's main rivals, in 2020. She suspected Novichok because of the combination and progression of Ms. Barton's symptoms. She complained of dizziness, sweating, a severe headache and vomiting during her distress call to the Coast Guard Sunday, then she lost consciousness and started suffering respiratory failure and bronchorrhea, ultimately becoming comatose. In examining Paul Barton's lungs and diaphragm, I observed that he also had respiratory paralysis but much more severe, likely contributing to his death. In essence, he suffocated to death. But because of Dr. Nguyen's astute observations and background, she and her team started Ms. Barton on atropine to reverse the effects of the deadly nerve agents and give her a fighting chance to survive.

"The last thing I'll point out before ending my preliminary report is that it's impossible to overstate the toxicity of these compounds. Once we had a hypothesis that Novichok agents were involved, we went out to Barton's boat with Sheriff MacDonald and carefully took samples of foods and beverages that could have been tainted. By late last night we had a definitive answer. It was the water supply." Dr. Higgins gave MacDonald a subtle nod and sat back in his chair.

"Thank you, Doctor," said Wilson. "As most if not all of you know, there are only a handful of actors that have a documented history of using this awful stuff. A few terrorist organizations, mostly in the Middle East and Southeast Asia, and, as Dr. Higgins pointed out, the Soviet Union and Russian Federation, though they would vehemently deny it. The key questions, then, are one, who is messing with these deadly agents in northern Minnesota? And two, why?

"The only known connection between the events of the past several days and Russia is the apparent assassination of Evan Andresen, formerly KGB Agent Ivan Andropov, at a rest stop near Grand Rapids. Based on a park ranger's tracking and observation skills and Sheriff MacDonald's international experience, we believe that the person who killed Andresen could be the same perpetrator who murdered Larry Osgood, the Tri-Metals CEO. This potential Russian connection together with the introduction of these lethal nerve agents make it plausible that this same person or persons working together poisoned the Bartons. Once the autopsy report or any disclosure of the use of Novichok becomes public, we could have mass hysteria and who knows what else until we quell the threat. So, we're going to commit some serious assets to identifying and apprehending whoever this is and to trace the origin of these chemical weapons. Sheriff MacDonald, do you have anything to add?"

MacDonald stood, not for effect, but because he was developing a charley horse in his right thigh. "We do appreciate all the assistance we can get, especially if there are foreign actors and chemical weapons involved. I have a couple of observations. Craig Darrow, the resident park ranger who knows the BWCA better than anyone in law enforcement, has provided a general description of the man he saw get into a Mercedes sedan with North Dakota plates. Oddly enough, his description of a man over six feet tall dressed in black with unusually broad shoulders could also be applied to the man captured on video footage stealing the pickup truck that was used to murder Oscar Fawcett near Two Harbors last week. Darrow also got a glimpse of the man's face, enough to see a trimmed white beard and abnormally large ears. It's possible then, I say possible, that all the mayhem that's occurred in Lake County this past week has been committed by the same person, whether he's alone or has help. My office will concentrate on the Fawcett case and ruling out other persons of interest. We'll let the FBI take the lead on Osgood and the Bartons. For all we know, whoever committed these crimes may be long gone. We do have experience dealing with undocumented aliens, including Russians, crossing our border with Canada in the wilderness area. We will have our deputies alerted and prepared. But please keep in mind that it's my job to keep the citizens of Lake County safe, so if my staff and I conclude that we need to warn our folks about an imminent threat of nerve gas exposure, we'll at least give you a heads-up before we do it."

After those remarks, the meeting was essentially over, but Wilson felt obliged to let his counterparts at the FBI and CIA say a few words about the seriousness of the threat and the expertise of their respective organizations in tracking down the killer and recovering any chemical weapons.

MacDonald and Barnes had driven to the field office separately and decided to meet at Duluth Coffee Company to compare notes over the java of the day, a flavorful Colombian. They sat at a corner table for two near the entrance and a picture window overlooking a bustling Superior Street.

"You and Dr. Higgins seem to be pretty good buds," said Barnes, never completely comfortable sitting with her back to the door of a bar or restaurant.

“We met shortly after I moved back to Two Harbors. As you just witnessed, he’s painstakingly thorough and one of the smartest people I know. Plus, he lets me win a set now and then when we have our monthly tennis matches.”

“In Chicago and Minneapolis, I dealt with all kinds of blades and guns and even firebombs but never chemical weapons. I don’t understand why a foreign terrorist or Russian spy would want to poison a guy who owns convenience stores. And if the same person or group took out Oscar Fawcett, it makes even less sense. At least Barton was rich and might have some foreign connections, but Oscar?”

“I agree. The feds have more resources to track down Barton’s business connections. Maybe we interview his sister and his wife if she comes out of the coma. There may be a personal relationship or incident that sheds some light on this. I know you were going to try to contact Jared Cheslak, Oscar’s partner. Any luck?

“I met him at the campaign office in Lakeside last night. He’s distraught and angry and at a total loss for answers. He said Oscar was a teddy bear; that he’d never witnessed him in a heated argument with anyone. He’s ninety-nine percent sure he had no enemies. Before he heard about Barton’s death, he was as convinced as Becky Fawcett that Barton was involved in Oscar’s murder.”

“Even though that’s a dead end with respect to any new information, it’s certainly no surprise. Thanks for the quick follow-up.”

“It was kind of a two for one,” said Barnes. “While I was meeting with Jared, Becky Fawcett and her lawyer showed up. Becky had just been released from the St. Louis County Jail after posting bond, and the three of them were going to dinner. I got to meet the infamous Charlie Fallon. He reminds me of Kenny Rogers with chubbier red cheeks and no southern drawl.”

“I’m surprised you know who Kenny Rogers is,” said MacDonald, savoring the last swig of his coffee and contemplating getting a refill. “Fallon was one of the most respected judges in the state before he retired. You already know that story. I’m sure he’s still an effective lawyer when he wants to be and when he’s not selling bikes and skis.”

“He was a lot more talkative than his client. Apparently, she still thinks Barton had something to do with Oscar’s murder. She didn’t say a word to me. She held Fallon's hand and hid her face in his shoulder until I left. Jared asked Fallon whether he'd made a deal with the prosecuting attorney. Fallon wouldn't get into details, especially with me standing there, but I gathered that Billy Slocum is getting in the way of a plea deal. He's adamant that Becky serve time in state prison. Fallon wants no jail time."

"That's a tough one," said MacDonald. "With a murdered son and the humiliation Barton made her endure, I think she's a sympathetic defendant, but her use of the concealed pistol is damaging. Not to mention the assault with a deadly weapon against Slocum. If I had to guess, I'd say she spends at least six months in prison. If she gets probation with conditions, Fallon is a magician."

"I asked him about his bike shop in Grand Marais just to make small talk before asking him about Robin, and he wouldn't shut up. Apparently, it's become a hot spot for seniors looking for love."

"So, did you ask him about Gildemeister?"

"I did, and he looked like he'd just swallowed a yellow jacket. He said Robin was a good friend when he lived in the Cities, and was one of the few jurists who stayed in touch after he was charged with murdering his former partner. When I asked whether Robin had sought his advice before he left the North Shore, he got weird."

"Weird?" MacDonald asked.

"He said 'I have faith in Judge Gildemeister, no matter what, and you should as well. I had lunch with him a day before he left. He mentioned your name, Detective. Said he hoped you wouldn't give up on him. That's all I can say about it.' And that's all he did say."

"What do you think about that?"

"It makes me want to do some serious research into Charlie Fallon and his relationship with Judge Robin Gildemeister. Two former judges and maybe two killers."

TWENTY-SIX

Mickey Kaye drove his rusting Tacoma pickup into the state of Pennsylvania a few minutes before 1:00 in the afternoon. Erie would be the next exit on I-90, but he'd filled his tank and bought a Diet Coke at a thruway plaza near Buffalo and wanted to reach Elkhart, Indiana, spending an abbreviated night at a Hampton Inn that served a hot breakfast at 6:00 in the morning and would allow him to have Roger in his room for an extra fifty bucks. He hadn't been out of the state of New York since 2019, when he and his then girlfriend spent a wonderfully decadent long weekend at the Nobu Hotel in Cabo San Lucas.

He was twenty-eight back then and attending Cornell University in Ithaca as a graduate student in chemical biology with the original intention of preparing for a career in medical research. They'd pooled their meager resources from his job as a teaching assistant and hers as an admissions officer to escape snowy Ithaca during his holiday break a week before Christmas. He'd already decided to attend medical school in 2020 instead of getting a Ph.D. in biochemistry, a decision that had made his mother very, very happy.

But her happiness had been short-lived. Mickey never attended medical school. He didn't even get his master's in chemical biology. His mother died a week after the Cabo trip, and he entered Auburn

Correctional Facility, an ultra-max security state prison in Auburn, New York, on February 14, 2020, where he spent the worst thirty months of his life.

As soon as his parole officer gave him the green light to leave New York, he started applying for jobs in Minnesota, a state he'd never visited but the only state where he had family. Even with a glowing recommendation from his current employer, it took over a hundred applications to get one interview. He'd always believed once a prospective employer gave him the opportunity to tell his story, he could overcome the criminal conviction. A team captain with the St. Paul Fire Department had a son who'd served time in Stillwater Prison for aggravated assault. Mickey had little doubt this captain was the person who'd convinced the chief to give him a chance. He'd read over two hundred books during his stint at Auburn and even started writing a book about the tragic experiences in his life, but to most people, he was just a well-educated convict.

1471 Grand Avenue. That was the address of the rental that had caught Mickey's eye. He had docu-signed a one-year lease for a furnished, two-bedroom/one bath upper unit in a mixed-use, middle-class neighborhood in St. Paul known as Macalester-Groveland, a stone's throw from Macalester College and two miles from his new workplace in downtown St. Paul.

He hadn't talked to his sister in over a year. They'd had a major blow-up shortly after their mother died. She'd earned a law degree from Georgetown and passed the New York bar exam while he was in prison. After accepting a position in the litigation department of the largest law firm in Albany, she'd abruptly quit after a year and moved to the Twin Cities.

Their communication had been one-sided since before his conviction. She'd send him texts and emails, and he wouldn't respond, though he always read them and digested the information. She knew about his release from prison and career as an EMT and had encouraged him to visit Minnesota when he could, but she didn't know about the new job and apartment in St. Paul or that he was on his way to Minnesota. At least he didn't think she knew.

TWENTY-SEVEN

Nancy Whitman was on her way to California for the long Labor Day weekend to visit their oldest daughter and her husband before their grandson started first grade on Tuesday. Normally, Jack would have accompanied her on the trip, but, given the recent death of his long-time friend and client, they had agreed he should stay in the Cities.

After dropping Nancy off at the airport on Friday afternoon, Jack returned to the office with hopes of escaping to the family cabin in Wisconsin for a few days of fun and relaxation with Donna. Though he knew she'd been busy preparing the Barton estate documents, he didn't understand why she hadn't returned any of his calls or texts since he'd shared the news about P. J. earlier in the week. When he arrived at the Cooper Harding offices, most of the staff had already taken off for the long weekend, but he was surprised that Donna wasn't at her desk. In fact, not only was she gone, but her cubicle looked empty, not just neat/empty, vacated/empty. His surprise changed to concern when he entered his office and found a yellow sticky note stuck to the seat of his high-back leather chair.

Jack—

Please come to my office. I'm leaving around 6:00,
but we need to talk ASAP.

—Gretchen

Gretchen Perkins wasn't a lawyer. She was the manager and human resources director of the firm's Minneapolis office. She mostly left senior partners alone unless there was a complaint about them from another lawyer or staff member. Whitman saw a note in Donna's handwriting clipped to the top of a manila folder in the center of his desk. It said she'd completed all of the paperwork for the initial filings for the Paul Barton estate, including procuring Amanda's signature on the petition. He could review and sign the paper documents and give them to their admin for scanning and filing on Tuesday, or he could review everything in the new Barton Estate drive she'd created and make any changes (he knew there wouldn't be any) before signing electronically and filing today. To expedite matters, he chose that option.

Donna usually signed notes to him with a singular "D" surrounded by a heart. This note was signed *Donna*. He wondered whether Gretchen's note had something to do with his paralegal. He didn't have to wait long to find out. Gretchen knocked on his open office door and didn't wait for a response, sitting in one of the two upholstered leather guest chairs facing his desk.

"Why don't you have a seat, counselor?" she asked, crossing her legs and setting an open laptop across her knees. Perkins was a fifty-something, no-nonsense HR veteran. She'd been the director of hiring for a Fortune 500 manufacturer headquartered in Bloomington for ten years before shifting gears a year ago to be a combination office, benefits and personnel manager for a hundred employees, including forty lawyers. She'd been seeking a position with more collegiality and less stress. She didn't find it. Barely five feet tall and a hundred pounds with ultra-short brown hair streaked with gray, small facial features, and emerald-green eyes made greener by tinted contacts, Perkins also had a big, beautiful smile that she rarely flashed at work, believing she needed to be extra tough and businesslike to gain the respect of the lawyers and to keep their huge egos in check.

"Sure, Gretchen," said Whitman, slowly sinking into his chair while distracted by the sound of multiple sirens rising from Marquette Avenue twenty-five stories below. "Are they coming for me?"

"Funny, but maybe," said Perkins, the smallest of wry smiles appearing for an instant. "Donna Morgan quit earlier today. She's not coming back. Do you have anything to say about that?"

"I'm shocked," said Whitman, which was true. "She was doing great work. You tell me why." He thought their affair had been consensual, and he didn't want it to end. She'd initiated it, after all. But he braced himself for something bad.

"She claims the two of you have been having an intimate affair for over two months. She said after the events of this past weekend, the death of your client, Paul Barton, and the way she was treated by your wife at the Barton dinner made her realize it was time to end the affair and move on personally and professionally. Do you admit the affair, Jack?"

Whitman wanted to deny it but was smart enough not to. "I do," he said. "I also admit that I really like Donna and was short-sighted and stupid to get involved with her. She could have been a long-term asset for us."

"I don't disagree that it was stupid, but it looks like you and this firm might be able to move on from this mistake with minimal fallout. Donna wasn't going to stick around long regardless of any relationship with you. Did you know she's a lawyer?"

"What?" He didn't but for several reasons wasn't surprised. "I had no idea."

"When she applied for the paralegal job at Cooper Harding, she submitted what I would call a partial résumé. Her education ended with a B.A. degree and paralegal certificate from a community college when in reality she was first in her class at Georgetown Law."

"That's fraud," Whitman said.

"Well, you're the lawyer," said Perkins, "but everything in that résumé was accurate, except for the amount of time she claimed to have worked as a paralegal and the leave of absence she said she took to travel in Europe and China before moving to the Midwest. Usually, we see applicants embellish their credentials and job history; Donna downplayed her education and experience in order to get a job for which she was overqualified. Maybe it's fraud, but for me, the big question is why?"

It hadn't been a good week for Jack Whitman. The murder of a long-time friend and client, the loss of the best paralegal he'd ever had, and the end of a relationship he never should have started, which today felt like it was worth more than his thirty-year marriage to Nancy.

"I'm asking myself that question a lot his week," said Whitman. "Did she say where she was going? For work, I mean."

"She did not. She said she had a new position in the metro, but wouldn't be starting for a few weeks. She promised to let me know after she started. Smart woman. We'll be posting for a replacement next week. I'll be personally involved in choosing her replacement. I assume you're good with that."

"Of course," said Whitman. "You have a good weekend, Gretchen."

"Sure. You, too, Jack."

"And Gretchen, thanks for handling this."

Perkins raised her hand in mock salute as she left his office thinking he was just another entitled, arrogant chauvinist who got lucky, this time.

After she was gone, Whitman spent over an hour contemplating his future and gathering all of the handwritten notes and cards Donna had sent him over the past few months, a few of which had been sprayed with her perfume. Then he grabbed a lowball crystal glass and bottle of Weller's from the sliding door in his credenza and poured himself a triple shot of the golden bourbon. He ambled over to the suede love seat abutting a west-facing wall of windows in his corner office in the iconic skyscraper known as the IDS Center. Looking out over the city and the western suburbs, he squinted for a few moments at bright rays of the setting sun slashing through gaps in a bank of cumulus clouds. The rays disappeared over the horizon as the dark shadows of a cloudy night commandeered the sky exactly two minutes before eight. Some would have marveled at the reliability and inevitability of the earth's cycles. Whitman turned away from the window, sat on the couch, and guzzled his whiskey.

When it was gone, he flipped the glass onto the couch, grumbled, "Fuck me!" to himself, and left the office in a deep, depressed funk.

TWENTY-EIGHT

"I want to know who ruined my life, and I want to know now, you understand, Detective Barnes?" Melanie Patton was definitely awake.

Lincoln Barnes had planned to take Saturday off from the investigations of the Oscar Fawcett and Paul Barton murders, but when Sheriff MacDonald called her an hour before sunrise with the news that Melanie was awake and wanted to talk to the "authorities," she'd decided to revise that plan, especially when MacDonald added that a team from the FBI's Minneapolis office would be in Duluth by 9:00 to interview her. According to MacDonald, Melanie had suffered permanent injuries to her lungs and other internal organs and faced an uncertain road to recovery. The next two to three days would be critical, according to her doctors at St. Luke's and a specialist from the University of Minnesota. Nonetheless, once conscious she wanted answers and demanded access to her cell phone. Barnes had arrived at the hospital at 7:30. She'd met briefly with Patton's care team and immediate family, consisting of an older sister who'd flown in from San Diego and had been spending nights on a daybed in Melanie's room for nearly a week. They were all in agreement that, regardless of Melanie's wishes, Barnes should spend no more than twenty minutes with her.

"First of all, the sheriff and I want to express our condolences for the loss of your spouse. We'd certainly understand if you'd like to wait a few days before talking about this." Barnes knew Melanie would not react well to the perfunctory show of sympathy, but she also knew her boss would never dispense with it, so she would suffer the consequences.

"That's fine, but let's get on with it. What do you know?" Agitated and impatient, Melanie's voice was weak and raspy but insistent. Her skin was pale with a bluish tint that made it look translucent. Though she'd never needed to be ventilated, she was wearing a canula for oxygen support, and an IV kept her hydrated and infused with a long list of antibiotics and supplements to combat the effects of Novichok poisoning.

"We know that you and Paul Barton were poisoned," Barnes replied. "We don't think Rebecca Fawcett was involved. She was in jail from the night of the Barton celebration until last Monday night. Besides, only a few international terrorist groups and the Russian secret police and government assassins are known to have access to the kind of nerve poison that tests found in the water supply and in bottles of gin, vodka and bourbon. No one we've interviewed or researched at Barton Industries has a connection to any of the known users of chemical weapons. We're hoping that you might be aware of some relationship that Mr. Barton had to a person or organization that might have a history of using these agents as murder weapons."

"I've already covered some of this with the doctors, but you should know it too. I drank a couple of gin and tonics and some white wine on the boat and maybe a half a glass of water. P. J. drank sparkling wine and vodka tonics followed by some expensive bourbon from a bottle that had already been opened. He said he was feeling dehydrated and guzzled three or four big glasses of water, so, if that poison was in the boat's filtered water, he was totally fucked. Within twenty minutes of drinking all that water, he started vomiting. Awful, awful things happened to both of us after that and then the boat stalled, and you know the rest. They said I made an SOS call, but I don't remember doing it; I remember feeling my lungs and gut were on fire and my vision was blurry. To answer your question about foreign enemies, if P. J. had any, I didn't know about them. Barton Industries doesn't have operations in any foreign country except Canada. He may have had Russian friends from college or grad school that I didn't know about, but I doubt they had cause to kill him. He could be a royal asshole as a person, but he was a sharp businessman who learned from his father to take carefully calculated risks and to treat his employees well. Nothing and no one was more important to him than Barton Industries.

"I feel nothing but pity for Becky Fawcett. P. J. used her to get his kidney. He never intended to marry her, and then he was incensed when she and Oscar hired a lawyer and went public with their claims against him. If she had simply asked him for financial help, he would have given them a couple million, but once the lawsuit began, he became irrational. I told him to give Oscar the five million and be done with it, but for him it became a business transaction. Why should he pay the kid that kind of money before he knew whether the kidney was going to keep him alive? And, unfortunately, it didn't help that Oscar was gay. But, despite all that, I would be shocked if Becky hired a Russian assassin to poison us."

"Thanks," said Barnes. "That's all good to know. Can you think of anything else that might aid our investigation? You mentioned these killers have ruined your life. You've lost your spouse and at the very least your health has been compromised. Are there other ways your life has been ruined?"

"P. J. had controlling shares in the companies. His dad left sixty percent to him and forty percent to Amanda, so P. J. had the power to make major decisions without consulting her, though under the law he could only go so far. For the most part he shared power, letting her run parts of the company and consulting her on major changes. But when she discovered he intended to appoint me chief operating officer of Barton Industries at the next board meeting, she was furious. She has grown to detest me for sticking my nose in her businesses, criticizing her management style and recommending changes to P. J. Now, I have no doubt that she'll fire me as soon as the lawyers tell her she can."

"I don't get it," said Barnes. "Paul Barton had no children, so won't you inherit his shares?" Even before she finished asking the question, Barnes anticipated Melanie's answer.

"The Bartons are suspicious and distrustful by nature. P. J. asked me to marry him on a Sunday, and his lawyer sent me a draft of a prenup agreement on Monday morning. At first I was angry and hurt, but when your family builds a business empire, you don't want an outsider, even your wife, to take control. Don't get me wrong, I'll get a mansion, some toys and more cash than I'll ever need, but I love my job, and if Paul had lived, I'd eventually have been the CEO."

Barnes couldn't generate a lot of sympathy for Melanie's financial prospects but sadly gave her no better than a 50/50 chance to survive long enough to enjoy them. She wondered how someone who appeared to be so ill could talk so much. Even though her twenty minutes were up, she needed to know one last thing.

"So, if your husband was so quick to demand a prenup, he must have had a Will as well."

"Oh no. Jack Whitman was always badgering him to create an estate plan, but Paul never wanted to think about his death. Besides, he knew Amanda or her kids would get everything outside the prenup if he didn't have a Will, and he was fine with that."

"What about Amanda? Could she have wanted Paul dead enough to act on it?"

"As much as I loved him, P. J. was a know-it-all with a huge ego. That, coupled with his control of the companies, drove Amanda crazy. But he was her brother, the only other living Barton. In the end, she loved him too much to be involved in his murder. On the other hand, if she could have snapped her fingers and had me vaporized, she'd have happily done it."

"Okay, I get it. So, you can't think of anyone with the motive and connections to hire a professional assassin, most likely from a foreign country, to plant a very deadly chemical weapon on your boat."

Melanie was exhausted. Her eyelids fluttered as she tried to stay awake, but all she could muster was a quick sideways shake of the head.

Taking that gesture as her cue to leave, Detective Barnes gave Melanie a nod and turned toward the door.

"Except maybe Billy." It was barely audible.

"Billy?" Barnes turned back to the patient. "Billy who?" The reason Barnes moved up the ranks at the MPD so quickly had nothing to do with her gender or race. In fact, some would argue both were hindrances. It had to do with her compulsion to research every aspect of a case so she knew all the facts better than the perpetrators and her peers. She knew who Billy was.

"Amanda's husband, the biggest prick I know. A power hungry, unethical prick. His business partner is a wealthy Russian who runs a network of chiropractic clinics. I'm getting dizzy, Detective. Just check it out."

TWENTY-NINE

"It's me."

"Are you home?"

"No. I told you I needed to take care of a few things. I went to St. Paul to make sure I got paid. I have my money now."

"How much did they pay you?"

"Not for you to know. It was enough. I'm in Duluth but heading north. One more thing to do and then I'll drive to the border. Friends will meet me with boat on the Crooked Lake. In six days I'll be home and never coming back."

"That's probably a good idea given recent events."

"But you know I will come back if I don't get fair share."

"And you know I'm not totally in control of that but you will get paid."

"No need for these burner phones at home."

"I'm sure. But I don't understand what else you need to do?"

"I'll call you when I'm home."

THIRTY

With all the craziness surrounding the recent crime wave, the Lake County Attorney had decided it was the perfect time to pack up young George and spend Labor Day weekend with her baby sister, an assistant professor of English literature at the University of Wisconsin in Madison. Sheriff MacDonald would miss them, but their absence made him feel less guilty about spending most of the holiday weekend at work. He and Fred had embarked on a Saturday morning run from home to the Gitchi Gammi Trail and then up to Split Rock Lighthouse and back, about six miles in total. After the hottest summer on the North Shore in decades, a breeze off the lake and cloudy skies had combined to make it a cool, comfortable day for a brisk run, a day that made MacDonald think of fall things, like football, bonfires and pumpkin pie.

Back home, he filled Fred's water bowl and shared a skillet of bacon and cheesy scrambled eggs with his furry companion. He enjoyed his breakfast on the wicker couch on the screened-in back porch while Fred sat on the floor, patiently waiting for whatever came his way. Hallie would not have approved, but if she needed a change of scenery, maybe Fred needed a temporary change in his diet. The sheriff wondered how the Melanie Patton interview was going, so when his cell phone started buzzing in the side pocket of his running shorts, he figured it was Detective Barnes. It wasn't.

"Mr. Wilson. Calling a small-town sheriff on a Saturday; this must be important."

"Hi Mac. I'm not sure about that, but I've received some information that might be related to the multiple murders in your neighborhood, so I'm sharing what I know. You certainly had my back at the service, so I'm just trying to return the favor."

"And I appreciate it. What's up?"

"After the Larry Osgood and Paul Barton murders, the agencies started monitoring foreign wire transfer activity coming out of two Santiago, Chile, banks associated with the parent company of Tri-Metals. None of the activity was suspicious until two days ago. There was a wire in the amount of about a half-million euro that went first to a Swiss bank, and then that same amount minus a transfer fee was sent to Rossiya Bank in St. Petersburg, the bank that Putin and many former KGB have used for years to move money and hide assets. We haven't been able to track down the name of the account holder, but it's more than suspicious and to me looks like a payoff of some kind."

MacDonald's head was spinning. "Why would an international conglomerate hire a Russian assassin to take out one of their own CEOs? And while that's at least somewhat plausible, what connection did the Chileans or a Russian assassin have to Paul Barton or Barton Industries?"

"All questions Homeland and the agencies are asking," said Wilson. "For now, I'll continue to be a liaison between the FBI, CIA and local authorities. We'll concentrate on the Larry Osgood kidnapping and murder and the involvement of Tri-Metals and the Chileans. We're also working on the connection between this possible Russian assassin and the murder of the former Ivan Andropov. I think you're aware that the FBI is going to question Barton's wife, but otherwise we'll leave the investigation of the Fawcett and Barton murders to you."

This was a change in strategy, but MacDonald knew it's what Barnes wanted. "I'm good with that plan, Woody, so long as we share critical information. I know I can count on you to do that, so let's keep in touch. My detective is with Melanie Patton right now. I have a feeling we're close to discovering a link between this Russian and all of these crimes."

"Really Mac? Anything you'd like to share?"

"Just an old soldier's intuition, Woody. An old soldier's intuition."

THIRTY-ONE

Lincoln Barnes had originally planned to spend Labor Day weekend with her sister's family in St. Paul. Her sister and brother-in-law were both teachers. He was also the head boys' basketball coach for a St. Paul high school. Their two energetic young boys liked nothing better than playing baseball, soccer, basketball or anything else, including video games, with "Auntie Lee" or eating pizza and ice cream with her on a movie night. It would have been a welcome shot of sanity in Barnes's crazy life. Her sister's family was the reason her mother had moved from Chicago to St. Paul eight years ago and then had retired from her job as a flight attendant with United Airlines in July. In fact, the family would celebrate her retirement with a backyard barbeque on Sunday, but Barnes wouldn't make it, except maybe for a brief cameo via FaceTime or Zoom. When she'd accepted the Lake County job, she'd never imagined a week like this, when she'd be so wrapped up in murder investigations that a weekend trip to see family was unthinkable.

Barnes felt empty after the Melanie Patton bedside interview. Melanie looked awful. Barnes couldn't get the image of her pale, sallow face out of her mind. She'd left Sheriff MacDonald a long message summarizing their conversation and suggesting the possibility that Amanda Barton's husband, Billy Slocum, might have some foreign connections and plenty of motivation to eliminate his brother-in-law.

In an effort to improve her mood, she'd called Deputy Sams to see whether they could spend Saturday night doing something unrelated to work that would include spicy food, loud music and adult beverages. Sams and Ranger Darrow had been in Duluth when she'd called. They'd been shopping for a new king bed, but as usual they were interested in partying with Barnes. They'd agreed to meet at Darrow's home in Finland Township at 5:00 for a hike on a leg of the Superior National Forest near the Sawtooth Mountains, followed by an extended happy hour on Craig's deck, where he'd prepare pork ribs and grilled potatoes and vegetables on his pellet smoker, and then Barnes would probably spend the night in the guest bedroom. Sams had indicated they might not make it back by 5:00 and reminded Barnes of the spare key under the welcome mat.

Barnes had only been to Craig Darrow's house in the woods one other time. Fortunately, she had a sixth sense for directions and remembered how to get there from Highway 61 without the use of GPS. She was dressed in nylon sweatpants and an Illinois State Redbirds T-shirt, with Hoka trail runners and a red Nike baseball cap completing the outfit. Fearing evening temps could drop into the forties, she stuffed her Lake County windbreaker and a sweatshirt into the duffel bag she always kept in the back of the Jeep.

A city girl who'd quickly learned to appreciate many of the natural sights, creatures, smells and sounds of her new environs on the North Shore, Barnes would never get used to the biting black flies and blood-sucking mosquitos, even though their ranks tended to diminish this time of year. She'd already slathered herself with a deet-based repellent to keep them at bay.

Leaving Castle Danger at 4:15, she drove north on 61 to Beaver Bay and then headed northwest on Lax Lake Road. The forest became denser as she drove on a steady incline away from Lake Superior. Passing Lax Lake on her right, she glanced up at the picturesque Sawtooth Mountain range that framed the lake and contained some of the best hiking and Nordic ski trails in Tettegouche Park as well as the remnants of some century-old logging camps. She had fleeting yet pleasant thoughts of her North Shore adventures with the judge and, if she were honest, would have to admit that she was envious of Sams's relationship with Darrow, feeling robbed of the life she thought she'd have with Robin Gildemeister.

The farther north and east she drove the fewer homes she passed until the road came to an end where it intersected with Highway 1, also known as Voyageur Highway because it led north to Ely and the Boundary Waters wilderness. She passed over the Baptism River and through the tiny community of Finland, one of the last places in Minnesota to be settled and aptly named because many of its early inhabitants were of Finnish descent. A bar, grocery store and community center were about the only commercial establishments, and if you blinked or changed the station on your radio, you might miss it entirely.

Barnes had to drive even farther away from civilization to get to her destination. She veered right onto Lake County 7 and then left onto Airbase Road for a couple miles, silently congratulating herself for remembering the route but relieved she didn't have to drive it in the dark. The final turn was a left at Lookout Road, a recently paved asphalt road that dead-ended less than a mile into the deep woods. Darrow's place was on the east side, a winding gravel driveway lined with pine, spruce and fir trees leading to a cleared, one-acre homesite at the crest of a gradual incline with views of Lookout Lake to the west and Egge Lake to the east. The driveway ended at a detached two-car garage.

Not seeing any vehicles in the driveway, Barnes assumed Craig and Michele hadn't returned from Duluth. She parked the Jeep in a visitor parking area adjacent to the driveway and retrieved her duffel bag from the back seat. She scanned the property to see whether any changes had been made since her first visit about a month earlier. Darrow had purchased the two-story, two-bedroom house a year ago. It was supposed to be the model for a ten-home development, but the Duluth builder who came up with the idea to build homes with five-acre lots on the outskirts of nowhere in the midst of the pandemic became overextended before completing the first house, so Darrow bought it from the bank for under two hundred grand. Barnes agreed with Sams that for that price the property was a steal. The exterior consisted of slate blue cement siding with rust-colored shakes on a partial second story. There were two spacious bedrooms, two full bathrooms and a woodburning stove in the great room.

Conveniently, Darrow's older brother was a carpenter, and the two of them had built the garage and replaced the cement steps leading to the front entrance with a large front porch with charcoal composite steps and decking and a black aluminum rail. Darrow had added a stone fire pit in the backyard along with some outdoor furniture to go with his pellet grill.

Barnes walked up the steps and bent over to lift up the welcome mat to get the spare house key. When it wasn't there, she didn't think much of it and tried the front door. Unlocked. Thanks, Michele. She entered the foyer and set her duffel bag on a wooden bench sitting below a row of antique hooks. Suddenly thirsty, she walked through the great room to the kitchen and got a bottle of water out of the refrigerator. As she twisted the cap, she was startled by the sound of a heavy-footed person clumping down the steps between the upper hallway and the great room. Before she could react, he was standing in the archway between the great room and the kitchen, facing her. He wasn't much taller than she, but twice as wide. He wore a black long-sleeve T-shirt, black jeans with a black belt adorned with a silver wolf-head buckle, and black work boots. His white crew cut was mostly covered by a black ballcap with a tiny gray skull and crossbones across the front. He had a swarthy complexion with multiple pock marks on his cheeks and a raised purple scar on his neck running from just below his right ear to his Adam's apple. Barnes was struck by the sheer size of his ears and long nose as well as the thickness of his hands and fingers. But, more than anything else, she was bewildered by his presence and on edge because of the menacing look in his big gray, bloodshot eyes.

"Who are you?" she asked. "And what are you doing in Craig Darrow's house?"

As soon as she asked the questions, Craig Darrow's description of the man getting into the Mercedes sedan near Fall Lake and Deputy Hokanen's description of the man in the video stealing the truck that killed Oscar Fawcett flashed across her cerebral cortex: *A huge man dressed in black.*

"You fucking bitch!" the man bellowed in a bass register, spit spewing from his lips and distracting her momentarily from seeing the motion of his right arm reaching behind his back to grab a black-handled weapon with a silver blade, perhaps a machete, that had been sheathed somehow across his wide ass.

Her Glock, resting in a holster in the glove compartment of the Jeep, wouldn't do her much good now. Standing her ground against this armed behemoth was suicide. Her only chance was to run. She threw her bottle of water in his face, turned away from the bear of a man and scurried through a laundry room to the back door. By the time she unlocked and opened it, she could hear him cursing in a foreign language. She leaped off the back porch and ran toward the woods, afraid he would have a better chance of catching her if she stayed in the open and made a run for the front yard and the Jeep. She was fast and in good shape. There was no way this old man could keep up with her in the forest.

She took her phone from a front pocket of her pants and hit the speed dial for Sams while picking her way through the dense woods. Using the sun in the western sky as her guide, she couldn't decide whether to head east toward Egge Lake or south and then west to get back to a public road. Sams didn't answer, so she left a message.

Michele, hope you're close to home. There was an intruder in the house. Huge guy dressed in black with a machete. He's after me now. I'm unarmed, trying to pick my way through the woods. Heading south, I think. Gotta go.

Barnes was moving as fast as she could, brushing and banging her limbs against branches and nearly tripping on tree roots and raised vegetation. Stopping for a moment to gauge the progress of her pursuer, she was stunned. He appeared to be running through, not around the brush and small trees and was closing the gap between them. How could he keep up with her?

She needed to alter her course and get out of the forest. This beast of a man clearly had an advantage in the dense woods, but if she could find a road or trail, her speed might save her. Locating the sun again through the trees behind a bank of white clouds, she decided to head due west and ran toward the light. She was getting acclimated to darting quickly through narrow openings between the trees and high stepping as much as she could to avoid unseen hazards growing up from the ground. But he continued to stay with her, to track her down like a grizzly bear chasing a fawn. Though it may have been her imagination, she thought she could hear him huff and grunt as he bore down upon her.

Hearing the familiar growl of a semi-tractor re-energized her. But then she made the mistake of looking up momentarily, taking her eyes off the terrain to peer into the distance searching for the road. She tripped on a poplar root and fell hard onto a downed birch tree, hitting an elbow first and skidding along the uneven ground. She knew she had to get up and run, but she also felt a combination of fear, hostility, and doom. He was on her before she could even get to her knees, over two hundred forty pounds pouncing on top of her, pinning her shoulders to the ground with his hands and then keeping them there with his knees.

"Now I got you, you fucking bitch!" he yelped with a thick Russian accent between heaving breaths that were as foul as the stench of his sweat.

"Get off me you pig!" Barnes screamed, struggling with every fiber of every muscle to extricate herself but quickly comprehending her fate.

Instinctively, she covered the back of her neck with her hands as her assailant unsheathed his razor sharp weapon.

"Keep hands there and I'll slice your fingers off with your fucking head!" he bellowed as he raised the machete high above his head.

In disbelief of the horrifying turn of events but anticipating the inescapable pain and finality of this monster's hand-held guillotine, Barnes instead heard the familiar sound of a Glock 22 firing multiple rounds followed by her captor's tumbling off her back with a thud, deathly still and bleeding from multiple wounds to the head, his weapon now impotent between his legs. In disbelief again, Barnes looked up and to her right and left, and then she actually managed a crooked little smile.

Sams.

PART II

It was this day that her life changed. And not because of a man or a job, but because she realized that life is way too short to leave the key to your happiness in someone else's pocket.

—Unknown

THIRTY-TWO

It was Saturday night on a holiday weekend, and if Mickey were honest, he'd have to admit he was lonely, a condition he'd endured for the last three or four years, mostly because of the unshakable shame and embarrassment he associated with his criminal record. He thought about calling his sister to let her know he was sitting in his new home in St. Paul, less than ten miles from her place in South Minneapolis, but he wasn't quite ready for that. He'd start his new job in a few days, but tonight he had far different matters on his mind. At least he had Roger, who was asleep next to him on a blue suede couch, snoring softly.

Thoughts of his mother and the events that led to her death and his incarceration haunted him, despite his ongoing efforts to block them out and move on with his life. His childhood had been tumultuous, mostly because of his stepfather.

Raymond Rossi was the grandson of Italian immigrants who escaped fascist Italy and settled in Schenectady, New York, in the 1930s. His grandfather was a laborer for a home builder, and his father started his own home remodeling business in Albany, which Raymond inherited at the age of thirty after his dad died of a massive coronary. Thanks to his father's guidance and a business degree from a community college, Raymond became a capable contractor who managed his father's successful business well enough to increase its customer base and revenue for a handful of years. Unfortunately, his volatile temper, abusive personality and addiction to alcohol all contributed to the eventual alienation of his family and disintegration of his business.

Raymond married the daughter of one of his project managers shortly after his father's death, but she divorced him six months later, alleging verbal and physical abuse. A trip to Boston to attend a home show didn't help his business much but forever changed his life. He had dinner and several drinks with a couple of his employees at a sports bar near Cambridge and became infatuated with their attractive young server. So infatuated that he gave her a five hundred dollar tip and asked her out. Under six feet tall, Raymond was stocky, muscular, and not unattractive. With olive skin, curly black hair, a neatly trimmed black beard and straight white teeth under a Roman nose, he looked like a tough guy—a union boss, a shop foreman or a small business owner, which is what he was.

He was pleasantly surprised when the server agreed to have dinner with him, and even more surprised when she agreed to marry him near the end of a whirlwind ten days of dinners, movies, concerts and lots of sex. He may have exaggerated the size of his business, the beauty of his house in Schenectady and his net worth, but he didn't need to; Elena Krasikova needed him as much as he wanted her. She was nine weeks' pregnant, and her student visa would expire in May. She couldn't go back to Russia or, heaven forbid, Kazakhstan, where her mother now lived with her stepfather. Raymond knew none of this until he told her he loved her and wanted to get married. She knew she couldn't hide the pregnancy for long, so in response to his proposal she disclosed her condition while sobbing, saying the father had abandoned her and demanded she get an abortion; that she wanted nothing to do with him but would not end the pregnancy under any circumstances.

Blinded by Elena's beauty, Raymond regarded himself as her white knight, her savior, even though he'd told his first wife he didn't want kids. Amazingly, they were married for ten years. Elena became a U.S. citizen, earned a degree in marketing at SUNY Albany, and became the office manager for a temp agency in the Capitol District. She was also the primary nurturer and caretaker of her two children, Mikhail, born six months after their marriage and never adopted by Raymond, and Donna Rae, born two years later.

Raymond curtailed his drinking for a while, and, though he never developed an interest in being a parent, his love for Elena never wavered. Though she was never in love with him, she appreciated him and was grateful for the family life and opportunities she had in upstate New York. He on the other hand was insanely jealous of her and seethed inside whenever he saw her talking to another man.

Elena had worked part-time as a hostess in a classic downtown steakhouse in Albany while taking classes at SUNY. Even though the extra income was appreciated, once Elena graduated and started working full time, Raymond started drinking heavily and demanded to know her whereabouts at all times as well as the identity of each of her colleagues and friends. When she refused to comply with his unreasonable rules, the abuse began. From locking her in their bedroom to beating her with either a belt or a closed fist, Raymond devolved into an irrational, drunken monster. The children were nine and seven when Elena moved out and took them with her. She rented a condo in Delmar, got an order for protection against Raymond and retained a family lawyer to assist her in ending the marriage and preserving her family. Afraid to use her maiden name for fear that her family in Russia would find her, she changed the surname of Mickey and herself to Kaye. She wanted to change Donna Rae's name as well, but since she was Raymond's child, Elena was too afraid of his reaction to do it.

Raymond's personal and professional lives moved in tandem in a downward spiral. He neglected his business, didn't contest Elena's divorce petition and was arrested and convicted of driving under the influence. He was forced to file personal bankruptcy and to move in with his mother in Schenectady. He started seeking handyman jobs for cash to avoid paying child support and never visited the kids, who were both afraid of him, especially when he was drinking. But one thing never changed—Raymond's obsession with Elena. He sent her letters, presents, cards, flowers and called her several times a week begging for forgiveness and asking for another chance. Elena did not date or have male friends after divorcing Raymond because she was afraid of his reaction. When Raymond's mother died after a bout with pneumonia a week before Christmas in 2019, his only connection to reality was gone. He followed Elena home from Christmas Eve services at a Catholic

Church in Albany and accosted her as she was unlocking the front door of her townhome. It would be their last argument.

When Mickey came home early from Cabo and arrived on the scene to surprise his mom on Christmas Eve, he was the one who was surprised. His mother was face-up, sprawled on the tiled entryway. She'd nearly been decapitated, blood still oozing from her neck, arms and torso. Raymond was on his knees in the middle of the bloody mess. He was delirious, crying and telling Elena how much he still loved her, a bloody oversize butcher knife on the floor between them.

Elena had been everything to Mickey and his sister, creating a safe, happy and loving family life as a single mother and constantly stressing hard work and education as the only path to a successful life. Mickey's brain exploded with a combination of unfathomable grief and uncontrollable rage. In hindsight, he understood he should have called 9-1-1 immediately. Instead, he reflexively picked up the knife and slashed Raymond across the throat. Then he called 9-1-1.

Raymond survived the slashing but faced a first degree murder charge. Mickey was charged with attempted murder and assault with a deadly weapon. His sister, in her first year of law school, urged him to hire a top defense lawyer and fight the charges. Mickey deeply regretted his violent act within seconds of committing it. He believed he deserved to be punished for his actions. He retained a young lawyer who was a college friend to negotiate a plea with the district attorney. She arranged for him to plead guilty to the assault charge in exchange for the state dismissing the attempted murder charge and recommending a sentence of no longer than three years. His sister was irate; she'd never been close to her father—in fact, she had grown to despise him. She insisted that, given the circumstances, three years in prison was an unfairly high price to pay for lashing out at the man who had violently murdered their mother.

Raymond never stood trial for Elena's murder. On the morning of his arraignment, a month after the murder, he was handcuffed, being escorted from the back of a squad car to the courthouse, when a stolen yellow Freightliner dump truck traveling fifty miles an hour on Columbia Street ran a red light and literally flattened Raymond and the unfortunate officer next to him. The truck was abandoned less than a mile from the courthouse. The driver was never identified.

Mickey read and re-read Paul Barton's obituary in the online edition of the *Star Tribune*. It was nearly two columns long and recited all of the accomplishments of a man who was the chairman, chief executive officer and principal shareholder of Barton Industries, a holding company that controlled billions in assets, including convenience stores, local newspapers and an investment management firm. The paper said Barton was survived by his wife, Melanie, a sister, Amanda Barton, and her spouse William Slocum, and a niece and nephew. Mickey knew most of this. He'd had plenty of time to do research on Barton during his time in prison, and these days there was a surplus of financial, business and even personal information on a guy like Barton in *Forbes*, *Bloomberg*, and the *Wall Street Journal*.

Mickey grabbed an Axe Man IPA from the fridge and sat at a compact mahogany secretary that was the nicest piece in the furnished apartment. He unlocked an old leather briefcase that he'd placed on the desk earlier in the day and removed a manila file labeled *Barton Letter*. When he was eighteen and preparing to leave for college, Elena finally provided answers to questions he'd been asking since he was ten. She explained why she left St. Petersburg, Russia, twenty years earlier and could never return. She told him about her parents—her father, who was a Soviet military officer who'd died fighting in Afghanistan when she was twelve, and her mother, who then married one of his three brothers, all of whom were KGB and, according to Elena, not to be trusted.

Elena's older brother was also in the Russian military and had been an outspoken critic of Gorbachev and Perestroika. But the most important disclosure on that day was the identity of Mickey's father. Elena told her son about her relationship with Paul Barton Jr., the man who unquestionably was his father and, in her opinion, a coward, and about how his grandfather, Paul Barton Senior, had threatened to have her deported if she didn't end her pregnancy.

According to Elena, Paul Senior was a self-made man and an arrogant, sexist bully. On his own, he drafted a letter agreement and presented it to her along with his personal check for a hundred thousand dollars. She accepted the letter and the check because she could never, ever return to Russia, but she assured her son that she'd never intended to get an abortion. Barton had someone follow her in a car on the day of her appointment at the Planned Parenthood clinic, but he left as soon as she entered the building and, fortunately for her, the clinic refused to divulge any information about the status of her pregnancy after her visit. Two weeks later Elena met Raymond Rossi, and she'd not had any contact with the Bartons since. She told Mickey that Paul Senior was long dead and that it was up to him whether he ever wanted to contact his father. In any event, she thought he should have the original letter, which he now pulled from the file and read once again, but this time it had new meaning.

March 16, 1992

Dear Elena Krasikova:

As you know I am the father of Paul Barton Jr. Paul has told me about his relationship with you and the predicament (his description) the two of you have created. I can't tell you how disappointed I am that you have jeopardized my son's future (and yours as well) by not taking appropriate precautions given your precarious status in this country. I will give you the benefit of the doubt that you didn't intentionally become pregnant to trap my son and guarantee citizenship for you and your child.

I am not going to mince words or negotiate with you. I am offering you $100,000. In exchange for this payment, you will terminate your pregnancy and will share with my office the time and place of your medical appointment. I believe it's in your best interest at this point to take these funds and return to your home in Russia, but that's not a condition of this payment. However, there is a second condition of giving you this money: you must never contact my son or anyone in my family at any time in the future and never tell anyone about this transaction. If you do, I promise you, the consequences will be severe.

My personal check made payable to you is enclosed with this letter. By cashing it, you agree to abide by the terms set forth above. Unlike my son, Elena, I am not someone to be manipulated or deceived. Please don't test me.

Paul Barton

Mickey had been contemplating whether to contact his birth father since the death of his mother and his release from prison. Elena hadn't told him much about P. J. Barton, but any man who would abandon someone as vulnerable as his pregnant mother and hide behind the wealth and power of his father must have been as bereft of character as his stepfather, a man who'd often told Mickey that he'd "married your mother, not you."

When Elena had disclosed the identity of Mickey's father, she'd also given both Mickey and his half-sister a brief history of her family in Russia, including the dark, evil résumé of her older brother. Unlike Mickey, his sister was fascinated by the sordid past of the Krasikova family, and at one time had confided in him that she intended to contact them and hoped to visit them in Russia. She also changed her surname from Rossi to Morgan when Mickey was in prison. He had no idea why she picked that name, but her effort to disassociate from her father's name and memory did not surprise him, though her fascination with Elena's Russian family did.

Part of him wanted to destroy the letter and move on with his life without the legal complications and messiness of establishing his birthright and entitlement to a piece of the Barton fortune. But whenever he thought about Elena's struggles to create a decent life for herself and her children, her willingness to marry a man she didn't love to ensure a life in the States for the two of them, and her brutal murder at the hands of a sociopath, he knew what he had to do. For him, vengeance might be the only path to peace. He would contact Donna. She would be only too happy to help him.

THIRTY-THREE

It took Detective Barnes a minute to get to her feet after nearly losing her head. "Jesus Christ, Michele, I'm still shaking. Holy shit. Nice shooting. I owe you my life, woman."

Deputy Sams gave Barnes a one-armed hug while keeping an eye on the man in black, the man she'd put down with three to the head. She knelt next to his body, tossed his weapon beyond his reach and checked his vitals, though the closer she got, the more certain she was of his status.

"Definitely dead," she said. "I don't want to touch the fucker any more than necessary."

Ranger Darrow thrashed his way onto the scene from the south, he and Sams having split up to cover more ground. Unlike Sams, he had no weapon other than a five iron he'd pulled from his golf bag.

"I heard shots," he exclaimed, out of breath but relieved to see the two women standing. "You two okay?"

"We're good," said Sams. "He's not so good," she added nodding toward the prostrate body on the forest floor.

"That's one big, ugly man," Darrow said. "I guess I missed all the action."

"Lincoln's lucky you did," said Sams, picking up the machete. "That golf club may not have stopped this animal from using this. I guess we're all lucky that my Glock was in your glove box on an off-duty Saturday."

"Hey, we need to call Mac and try to get some ID on this guy," said Barnes. "I have a feeling he's not from around here."

"You're right, but are you sure you're okay to be a part of this? You might need some professional help to deal with what just went down, my friend."

"We both might, but that will have to wait. I've got some latex in the Jeep. Craig, maybe you could walk up the road past your place to search for this guy's vehicle. Let's photograph and bag everything in it. Michele, I'll take some photos of my new friend if you want to make the calls."

"You're sure about all this."

"I'm sure."

"What do you think this guy was after in our house?" asked Darrow, leading them out of the woods to his truck parked on the shoulder of Lookout Road.

"Does he look familiar to you?" asked Barnes.

"Yeah, he's the guy I saw at Fall Lake."

"I think he knew you'd made him and didn't like it. He was planning to use that barbaric weapon to eliminate the only person that he thought got a good look at him."

Darrow rubbed his throat with his hand.

"I think we might be even on the life-saving score," said Sams.

THIRTY-FOUR

Donna Morgan would start her new job as a deputy U.S. attorney in the civil division in Minneapolis in eight days. Fortunately for her, the head of that division was a graduate of Georgetown Law School and had just left her apartment on Fremont Avenue South after spending a Saturday evening enjoying Donna's homemade spaghetti marinara, sharing a couple of bottles of Brunello di Montalcino and swapping bodily fluids and other carnal delights. Though Donna preferred that her guests leave before sunrise, she felt this one deserved special treatment, so she even made some Turkish coffee and served him fresh strawberries and egg bagels for breakfast. He was ten years her senior, recently divorced and not really her type, but she needed additional leverage to protect herself in case things didn't work out as planned, not to mention a steady source of income now that she'd quit her job at Cooper Harding.

She'd been relieved to get a message from her brother earlier this morning. She'd been paying a former boyfriend to keep tabs on him in upstate New York, so she already knew he'd quit his job in Schenectady and accepted an emergency tech position in St. Paul. Her brother was highly intelligent and the kindest person she knew, but he was like their mother, totally guileless, even after spending nearly three years in prison for trying to avenge Elena's savage murder at the hands of a man she'd despised with every fiber of her being.

What she hadn't known was whether Mikhail, or Mickey as he preferred to be called, would be interested in pursuing his rightful inheritance from Paul Barton Jr. Donna knew a lot more about the priority, validity and value of Mickey's claim against his birth father's estate than she could admit, at least for now. She'd always had the utmost confidence that, even if Mickey were reluctant to make the claim, she could ultimately convince him to do it. She'd spent the past few years of her life executing a plan that counted on it.

Mickey didn't like texting; he didn't trust the security of any transmission that relied on the World Wide Web. He'd left her a short voice message requesting the name of a competent probate lawyer. She'd already researched all of the usual suspects and could provide her brother with the names of the best and brightest, but she believed the optimum strategy would be to retain a lawyer familiar with Lake County and, even better, a lawyer who had added incentive to ensure that his claim was successful. Perhaps the lawyer who was not only representing a woman who hated P. J. Barton so much she'd tried to kill him, but who was also sleeping with that woman. She'd give Mickey the contact information for Charlie Fallon. Then she'd wait for the shit to hit the fan.

THIRTY-FIVE

Sheriff Sam MacDonald sat in his office in the Lake County Law Enforcement Center and sipped cold vending machine coffee from a paper cup. It wasn't quite 7:00 on a cool, cloudy Sunday morning, and he'd been up all night. He was worried about his two most talented employees, Barnes and Sams. He was all too familiar with the emotional and psychological trauma that can haunt anyone, whether law enforcement or victim, involved in a violent crime. He had to order them to take a few days off. He'd ensure they'd get professional help, but he knew they'd both resist accepting it.

He'd texted Woody Wilson at 2:00 this morning, 3:00 Woody's time, so he wasn't surprised to see his number displayed on his cell phone.

"Good morning, Mr. Wilson. I hope I haven't ruined your Sunday."

"We just do what the job requires, right Mac? Your text said you had information that might be vital to the feds. I know how good you are at saying a lot by saying almost nothing."

MacDonald told Wilson about the man in black lying in wait in Ranger Darrow's home in rural Lake County and about his pursuit of an unarmed Lincoln Barnes with a machete.

"I believe this guy is a professional killer," said MacDonald. "He appears to be in his early sixties, about six feet, two inches tall and two hundred fifty pounds, but very well-muscled, not obese. Barnes is a triathlete and very fast, and this guy closed on her in deep woods, basically running through what she had to run around. But for Deputy Sams and Ranger Darrow arriving on the scene, Barnes would have been a very unsightly murder victim and the man in black would have been in Canada and, ultimately, back in Mother Russia."

"So, Darrow shot him? I didn't think rangers carried firearms."

"They don't and he didn't. Sams is the best shot in my office, and it's not close. She put one in his temple and two in his neck with her service Glock from about twenty-five yards."

"Wow. Where do you find these people, Mac?"

"She's half Ojibwe with a Ph.D. in psychology and incredible instincts for the job, not to mention special levels of compassion and empathy, but it's tough to overcome bigotry sometimes. I'm lucky to have her."

"What else have you learned about this guy? Any confirmation that he's Russian?"

"He didn't leave us with much in the way of evidence. A stolen pickup truck, a rucksack filled with black clothing, a shaving kit, a burner phone, and a Russian passport with the name Ivan Serov and an address in Kazan, but I'm sure that's not his real name or address. In his pockets we found a money clip with a couple grand U.S., a mini-legal pad with directions to Crooked Lake on the Canadian border and a name and number that we've traced to the Russian embassy in Ottawa. I'll send you an encrypted message with the details. And you'll love this: He had a mini silver PSS silent pistol in a sleeve inside the cuff of his black jeans. That's a real blast from the past."

"You mean one of those sealed cartridge, double-action jobs?"

"That's right. Putin probably still carries one in the vest of his suit."

"Any evidence related to the nerve gas or chemical containers?

"Nothing on him or in the truck," said MacDonald, "but he must have been staying in this area for a few weeks, so there might be more in a motel room, abandoned cabin or who knows where."

"And at this point what local mayhem are you attributing to him?" asked Wilson.

"We had a long discussion about that at Darrow's house when I was fully awake. It's conceivable, even probable, that the man in black is responsible for the deaths of Larry Osgood, Paul Barton, Ivan Andropov, and Oscar Fawcett."

"Oscar Fawcett?"

"Yeah. He's the young man who gave Paul Barton one of his kidneys a few years ago when his mother was engaged to Barton," said MacDonald. "He was supposed to get five million if they both survived until right about now. Didn't I tell you about that?"

"Right, right. The jilted mom tried to shoot Barton because she was convinced he was the killer. But Mac, what connection could there possibly have been between whoever this Russian killer is and Fawcett and Barton? You think Barton could have hired him to kill Fawcett, make it look like an accident?"

"It's possible, but that's a lot of trouble to go to, not to mention expense, just to save five million bucks, especially for a guy with Barton's money."

"Maybe Barton refused to pay him and the Russian deployed the nerve gas in retaliation,"

"That's funny. That was Detective Barnes's theory last night."

"Wait a minute. You said this guy always dresses in black, right?"

"As far as we can tell. Pants, shirts, jackets, hats, even underwear, all black."

"Oh my god, Mac, I think we're going to need to bring the CIA into this and maybe even the State Department."

"And that is because?" asked MacDonald, getting up from his desk in search of more bad coffee.

"Why do you think this guy was hiding in Ranger Darrow's house last night instead of driving up to Canada to meet his pals?" Wilson asked.

"Because he believed that Darrow got a good look at his face and could ID him."

"But in reality that ID would be worthless once he left the country, and certainly once he returned to Russia."

"I don't deny that. Especially given our current relationship with Moscow and the war in Ukraine. But you think you know who this is, don't you?" MacDonald lifted the plastic door on the vending machine in the cafeteria and grabbed the steaming paper cup of nasty but caffeinated liquid. He took a quick sip and nearly spit it out.

"When I worked at State five years ago, we had a team that worked with the CIA researching the targeted killings carried out by former

KGB officers who were then with the FSB. Several of these assassinations outside Russia involved some type of chemical agent or nerve gas, and many were allegedly committed by a guy who the CIA called the Ghost. In fact, I think that's what Putin named him. Anyway, he was always dressed in black, but no one on our side knew his name or ever got a good enough look at his face to photograph or identify him. The story was that he was Putin's favorite hit man and that his only weakness was a lust for money. Apparently, Putin gave him a long leash in terms of doing private kills for hire in Europe and even South America. He had a knack for getting the job done and leaving no trace behind. He'd be in his early sixties by now, so your killer certainly fits his profile."

"His body is in the morgue at St. Luke's. About an hour ago I gave your friends at the FBI in Duluth a heads-up on what we've found, though I think I might have been talking to the night janitor. I assume someone in your world will be interested in his DNA, body markings, dental work, etc., to provide information to the Russian embassies in both D.C. and Ottawa."

"If this is who I think it is, Moscow will want the body ASAP but won't want to give us an accurate ID," said Wilson. "I'm sure we'll condition his return on proof of identity."

"Of course," MacDonald agreed, pouring the horrible liquid in the cafeteria sink and resolving either to head out to a coffee shop or go home and make a fresh pot of Italian roast. "Once the press gets wind of this guy's killing spree and presumed nationality, they might do some of the legwork for you. From the perspective of the Lake County Sheriff's office, our investigation might be close to complete on the Oscar Fawcett and Paul Barton murders, though we're still interested in why a Russian national with no known connection to the victims was involved. The feds have taken jurisdiction of the other two cases."

"What about Barton's wife?" asked Wilson. "The FBI agents who interviewed her say the only lead she gave them was a Russian businessman who worked with her brother-in-law, a guy named Slocum. Could that be a connection?"

"That's the same story Lincoln Barnes got from her. Lincoln will follow up, but it's likely a dead end. Slocum's a big-time ambulance chaser, and my guess is this so-called businessman is nothing more than a referral source for personal injury cases. Barnes said Melanie detests Slocum's wife, Amanda Barton. She's Paul Barton's sister and stands to inherit everything outside of about thirty million in cash and property going to Melanie under a prenup."

"Thirty million. My sympathies to Melanie, although she might not be well enough to enjoy it. Thanks for the update, Mac. This case won't be handled by anyone local going forward. I'm thinking a trip to Minnesota with D.C. personnel from the agencies is in my future. In the meantime, if you uncover anything else that might be of interest, you can call my cell at any time."

"Roger that. It will be good to see you again in person, Woody, in spite of the circumstances."

MacDonald had received two voice messages during his call with Wilson. The first was from a reporter at the *Star Tribune* who wanted to interview him about the Larry Osgood murder. Apparently, there was a story in *El Mercurio*, the largest print and online newspaper in Santiago, Chile, reporting that Tri-Metals' parent company had terminated its director of security because of his alleged involvement in the Osgood kidnapping and murder. The fact that someone related to Tri-Metals staged the kidnapping did not surprise MacDonald. That they'd arrange for the murder of their own seemed a bit bizarre.

The second message was from his friend Dr. Higgins from Midwest Medical Examiners.

Melanie Patton Barton was dead.

Lincoln Barnes opened her eyes and stared at the lighted digits on the clock radio on the nightstand. She couldn't remember the last time she'd woken up at 1:25 in the afternoon. She'd taken a couple of Xanax at 8:30 in the morning to calm her nerves and allow her to get at least a couple of hours of sleep before she had to relive the events from the night before in the Finland woods. She also couldn't remember a more menacing human being than the monster who'd pursued her and nearly broke her back before Michele had blasted him back to a Stone Age Hell, where he belonged for eternity.

After the paramedics had picked up the ghastly body, and she and her colleagues from Lake County had discussed the evidence they'd gathered at an impromptu meeting at Darrow's place, Sheriff

MacDonald could go home to Hallie and George, and Michele and Craig could talk things out and salve each other's emotional wounds. But, as usual, Barnes was alone, which was fine with her most of the time, but not today. She sat on the edge of a king bed in the former home of the former judge known at times as Robin and at other times as J. R. But by any name, she wished the man she thought she knew was sitting next to her now. In the long run, she didn't want his perfect cottage without him, or at least without knowing the truth about him. Why did he feel compelled to run and hide rather than explain the contents of that diary? Because he was guilty of murder? She couldn't live in this house and simply forget about him. She needed to confront him. As soon as she could take a week off—not anytime soon, she feared—she would head to Madeline Island and track him down. She was savvy enough to know that anyone, everyone was capable of murder. But she didn't really believe it.

She grabbed her cell phone from the nightstand and a sweatshirt from a dresser and padded down the stairs in her bare feet. This would be her first autumn on the North Shore, where the weather could change dramatically by the hour. Looking out the sliding glass doors in the great room, she saw no trace of the sun, nothing but puffy gray and white clouds moving quickly from left to right across the afternoon sky. A typical northeast wind was shaking branches of the birch and aspens that dotted the backyard. She pulled the sweatshirt over the tee and gym shorts that were her customary nightclothes, made herself a cup of French roast on her Keurig and slathered the halves of a toasted English muffin with peanut butter. Carrying a plate of food that also included a honey crisp apple in one hand and her coffee mug in the other, she used her elbow to open the unlocked slider that led to the deck overlooking the sloping backyard and the endless lake. She figured the temp was low sixties at best, so she was comfortable in the cotton sweatshirt as she set her mug and plate on the arm of one of the two ancient Adirondack chairs that the judge's grandmother had purchased thirty years ago. She retrieved her phone from a side pocket of her shorts before sitting down to enjoy a late breakfast and a view that included occasional whitecaps atop the green-hued waves of Lake Superior and a lone osprey making repeated unsuccessful dives for a lunch of whitefish or salmon. She wondered whether she could really give this place up. Her reverie was disturbed by a single ding of her phone, signaling a text message. It was from her sister.

Just making sure you'll be able to FaceTime us for mom's party this afternoon, maybe about 4? Hope you're safe up there in the wilds!! Love you. Wanda.

She was thankful for the text, as she'd completely forgotten about the soiree Wanda was hosting for their mom, retiring from United Airlines after more than forty years as a flight attendant. Before she put the phone down, she noticed there was a voice message from Sheriff MacDonald, which really surprised her, given his strict orders to get some rest and not think about work today. The message was short and to the point.

"Melanie Patton is dead. We'll talk tomorrow."

THIRTY-SIX

Melanie Patton Barton died early Sunday morning. Despite the administration of atropine, lorazepam and other potential antidotes by her medical team, the level of poison in her system was much higher than the toxicologists had originally estimated based on her symptoms and other documented cases. Her respiratory system started failing early Saturday night, and shortly after midnight she had a fatal heart attack, but in reality she suffocated first and then her heart gave out. Her death was front page news in the Labor Day editions of the *Duluth Tribune* and the Minneapolis *Star Tribune*. But the front page headline in those papers as well as in every major newspaper in the U.S. from the *Los Angeles Times* to the *Washington Post* went something like this:

RUSSIAN SPY MAY BE RESPONSIBLE FOR MULTIPLE MURDERS IN MINNESOTA

The original article was written by two well-known reporters on the international desk at the *New York Times.* Information about the Oscar Fawcett murder and Larry Osgood kidnapping was readily accessible, but this article referenced a reliable source at Homeland Security for detailed and mostly accurate facts about Osgood's slaying, Ivan Andropov's murder at a rest stop and background as a KGB agent, and the suspected poisoning of billionaire Paul Barton Jr. and his spouse

Melanie, now dead as well. Only a handful of people knew anything about the hulking Russian man in black or the rare and deadly use of a Novichok nerve agent on Barton's boat. But now it was all in print, across the newswires, online, on network and cable news channels and, of course, misquoted and misinterpreted on social media. It was all out there except for the identity of the off-duty peace officer who shot and killed the Russian in self-defense. That fact, if known by the journalists, was omitted.

After an early morning run on the Gitchi Gammi Trail with Fred, Sheriff MacDonald made a pot of strong coffee and sat in his screened-in porch to enjoy his customary morning ritual—reading the *Star Tribune* and *Wall Street Journal* online editions on his iPad. After a crazy weekend, he'd planned to spend Labor Day at home watching the Twins and deep cleaning the kitchen and master bathroom, since he was primarily responsible for anything disgusting in both. Then he'd make a pan of vegetable lasagna, one of his two culinary specialties, to have with a bottle of Sangiovese for dinner when Hallie and George returned from Madison.

When he saw the headline in the *Star Tribune,* he was in semi-shock, but that reaction quickly turned to anger when he read the article that was attributed to the *New York Times*. He knew that neither Barnes nor Sams would have shared any of these details with a reporter without talking to him first, and no one else on his staff or the FBI knew all of the facts from all four of the cases. In fact, other than MacDonald himself, only one other person was privy to all of the mostly accurate details contained in the article. That person was Woodrow B. Wilson, who, MacDonald concluded, must be the "reliable source at Homeland Security." The sheriff believed his former colleague must have had a good reason for divulging everything about these cases to the world; he just wished Woody would have given him a little advance notice and maybe the rationale as well.

After checking in with Barnes and Sams, neither of whom had read the article or knew anything about it, MacDonald tried to call Wilson. When there was no answer, he left a brief message:

"Hey Woody, it's Mac. You must have a very good friend at the *Times*. Call me."

THIRTY-SEVEN

Mickey had done his own research on Charlie Fallon before he'd called him on Sunday afternoon. Fallon's credentials as a lawyer and jurist were impressive. He'd retired as a federal judge after his beautiful young second wife, also a lawyer, had been murdered. Thereafter, Fallon had been acquitted of killing his former law partner, an overly ambitious narcissist who'd been having an affair with his wife. Apparently, Fallon had discovered irrefutable evidence that he'd killed her to cover up a laundry list of misdeeds, so, after a friendly game of golf and dinner with friends, Fallon had bashed his head in with a driver and dumped his body in the exact same spot in the Gooseberry River where his wife's lifeless body had been discovered.

Mickey wondered how one man who'd literally taken justice into his own hands had been acquitted, whereas another man who'd merely made an unsuccessful attempt had spent thirty months in prison. Regardless, he could work with an accomplished lawyer and respected judge who appreciated the fine distinction between justice and pure vengeance.

Mickey's first day at the new job was Tuesday, and Fallon lived in Grand Marais. He'd made the call late in the day in hopes of avoiding voicemail. The former judge had picked up after the first ring.

Fallon had been spending the long weekend with Becky Fawcett in

Silver Bay. He was intrigued after hearing about Elena's relationship with P. J Barton and tragic marriage to Raymond Rossi. He was hooked when Mickey read him the threatening letter from Paul Barton, Sr. He'd agreed to drive down to Tobie's Restaurant in Hinckley, the well-known halfway point between Duluth and the Twin Cities, on Labor Day to meet with Mickey, but only if they could meet at 7:00 in the morning or earlier and he could bring Becky. Mickey had no problem with either condition.

Looking out at the parking lot from the entryway at Tobie's, Mickey watched a black later-model Audi S7 turn into the lot and park next to his truck. He recognized the man who emerged from the driver's door from photos in online newspaper articles and a federal judicial website as Charlie Fallon. A big man, at least six-three with broad shoulders, he looked thinner and older than he did in photos from five to ten years earlier. Dressed in a navy cotton crew neck sweater over tan khakis, Fallon was carrying a leather portfolio. His thick, bushy hair had turned completely white, and he sported a trimmed white goatee. Mickey figured his companion, a compact, handsome woman wearing a maroon windbreaker over white jeans and taking her boyfriend's hand in hers as soon as she could, was at least fifteen years younger than Fallon. He opened the door for them with a welcoming smile.

"Hi, I'm Mickey Kaye," he said, extending his right hand and shaking each of theirs. "Thanks for meeting me on a holiday."

"Of course," said Fallon. "At this stage of my life and what's left of my career, I'm only interested in unique and compelling legal matters. I think your case fits that description. Besides, Becky wanted to meet Paul Barton's son." Mickey hadn't known anything about his birth father's kidney transplant or Becky Fawcett's relationship with him until he'd read an account of Becky's attempt to shoot Barton in the *Times*.

"Well, Becky, I hope I don't disappoint you. One of the reasons I moved out here was to meet my father, a man who didn't even know I existed. I had no idea he'd be dead before I got here."

Becky visually assessed the young man who was maybe five years older than Oscar. He wore an unzipped cotton jacket over a powder blue oxford cloth shirt and black pants. A few inches shorter than

Fallon, he had a tapered, muscular frame and was much better looking than his father, with expressive brown eyes and neatly trimmed black hair. He reminded her of a young Sean Connery.

Labor Day was "seat yourselves" day at Tobie's, so Mickey found a booth in a back corner for privacy even though there weren't ten customers in the place. The three made small talk over coffee about Mickey's new job, Fallon's bike shop in Grand Marais, and unusually hot summers in both northern Minnesota and upstate New York. Once breakfast was served, the Eye Opener for Becky and the Northwoods Walleye Breakfast for Fallon and Mickey, Fallon opened his portfolio and started asking Mickey questions about his mother, his family and his childhood in Schenectady, making occasional notes on a yellow legal pad. Becky stopped eating and started listening intently when Mickey described the night he came home from grad school and discovered his mother stabbed to death by his stepfather.

"It was at that moment that I made the biggest mistake in my life. I picked up the knife and literally lashed out at Ray Rossi. He didn't die, but my plan to be a physician did." Mickey noticed a change in Fallon's demeanor when he disclosed his felony conviction and his time in prison.

"What happened to your stepfather then?" asked Fallon. "Is he in prison?"

"No. He was killed in a car accident a few days before he was to stand trial."

"That's odd," said Fallon. "Wasn't he in custody pending the trial? How was he able to post bail?"

"I was in custody pending sentencing," said Mickey. "He'd spent a few weeks in the hospital, but on the day of his arraignment Rossi was being escorted from the county jail to the courthouse when a speeding dump truck smashed into him and the officer next to him, killing them both instantly. The driver abandoned the truck a few blocks away and was never apprehended or even identified."

"Sounds like your stepfather got what he deserved," said Becky, feeling herself drawn to the son of the man she'd hated so much it changed her very personality. It was like they had a common enemy. Barton had rejected both of them.

"The letter you read to me. Did you bring a copy?" asked Fallon, trying to stay on task.

"Of course," said Mickey, reaching into an inside pocket of his jacket and removing a folded piece of paper. "This is a photocopy," he said, handing it to Fallon. "Let me know if you need the original for any reason."

"You safekeep it for now," said Fallon, moving his plate of barely touched eggs, fish and hash browns to an empty table and taking a sip of his coffee. "Attorneys must file all documents into the courts' electronic filing system in Minnesota, so when I file your letter as part of your claim, it will be a PDF, not an original. That doesn't mean we won't be required to produce the original if there's a trial or if the court wants a handwriting expert to review it.

"Here's what I've found out about Paul Barton's probate proceeding. All of this documentation is available through the judicial website if you know where to look. He died without a Will, so the rules of what we call intestate succession apply, meaning Barton's estate would normally be divided between his spouse and any children. The Cooper Harding law firm is representing Mr. Barton's sister, Amanda. She's filed a petition to appoint herself as the personal representative of his estate. According to the petition, Melanie Patton Barton signed a prenuptial agreement that entitles her to a fairly small part of Paul's estate, if you consider thirty million dollars small, and the rest, including sixty percent of Barton Industries, would be distributed to Amanda as his only sibling and next of kin."

"And what's the rest worth?" asked Mickey, not caring about the amount but curious about the wealth his biological father had accumulated.

"Between nine hundred million and 1.5 billion dollars," Fallon replied. "At least that's the range quoted in the petition. By the way, did you know that Melanie Barton died early Sunday morning?" Mickey shook his head. "It wasn't reported anywhere yesterday, but a doctor friend of mine at St. Luke's in Duluth let me know. What this means, Mickey, is that if we can prove that you are Paul Barton's son, you will inherit one hundred percent of his estate. The prenuptial agreement was filed as an exhibit to Amanda's petition. It provides that Melanie's financial interest in Paul's estate dies with her, unless she survives Paul by at least sixty days. She did not."

"Will proving that Barton's my biological father in court be difficult?" Mickey asked. With his background in chemistry and biology, he knew that his blood and DNA should be an uncontroverted match to Paul Barton's but wasn't sure that would be enough.

"I assume that Barton's sister will deny that you're his biological son, whether or not she knows of your existence, especially since she has an incredible amount to lose if it's true. She's a very wealthy woman in her own right, but I'm sure it's control of Barton Industries that she's after. Paul Barton has not been buried or cremated yet; a date for any funeral hasn't even been set, so genetic testing to establish a DNA match would be done. We'll ask the court to order it as part of our objection to Amanda's appointment and separate petition to declare you as Paul Barton's biological son and sole heir."

"That sounds fine," Mickey said. "What do you need from me to start the process?"

"Just two things. I've prepared an affidavit for you to sign that simply recites certain facts about your mother, your birth and your interest in establishing paternity and the right to inherit from your birth father's estate. I'm a notary, so if you sign the affidavit, I can sign and stamp it today. I have also prepared a short retainer agreement that authorizes me to represent you in this matter and states that you will pay me an hourly fee for my legal work on your behalf at three hundred dollars per hour plus any costs or filing fees. I won't charge you anything for our meeting today."

Mickey quickly read the affidavit and agreement, took a pen from a front pocket of his jeans and signed both. "I know a few lawyers back in New York. They charge a lot more than three hundred dollars per hour and they don't have nearly your experience."

"As I said, I only take on cases and clients that truly interest me. I have a very simple lifestyle and plenty of resources to fund it. I charge a fee I believe is fair to both of us," Fallon said as he signed and applied his notary stamp to Mickey's affidavit.

"I'll file our documents with the Lake County court tomorrow," Fallon continued. "Give me your email address and I'll send you a copy of everything. It's also a good way for us to communicate about your case."

"It's mickeyk92@gmail.com. Here, let me write it on your legal pad."

Fallon handed him the portfolio. After handing it back, Mickey stood and said, "I need to go," extending his right hand first to Becky and then to Fallon. "I know I've already said this, but I really appreciate that you've come down here to meet with me. I took care of the bill for breakfast when I got here. Take care and we'll keep in touch." He turned and walked out of the restaurant without waiting for a reply.

Driving the Tacoma south on I-35, Mickey encountered very little traffic at 8:00 in the morning on a holiday. That would change dramatically in a couple of hours when the hoards who traveled north for one last weekend at the lake or in the Boundary Waters wilderness returned home after the final chapter of summer.

For most of his life, Mickey had been curious about his birth father, but more to understand who he was than to find a way to inherit his estate. He had a hard time believing that any man could have abandoned his beautiful mother and then remained silent while his overbearing father intervened with threats and essentially extortion. Now that Barton was dead, was pursuing his rightful inheritance an integral part of avenging his mother and her lifetime of struggles? Maybe. At the very least, her story and the true character of the Bartons might be revealed. And learning about Barton's treatment of Becky and Oscar Fawcett supplied more ammunition for his actions.

What if he became majority owner of Barton Industries? It was making his head spin, though with all that money he could do a lot of good in this messed-up world and finally go to medical school, which is something his mother had desperately wanted.

With these thoughts swirling in his brain, not to mention some anxiety over reporting to the St. Paul Fire Department in less than twenty-four hours, he turned on the FM radio and found the morning news from NPR on a Hinckley public radio station. The lead story was about Minnesota, indicating the *New York Times* had reported that an unidentified Russian operative might be responsible for several unsolved murders in northern Minnesota, including the suspected chemical poisoning of billionaire Paul Barton Jr. and his spouse Melanie while they were on board his yacht on a pleasure cruise turned deadly nightmare on Lake Superior. Suddenly, Mickey felt nauseated and furious at the same time. The last statement of the story made him cringe.

"So far authorities have been unable to make any connection between the Russian government or any Russian business and Paul Barton Jr. or Barton Industries, a conglomerate that has no operations outside of North America."

He tried to call Donna but went straight to voicemail.

"This is Mickey. We have to talk in person. I'll be at your place in two hours. You need to be there."

Suddenly, he was having second thoughts about making a claim against his father's estate. He'd figured that a disgruntled employee or business associate or even another jilted lover had been responsible for killing Paul Barton. After all, the guy was a first-class asshole. But what if the murderer were a member of his mother's family? He'd suspected Donna of contacting them after Elena's murder, but she'd denied it. Unlike Mickey and his mother, Donna had no boundaries if she wanted something, but if what he was thinking were true, this was way beyond anything he'd ever imagined she would do.

THIRTY-EIGHT

After reading the lead article in the *Star Tribune,* Donna Morgan had turned off her phone and left her apartment with a backpack filled with a change of clothes and a bottle of Blanton's single barrel bourbon. She was in a state of denial. She was incapable of accepting a major setback because she was too busy scheming, thinking about how to escape the precarious and potentially life-altering position she'd found herself in, while at the same time not totally abandoning her original plan, a plan that had been botched by a man she never should have trusted, a man who always had to do things his way. A dead man.

Based on information picked up during her last days at Cooper Harding, Donna knew Jack Whitman's wife, Nancy, would be in California until Tuesday evening. She also knew that neither of his children was in town over the Labor Day weekend, which meant he'd be at one of two country clubs, Interlachen or Edina. It didn't matter to her which one. She knew he'd arrive before 8:00, have a quick breakfast with a few of his buddies, and play eighteen holes before noon. She drove from her apartment in South Minneapolis to Whitman's sprawling brick colonial on Bywood Lane in the prestigious Rolling Green neighborhood of Edina. She'd been there once before—on a weekend in June when Nancy had been at a sales agents' conference at Grandview Lodge in Nisswa. Whitman had grilled steak kabobs with root vegetables on his huge gas grill on the stone patio adjacent to the lap pool. She'd contributed a spinach and strawberry salad and a Boston crème cake she'd picked up at Woulet's, a popular Edina bakery. After dinner and a leisurely swim, the June night air had become cool, so Whitman built a raging fire in the outdoor, wood-burning fireplace. They'd made love on a cushioned chaise lounge near the fire before spending the rest of the night in a guest bedroom on the second floor of the eight-thousand-square-foot home. Whitman had wisely decided not to tempt fate or arouse Nancy's suspicions by bringing his mistress into the master bedroom.

Donna remembered a key piece of information from that night. During their dinner conversation, Whitman had disclosed his longstanding practice of leaving a spare key to the home under one of the flower boxes on the front porch after his college-age kids had been locked out of the house a few times when they weren't expected home. She was hoping that he'd continued the practice, though she knew he didn't set the alarm system when his wife was out of town, so if the key weren't available, she'd find a way to get into his house.

She decided to park on the street near Interlachen Park, rather than on Whitman's paver circular driveway, and to walk the two blocks to the house. She was careful to make sure none of his rich, nosy neighbors saw her dart to the left and onto his lawn immediately after she'd passed one of two brick fence posts that framed the entrance to the driveway. As she'd anticipated, the key was hiding under the base of a flower box, so she let herself in and set her backpack on a glass-top cherry coffee table in the middle of the two-story family room, a comfortable but impressive room that included a stone fireplace above which hung an attractive family portrait in which both Jack and Nancy Whitman were at least ten years younger and twenty pounds lighter, and a wall of windows overlooking the pool and patio. She plopped down on a never-ending white linen sectional with down-stuffed cushions.

Dressed in stylish, torn denim jeans and an intentionally revealing cream Milano silk blouse, she took her phone from a side pocket of her jeans to check the time. It was 12:30, meaning Whitman should be home any minute, since he only ate two meals a day, and he always ate a big breakfast before a morning round. Seeing her phone reminded her of the message from Mickey. She hadn't called or texted him, and she knew he'd be royally pissed when he drove to her apartment and she wasn't around and hadn't contacted him. She also knew she needed to placate him, especially if she wanted him to follow through on pursuing his claim against Paul Barton's estate. She just hadn't devised the right story line, sometimes called deception, for a man who wasn't easy to manipulate.

She moved the backpack to the floor and removed the bottle of Blanton's Black, reading the label and pondering what made it worth a hundred dollars more than Woodford Reserve Double Oaked, her favorite bourbon. As she set the bottle on the coffee table, she heard a garage door open and braced herself for a confrontation with her former boss and lover. Fortunately, Whitman was an easy man to manipulate. At least for her.

"What the fuck, Donna, how did you get in here?" Whitman nearly yelled as he entered the family room from the kitchen with a leather briefcase in his left hand and a cell phone in his right. He had showered and changed into a long-sleeve polo shirt and light gray khakis.

"Please don't be upset with me," Donna replied, leaning back on the sofa and trying to look contrite. "I knew Nancy was out of town and remembered the spare key under the flower box after I rang the doorbell and no one answered. I was honest with Gretchen when I told her I decided to leave the firm after the way Nancy treated me at the Barton party, but I've been feeling horrible because I didn't talk to you first. It's just that I was afraid you'd talk me out of ending our relationship. So, I came over today with a peace offering and to let you know what I'm feeling in person." Donna wiped a few tears from her cheeks. Not full-blown crying but a convincing display for her audience, nonetheless.

Whitman set his briefcase on the coffee table and picked up the bottle of bourbon. Seeing Donna and inhaling the scent of her Girl Gone Bad perfume made him weak in the knees and, at least momentarily, thinking that a reconciliation might be possible.

"Okay," he said, "I'll grab a couple glasses, and we can talk." He walked into the dining room and set the bottle on a built-in buffet. Opening a matching hutch in the corner, he took out a couple of Waterford lowballs and filled them each with three to four fingers of the brown liquor. Returning to the great room moments later, he handed a glass and cocktail napkin to Donna and then sat next to her on the sectional but gave her plenty of space. She would have to make the first move and initiate any physical contact.

"Thank you," Donna said, taking a small sip and then placing the napkin and fancy glass on the table. Whitman took a healthy drink and kept the glass in his hand. He didn't bother with a napkin.

"Thanks for the wonderful bourbon," he said. "I have to admit that after Nancy's performance last week, I wasn't shocked when I saw your vacated cubicle and got the news from Gretchen that you'd quit. Very disappointed, but not shocked. And thanks for completing the Barton estate documents. They were perfect, as usual, and I filed them on Friday. The thing that did surprise me was learning that you're a lawyer. It made perfect sense after I thought about it for a while—I've had some good paralegals over the years, but none had close to your breadth of legal knowledge and communication skills. I have to admit, though, it really hurts to be deceived by someone you've trusted both personally and professionally."

Donna thought about that statement for a few moments before responding. She wondered whether Nancy would have a similar reaction if she knew about their affair. "I'm truly sorry about that," she said. She wasn't. "I wanted to get away from upstate New York and move to Minnesota, but I had very little in savings and needed to take the bar exam here and then start applying for jobs. I thought it would be easier to get a position as a paralegal while I got settled and passed the bar." Most of that was a lie, but it was the best Donna could do under the circumstances. "I didn't anticipate having an intimate relationship with my boss or being the target of his wife's suspicions. I also didn't anticipate falling in love with a married man. You and I both know that our relationship couldn't continue without either the firm or your wife finding out, and in either case, I'd be gone."

"I get it, Donna," Whitman said, inching closer to her. "In hindsight, you did the right thing by leaving the way you did. You were forthright with Gretchen, admitting our relationship was consensual. I think once she found out you were a lawyer, she decided that your exit resolved whatever issues the firm might have had with our relationship. And even though I know it can't last and you'll soon want someone younger, I would selfishly like to continue seeing you on a discreet basis if that's possible."

Without saying a word, Donna placed a hand on each of Whitman's legs between his knee and groin and leaned in to kiss him with an open mouth. In one motion, Whitman put the glass of whiskey on the table, cupped Donna's shoulders with his meaty paws and drew her closer as they shared a passionate kiss. Donna nearly lost her balance and moved her left hand to the middle of Whitman's crotch to steady herself and ascertain his level of his interest, which she determined to be high. When their lips separated, Whitman had a stricken look on his face.

"Oh shit," he said, his arms still wrapped around Donna. "I forgot that Nancy decided to come home a day early, and her flight from L.A. should land in about fifteen minutes."

"I'll be gone in ten," Donna said, handing Whitman his glass and unzipping his fly to relieve the obvious tension in his pants. She quickly took care of matters, then gulped down the rest of her bourbon and kissed the top of Whitman's head. He looked a little cross-eyed, his body completely limp on the sectional. She hoped the leverage she would gain by this visit was worth the vile act she'd just committed.

"I'll be in touch," she said. She was gone before Whitman could muster a response.

THIRTY-NINE

Sheriff Sam MacDonald started to worry when Hallie and George hadn't returned home from Madison by 8:00 on Monday night, especially because the National Weather Service was reporting heavy thunderstorms in northwestern Wisconsin. His calls went right to voicemail, but he knew she often turned her phone off when driving longer distances, and he couldn't argue with that. He was relieved when he heard the garage door open at 8:45.

Hallie carried a sleeping George from the car to the kitchen, handing him off to MacDonald, who happily accepted the final leg to George's bedroom. Fred followed him, resting his snout on George's bed while his master made quick work of getting his son out of play clothes and into pajamas before tucking him in and kissing his forehead good night.

When MacDonald returned to the kitchen, Hallie had changed into cotton sweats and was microwaving two generous portions of the lasagna he'd made earlier but stuck in the refrigerator pending her return. She handed him a glass of the Sangiovese while taking a sip from her own glass.

"Tense drive back?" he asked, clinking glasses with her and taking more of a gulp than a sip of his wine.

"Only for about an hour," she replied. "Between Tomah and Black River Falls there was a combination of heavy rain and strong winds, so I stayed in the right lane and kept the speedometer under sixty. It became pretty dangerous to pass because of a lack of visibility when spinning tires kicked up torrents of water across my windshield. As usual, a few assholes in pickup trucks had to be in a hurry, and, the absolute worst offenders, the commercial semi drivers. A few passed us going over eighty. Why are they even on the road on Labor Day?"

MacDonald left the rhetorical question alone, though he agreed with everything she said. "Glad you made it safely," he said, giving her a gentle hug. "You take a seat at the table, and I'll serve the lasagna. I bought a baguette and pre-made Italian salad to go with it."

Hallie sat at the round antique oak table that had been in Sam's childhood home and would probably outlast little George. "By the way, Sheriff MacDonald, I read Madison's version of the *Times* article about the Russian spy in our midst. I can't imagine you're too happy about it, but maybe that's mostly because you play everything pretty close to the vest until you have more answers than this so-called reliable source at Homeland Security."

MacDonald waited until he'd served all the food and sat next to his wife before discussing the ubiquitous *Times* article. "I was upset when I first read it, primarily because the only person who knew all of the proffered facts about each crime is Woody."

"You mean the only person besides you, right?" Hallie probed.

"Me and maybe Lincoln because she's such a sponge. I don't know if she knew some of the background stuff about Andropov, the former KGB officer who'd blended in as a model citizen over here for more than twenty years before being slaughtered at a rest area in Itasca County, but nothing gets past her, although she hadn't even read the article when I called her early this morning. It's got to be Woody."

MacDonald looked up from his plate of food and gazed at his wife. She'd eaten a few bites of salad but hadn't touched the lasagna. He'd never seen anyone except George fall asleep in a sitting position in the middle of a meal. Leaning on an elbow and using the table as a kind of fulcrum, Hallie's head was cradled in the palm of her right hand. Her eyes were closed, and she was snoring. Afraid to startle her, MacDonald quietly continued to eat and waited for her to open her eyes. Amazingly, it took nearly five minutes.

"Oh my god, Sam!" Hallie cried, her eyes wide open. "I can't believe I fell asleep. I'm so sorry, honey, but I'm too tired to eat. I need to head to bed. Please save my plate, and I'll have it for lunch at work tomorrow."

"I almost tried to carry you to bed," MacDonald said. They both smiled. Hallie was too tired to laugh.

"That would have been romantic," she said, "Thanks for making the effort on dinner. I'll make it up to you." She got up from the table, brushed his bare forearm with her hand and walked toward the stairs that led to their bedroom in the loft.

MacDonald finished his dinner and half the bottle of wine. By the time he'd cleared the table and loaded the dishwasher it was half past ten. As he flipped off the overhead light in the kitchen, his iPhone, sitting on a counter next to the dishwasher, played the familiar chime tones denoting a text message. It was Woody.

Got your message. Was in transit. In Duluth hotel with DC special agent and two CIA case officers. Sorry about the Times article. Explanation forthcoming. Can we meet for early breakfast tomorrow? Name the time and place. Woody.

"The feds have arrived," MacDonald said out loud. He wondered how "early" Wilson was willing to meet. He considered places in Two Harbors, or he could save Woody the trip and drive to Duluth, but ultimately figured Woody needed to do a bit of penance. He replied to his friend's text.

Judy's Café in Two Harbors. I'll be there at 6:30. Mac.

It was 6:35 on Tuesday morning. Two large men sat across from each other at a square table for four near the back of Judy's Café. One man was dressed in an expensive navy suit, buttoned-down oxford cloth white shirt, and red-and-white-striped silk tie. The other man, sensing heavy rains in the humid predawn air, wore a black windbreaker over his standard issue polyester Lake County sheriff's uniform. At his suggestion, both men had ordered the vegetable omelet with cranberry wild rice toast.

"I know it's not how we used to operate," said Woodrow Wilson, "but with all the information being traded on social media, sometimes we need to show our hand and then closely monitor and filter the responses." Wilson had assured Sheriff MacDonald that the decision to use the *Times* reporter to get the story of the Russian assassin into worldwide circulation and not to involve local law enforcement, including MacDonald, was made at the highest levels of Homeland Security and the State Department.

"I'm surprised the reporter agreed not to publish the names of the deputies who were involved in the Russian's demise," MacDonald observed. "That wouldn't have been good, regardless of the response."

"We didn't disclose their identities, and we cautioned the reporter against trying to discover the information. Let's put it this way: The guy is an old acquaintance of mine and knows he'll never get another lead if he violates our arrangement."

"Okay, so do you have a definitive ID on this guy?" MacDonald asked.

"We don't. But we've significantly narrowed the inquiry and come up with a lot of additional information about the man many Russian insiders know only as the Ghost." Wilson took a nylon portfolio from his brown leather briefcase, unzipped it and removed an iPad mini. "Here's the intel we've gathered so far and why I've got FBI and CIA personnel with me."

"Will you send me an encrypted email with everything you've got?"

Wilson hesitated. "Sure, Mac. For you, sure. Let's start with what we do have. First, your initial suspicion that the parent company was behind the kidnapping of Tri-Metals CEO Larry Osgood looks pretty accurate right now. They terminated their director of security on Friday. Apparently, when it looked like the environmentalists and Native American tribes weren't going to be blamed for the kidnapping, he decided to double down by assassinating Osgood and wanted to ensure that no one could tie the deed to Tri-Metals."

"How did you determine that?" asked MacDonald.

"After he was terminated, he contacted our embassy in Santiago and agreed to trade information for protection. We told him we'd meet with him but with no guarantees. To pique our interest, he said he'd met Ivan Serov at the 2022 World Copper Conference in Santiago. Serov attended as a guest of the majority owners, but he apparently told the security director, a man named Manuel, that he was interested in handling projects of a specialized nature for the company or the family where there would be terrible efficiency and never a trail. He said he had contact information through an intermediary in Kazakhstan."

"That sounds promising. Did anyone meet with him?"

"He was found in his car by Santiago police on Saturday afternoon, shot in the back of the head. The company issued a statement condemning the incident as a random act of violence. His briefcase and wallet were missing."

"None of that surprises me," said MacDonald. "I'm sure this Manuel didn't act alone or have the authority to pay the Ghost a pile of money without the approval of the ruling family. But what really confounds me is how utterly stupid it was to stage that kidnapping. First of all, they have to be totally ignorant about the opposition, and second, unless the MAGA idiots control the White House and probably Congress as well, copper mining in northern Minnesota is as dead as Osgood and Manuel."

"Probably," Wilson replied. "But I think the family knows that, and perhaps that's not the reason they wanted to get rid of Osgood."

Before MacDonald could reply, their server set a tray down on a portable stand and placed their breakfast plates and a pot of hot coffee on the table.

"Can I get you gentlemen anything else?" asked Meghan, their petite twenty-something server, her name printed on a badge pinned to her colorful Judy's Café T-shirt.

"I think we're good, Meghan. Thank you," said MacDonald.

"Thank you, Sheriff. I'll be back to check on you later."

After both men took a few minutes to attack their omelets and hash browns, MacDonald resumed the conversation.

"As you know, Ivan Serov is the name on this guy's passport, but it's not his real name, is it?"

"It's definitely not his name. But it definitely is the name he was using to do business in Europe, northern Africa and South America as well as the name he used for his bank and investment accounts at Rossiya Bank in St. Petersburg. The address on his passport doesn't even exist, but our operatives in Altana, Kazakhstan, think he might have been born there and moved to St. Petersburg after joining the KGB in the late 1980s."

"Any response or other noise from Moscow?" MacDonald asked, spreading peanut butter on the last piece of cranberry wild rice toast after devouring his omelet.

"Not what we expected. Apparently the so-called Ghost had gone rogue for a while, and Putin's lieutenants are relieved that he's been eliminated. They've told the State Department that whoever this man is he has not been acting under any kind of Russian authority, and no one in Russia wants the body. We've also had discussions with our contacts at INTERPOL. They've heard of the Ghost but have no detailed information on him. We do know that Ivan Serov's accounts at Rossiya Bank have been closed, and the Russian ambassador to Canada and their top two military liaisons have been recalled to Moscow. In other words, the Kremlin is distancing itself from the Ghost as much as it can. This guy was a killing machine, but he outlived his usefulness."

"I get that," said MacDonald. "And I can see how he got involved in the Osgood murder and killed Andropov because he always perceived as a traitor and thief in Moscow, but I still don't see any connection between Ivan Serov and the Bartons, or Oscar Fawcett for that matter. So, at this point, Woody, why are your guys here? What is it critical for you to find out?"

"Three things. First, did Serov leave any remnants or vials of the nerve agents wherever he was staying? Second, was anyone locally at Tri-Metals involved in conspiring to kidnap and kill Larry Osgood? In other words, anyone over whom we have jurisdiction. And third, we share your concern about the connection between this Russian assassin and Paul Barton and Barton Industries. Someone wanted Barton dead. His wife was probably collateral damage, and Oscar Fawcett was some type of sideshow to embarrass Barton and divert the attention of law enforcement. Ivan Serov probably didn't even know Barton until he got his assignment. The question is—who gave him the assignment and why use rare and ultra-deadly chemical weapons to carry it out?"

MacDonald waved to a couple of older gentlemen who'd entered the restaurant wearing maroon and gold UMD sweatshirts and were taking seats on the swivel chairs at the front counter. "You can certainly take the lead on the first two, Woody, but I'd like Detective Barnes to lead the investigation into the Barton connection. This Serov or whatever his name is nearly took her life. I'm trying to convince her to see a psychotherapist to deal with the trauma she suffered, but she's determined to discover the backstory behind the Fawcett and Barton murders."

"She'll have at least a week before we can even start that one, but she's welcome to meet with our team to compare notes and utilize our database. By the way, we haven't come up with a match for the Ghost's DNA. What about the deputy who shot him? Is she at least taking some time off?"

"She's seeing someone who's helped her before in Duluth tomorrow," said MacDonald, "and then she and Ranger Darrow are taking off for a week of hiking and camping in the Smoky Mountains."

MacDonald heard the familiar beep of his portable police radio and pulled it off his belt. There was a car/truck accident on Highway 61 about two miles north of Two Harbors, and both lanes of the highway were blocked, not solely as result of the accident, but because of an altercation. At least that was what dispatch had been told.

"There's an accident on 61 a few miles from here," said MacDonald, standing as he said it and flipping two twenties on the table . "I'm the closest peace officer. We're short-staffed today, so I need to head out."

"Do you want some help?" asked Wilson.

"Not from some dandy in a suit. You just make sure Meghan gets a big tip and have your best agent call Lincoln Barnes. Keep me informed this time, and I'll do the same."

"Ouch," said Wilson, watching MacDonald hurry out the door.

Northbound traffic on 61 was backed up over a mile, so MacDonald had to drive the Tahoe on the shoulder with his flashers on to get to the accident scene, one of the more surreal he'd witnessed. A Great Lakes Freightlines semi-tractor with a loaded trailer was jackknifed across the two-lane highway, and a late model silver BMW 7-series sedan with a crushed back end was on the southbound shoulder but facing north. At first glance, it appeared to MacDonald as if the Beemer had tried to make a left turn from the northbound lane into the parking lot of the Rustic Inn restaurant, even though the Rustic didn't open until 11:00. Several of the stopped motorists were honking, but, thankfully none had gotten out of their vehicles. He was about to see why.

MacDonald parked on the northbound shoulder and exited the Tahoe. He didn't recognize either of the two men yelling at each other in the middle of road. The semi driver was a huge man in every dimension, well over six and a half feet tall and maybe three hundred pounds with a long, curly brown beard. He wore a green and gold Packers cap and a grease-smeared AC/DC T-shirt with faded blue jeans and Timberland work boots that had to be at least size 15. The presumed driver of the BMW was well under six feet tall with a slim build. He was blond and clean-shaven, wearing a Ralph Lauren lavender polo with black pants and penny loafers. Both men looked to be in their mid- to late thirties. The smaller man was doing most of the talking, but he was also pointing a Ruger LCP at the semi driver.

MacDonald walked between the two men and pointed at the Ruger.

"Put that gun down right now!" he growled in his most authoritative baritone.

When the man complied, MacDonald extended his right hand in the man's direction. "Now give it to me, grip first."

The man also complied with this request, saying, "I've got a conceal and carry permit, Sheriff."

MacDonald slipped the pistol into his jacket pocket. "Right now, I'm more interested in why you two are holding up traffic in my county."

"This fuckin' little prick tried to make a left turn with his fancy car right in front of my fully loaded rig," said the semi driver in a voice even deeper than MacDonald's.

"You're the fucking prick, you overgrown piece of shit," said the Beemer driver. "I would have made that left turn if you hadn't been speeding. He had to be going at least eighty, Sheriff."

Before MacDonald could respond to either man, the semi driver shoved him aside with a meaty forearm and attacked the Beemer driver, knocking him to the ground with one push and then pouncing on him like Vern Gagne of All Star Wrestling fame.

After the shove, MacDonald nearly lost his balance and was, momentarily, in disbelief. He took two quick steps toward the action and crouched down, grabbing the big man's belt above the center of his buttocks with his right hand and, incredibly, lifted him two feet off the ground, turned him over onto his back and knelt with his full weight on the bearded man's chest. "You!" he screamed at the Beemer driver, whose nose and mouth were now bloody. "You go sit on one of the benches on the porch of the restaurant and wait for me!"

MacDonald then turned his attention to the man under his knees.

"And you, you're in trouble, but you could be in a lot more trouble if you don't do exactly what I tell you to do, do you understand?"

Even though the semi driver had MacDonald by sixty pounds and three inches, he could feel the raw power in the arms and legs of the man who'd picked him up like a sack of flour. He was also completely out of breath.

"Yes, sir, I'm sorry. I don't know what got into me. What do you want me to do?"

"I hear your engine running; is your rig drivable?"

"I think so."

"I want you to steer it into the parking lot and park between the restaurant and liquor store. Then you're going to sit next to your friend and exchange insurance information and pleasant conversation until I get up there."

"Got it."

When MacDonald stood and assisted the big man to his feet, he noticed that a Lake County sheriff's squad and a state patrol vehicle had arrived on scene. Deputy Ryan Hokanen had already exited the squad he'd parked behind MacDonald's Tahoe and couldn't suppress a smile observing that his boss had a chaotic and potentially violent situation well in hand.

"Good morning, Sheriff," he said, striding across the highway and stopping next to MacDonald. "I heard there was some kind of standoff up here, but it looks like you've diffused it. How can I help?"

Before MacDonald could answer, a state trooper approached the two men. "Morning fellas," she said. "As soon as this semi moves out, I can get the traffic moving if you two want to deal with the two drivers and issue whatever citations you think are warranted."

"Sounds good to me," said MacDonald. "I know most of the troopers who patrol up here, but I don't think we've met. I'm Sheriff Sam MacDonald and this is Deputy Ryan Hokanen."

"Good to meet you, Sheriff," said a tall, blue-eyed woman wearing the full state trooper garb, including a maroon, tech mesh fitted cap covering her short auburn hair. "My name's JoAnn Falk. I'm from Cloquet originally. I've only been a trooper up here for a few months, but I know Deputy Hokanen."

"That's great, Trooper Falk. Good to meet you as well." Seeing

Hokanen trying to suppress another grin, MacDonald wondered how well she knew his deputy, which also made him smile.

Once the semi was out of the road, MacDonald and Hokanen drove their squads into the parking lot of the Rustic. Hokanen got out of his squad while MacDonald stayed in the Tahoe and lowered his window.

"I'll let you wrap this up, Ryan. I need to run. Take statements from both men and tell them we could charge each of them with felonies but will consider not doing so if they both stay out of trouble. If they fully cooperate, let the trucker go first and then you can return this unloaded Ruger to the obnoxious guy with the BMW. Call me on the radio or my cell if you have questions or they give you any trouble.

"Absolutely, Sheriff. You have a great day."

"We're off to a good start, anyway," said MacDonald as the wind picked up and it started to rain.

FORTY

Heeding the advice, or maybe it was an order, from her boss, Lincoln Barnes had taken an extra day off to clear her head and regroup, if those overused metaphors meant anything or were even possible. She'd spent Tuesday morning kayaking on Lake Superior in a steady rain. Thankfully, there was barely a breeze and she'd worn a wetsuit, though she felt somewhat guilty using the judge's fancy equipment. She wasn't sure whether the contents of the house and garage were included with the judge's gift of the cottage. She felt confident he would want her to use the Trek bikes and kayak. Regardless, she would never be comfortable with the gift of the Gildemeister property, especially if it turned out the judge had murdered Kate Patterson, but she had no problem living in the perfect cottage on the lake until she knew the truth. Then, either way, she would leave the home and either transfer the title back to Robin or donate it to charity.

After a relaxing morning on the lake, Barnes made herself a grilled Gouda cheese and tomato sandwich and a pitcher of sweet tea, but she couldn't stay away from the detective work that energized her for a whole day. She returned calls to the FBI special agent who had traveled to Minnesota with Woody Wilson and to a detective from the Duluth PD assigned to the Becky Fawcett case.

Sheriff MacDonald had shared the joint CIA/State Department

report on the Russian, or maybe Kazakhstani, whose true identity was still unknown but who often used the name Ivan Serov and was known by many as the Ghost. The FBI special agent was focused on finding the place or places where the Ghost had been staying during his time in Minnesota. Barnes was focused on finding the person or persons who hired the Ghost to kill Paul Barton Jr., and maybe to kill Oscar Fawcett as well. They were both waiting for the Minnesota Bureau of Criminal Apprehension to analyze the burner phone that was found in the stolen pickup the Ghost was driving and to test the tires on that truck, which may have contained some unique or identifying soil or substance that would provide a clue about where he'd been living. It was likely in a remote area but with access to the internet. They agreed to work together to solve the mystery of the Ghost.

The Duluth detective thought Barnes would want to know that Becky Fawcett's lawyer had made a plea deal with the St. Louis County Attorney's office that would not include any jail time. He knew that Barnes and her boss, though not condoning Becky's attempt to shoot Paul Barton, were sympathetic to her plight. The cop didn't really care about any of it but had a major crush on Barnes, so an excuse to call her was his prime motivation.

It helped Becky's cause that Charlie Fallon had been a law school classmate of the sixty-something county attorney. It didn't help that P. J. Barton's brother-in-law, Billy Slocum, had been the unintended victim of Becky's errant shot, and that he and Amanda would scream bloody murder if a judge approved probation without a day in prison for Becky.

Late in the day she was surprised to get a text message from Michele Sams, who should have been on her way to the Smoky Mountains with her boyfriend. The text was short:

Hey GF, check out this YouTube video of our Super Sheriff. On my way to camping paradise with my Boy Scout. MS

Apparently, a couple of the motorists who'd been delayed by the morning incident on Highway 61 had posted videos on Instagram and YouTube of Sheriff MacDonald's interaction with the two idiot drivers who'd faced off after their accident. The title of the video was "Super-Sheriff subdues Mountain Man." Barnes felt a combination of admiration and pride as she along with over a hundred thousand others watched her boss make an incredible feat seem commonplace. It reminded her that her move to the North Shore was not strictly a move to be with the judge. Working for Sam MacDonald was special, and getting to live on the big lake had been a bonus.

FORTY-ONE

Mickey Kaye's first two days as an emergency medical technician with the St. Paul Fire Department had been successful, if uneventful. The first day was filled with paperwork, introductions and his assignment to a team working out of the downtown headquarters station on Tenth Street. He'd learned that one of the reasons he'd been selected out of the pool of eligible candidates, all of whom had the requisite licenses and certifications, was his score on the physical performance test—the highest recorded since the pandemic began in early 2020. What hadn't been a success—his attempt to contact his half-sister, Donna. After spending two frustrating hours sitting in his truck in front of her duplex in South Minneapolis on Labor Day afternoon, he'd sent her multiple voice messages and concluded that she was trying to avoid him, at least for now. He knew whenever that happened she'd done something she needed to rectify or at least cover up before he confronted her, which was why he needed to confront her as soon as possible.

At Hallie's insistence, she and her spouse scheduled a midweek date night at least once a month to keep their busy work lives and parenting responsibilities from overshadowing their relationship. Hallie's administrative assistant, who'd worked for the Lake County attorney's office for over thirty years and had two granddaughters under five, was their favorite babysitter, not to mention George's godmother. Getting paid twenty-five dollars an hour for doing something she loved didn't seem quite right, but since all of the money went into a Section 529 college fund for the grandkids, she'd take it.

Hallie had made a 7:00 p.m. reservation at the Ledge Rock Grille at Larsmont Cottages, a few miles south of Two Harbors on Old Highway 61, also known as Scenic 61. MacDonald had a late meeting in his office, so he'd meet her there. The place wasn't crowded on this Wednesday night, since school had started on Tuesday for most students in the area. She'd arrived a few minutes before him and ordered a bottle of pinot grigio to go with the Northwoods salad and a double order of walleye cakes, their customary order at the Ledge Rock. She knew MacDonald would need to order a stout IPA or other beer before being content to sip white wine, which is the first thing he did after arriving precisely at 7:00.

One of the reasons they liked this place was the great view of the lake from every table. Hallie pulled up the YouTube video of the Super-Sheriff on her phone and handed it to MacDonald.

"Have you seen this, Superman, I mean, Sheriff?" she asked, covering the smirk on her face with her hand.

"Unfortunately, yes," he said, returning the phone to Hallie after a brief glance. "Michele Sams sent it to me this afternoon from the Duluth airport. I say unfortunately because I felt sorry for the truck driver. I didn't witness the accident, but I have no doubt the obnoxious dude in the fancy car turned in front of the semi without a thought about how difficult it is to slow a full load moving downhill at fifty miles per hour. If he hadn't taken the handgun out of his glove box, the big man would have beaten the crap out of him, and that would have been justice."

"Sorry for bringing it up," she said half sincerely. "But you're still my hero, Sheriff MacDonald."

Their server brought a beer for MacDonald and uncorked the bottle of pinot.

"Here's to quieter days ahead in Lake County," Hallie toasted, clinking her wine glass against MacDonald's bottle of Bent Hop

Golden IPA. "I learned something today that might have a bearing on your investigation of the Barton murders."

"Really?" asked MacDonald, inhaling about half his beer. "I learned something today that might have a bearing on your enjoyment of your meal."

"I doubt that," said his wife, "but you go first, so I have more time to digest the information."

"A young couple discovered a severed head while walking on Burlington Bay Beach early this morning. Ryan responded to the call and had an EMT transport it to the morgue at St. Luke's in an ice-filled cooler. He snapped a few photos that I won't share but it's pretty clear it's Oscar Fawcett."

"Oh, my," Hallie sighed. "Has there been a funeral or memorial service for Oscar?"

"The service was postponed after his mom's arrest, but, as you know, the body was released by the medical examiner and cremated at Becky Fawcett's request, so I assume she'll want to do the same with these remains. I just hope she doesn't ask to see the gruesome thing. I have a call in to her."

"She doesn't need any more heartache in her life, though I heard that Charlie Fallon has negotiated a plea deal with St. Louis County that doesn't include any jail time."

"Is that what you learned today that might impact my case?" asked MacDonald, narrowing his eyes to scrutinize her response.

"Not even close," she said. "But I guess the suspense will have to build for a bit longer."

A young man carrying a platter of walleye cakes was the reason for the delay, followed closely by their server with the salads. Hallie immediately dug into her salad while MacDonald stared at her in disbelief.

"Really?" he asked. "You're really going to keep me in suspense?"

"I'm hungry," she answered coyly. "Just start eating and I'll get to it soon enough."

MacDonald finished his beer, gave Hallie's now empty glass a generous refill of the pinot and poured a glass of white wine for himself. He used his fork to spear one of the walleye cakes and deposit it on his plate. The second he took his first bite Hallie started talking.

"You don't have a lot of dealings with Sue Christensen, the clerk of court, do you?" she asked.

"On scheduling matters when someone in the office needs to testify in court. I know Sue—she's been the clerk forever, but other than mostly small talk around the courthouse, the answer is no."

"Well, she came to my office to deliver this bombshell: A young man named Mickey Kaye is claiming to be Paul Barton's illegitimate son. Apparently, Mr. Barton had a relationship that resulted in a pregnancy when he was in graduate school in the early 1990s. His father paid the woman to have an abortion and go away, but maybe she didn't. I haven't actually read the court file, so that's all I know. Sue also said Barton died intestate, so essentially this Mickey Kaye is asking the court not to appoint Paul Barton's sister as the executor because she's got a major conflict of interest. If his claim is valid and he is Barton's son, he would be entitled to about a billion dollars in assets and control of Barton Industries. Barton's sister would get nothing."

"That is a bombshell," MacDonald agreed. "I don't see Sue as any kind of a gossip, so she must have had a reason to disclose this to you as the Lake County Attorney, and I think I know why."

"Of course you do. This Mickey Kaye had a billion reasons to want both Paul and Melanie Barton dead. Therefore, we've got ourselves a new person of interest in the Barton murders."

"Impressive," said MacDonald. "Does this mean you'd actually handle the prosecution of this Kaye if he conspired to kill Paul Barton?"

"Oversee is the word I like to use," said Hallie. "I handle important civil matters for the county and oversee criminal cases. One more thing. Guess who's representing Mickey Kaye in the probate case?"

"If irony is the word of the day, it must be Charlie Fallon, the lawyer for anyone who wanted to see Paul Barton dead."

"Irony is the word of the day."

FORTY-TWO

Jack Whitman had been in a good mood from Labor Day afternoon, when he'd enjoyed an unexpected but welcome visit from Donna, until Wednesday morning, when one of the associates in Cooper Harding's probate practice informed him about Charlie Fallon's filing in the Barton estate. That news hadn't really diminished the renewed vigor he'd felt having Donna back in his life, especially now that Nancy knew she'd left the firm. He understood that continuing the affair was a prescription for disaster, but when he evaluated the current state of his life with and without Donna, he'd decided that his marriage, lifestyle, reputation, and net worth meant less to him than spending a few hours a week and an occasional out-of-town rendezvous with a beautiful woman half his age. He was a godless, horny old fucker, but at least he knew it.

He also knew that Amanda Barton would be furious about this development in her brother's estate and would press him to find a way to contest the claim. He wasn't terribly surprised that Elena had had the baby, but was surprised it took so long for the child to surface in Barton's life, or at this point, his death. But before his secretary had been able to schedule a meeting with Amanda, she'd left a message for Whitman demanding to see him first thing on Thursday morning, which for her meant before 8:00.

When Whitman arrived at the Cooper Harding offices and snuck in an employee entrance at 7:15, Amanda was already in the lobby, sitting on a brown leather couch reading the *Wall Street Journal* and sipping her second cup of coffee. The handwritten note on Whitman's chair simply read, "She's here." Whitman set his Starbuck's vente Americano on a prized coaster he bought at the 2011 Masters in Augusta and called the receptionist on his office phone.

"Bring her back," he said.

Amanda walked in and closed the door behind her before sitting on one of two upholstered leather guest chairs facing Whitman. Five years younger than her brother, she was an imposing physical specimen, much like her mother but with two healthy kidneys. At least five-foot nine and built like Charlize Theron, she was fastidious about her appearance—no gray strands in her dark brown, chin-length bob and a perfect tan year round, whether she was living in the Twin Cities or visiting her homes in Florida or Hawai'i. She'd undergone a few plastic surgeries for a tuck here and tightening there as well as several rounds of Botox injections to her face and dermal filler added to her lips. No matter what she did, or how attractive some might find her, to Whitman she was the embodiment of Cruella De Vil.

"What the hell is wrong with the St. Louis County Attorney?" she asked. "Billy's still in rehab and might never play tennis again, and apparently that old fucker has made a deal with his murdering sack of shit buddy to put that gold-digging Becky Fawcett on probation with no jail time. Billy said if that happens he will personally find and fund his opponent in the next election."

It was clear to Whitman that neither Amanda nor Billy Slocum knew anything about county politics in Duluth, Minnesota, or about P. J. Barton's relationship with Rebecca Fawcett. Besides, he couldn't stand Slocum, a man who had a network of shady chiropractors, orthopedic surgeons, and illegal immigrants sending him questionable accident cases in exchange for even more questionable kickbacks.

"Buck Letourneau has already announced he won't seek re-election next fall. He's sixty-seven years old." Whitman believed his friend's treatment of Becky Fawcett and her son had been appalling, but he needed to choose his words carefully or Amanda would surely fire him and the firm in an irrational rage.

"Oscar Fawcett's severed head has been discovered on a beach near Two Harbors, so his mother will have to deal with that at some point, Amanda. Clearly, the county attorney and any judge are going to have a fair amount of sympathy for her under the circumstances. Nonetheless, we can work with Billy to submit a witness impact statement and file it with the court before a plea deal has been accepted." He knew this wouldn't be enough to satisfy Amanda, but he had a new subject that he was certain would divert her attention and take precedence over anything to do with Billy Slocum.

"But there's something else that's come up that we need to discuss and deal with promptly."

"Oh?" she asked with a bit of an edge.

"Your favorite attorney has filed a petition seeking to appoint an independent fiduciary to administer P. J.'s estate and to declare that his client, a man named Mickey Kaye, is your brother's illegitimate biological son and sole heir." Though Whitman knew it wasn't physically possible, he thought for a moment that Amanda's head would explode and blood would be splattered all over his office.

"Sole heir?!" she screamed so loudly that Whitman expected a wellness check at his closed door at any minute. "And who's the mother of this fraudster?"

"A woman named Elena Krasikova, though she'd changed her last name to Kaye. She allegedly had an intimate relationship with P. J. when he was in graduate school in Cambridge, and Mickey is her son and allegedly P. J.'s son. She died a few years ago."

"Why haven't I ever heard of her or this child? I mean when P. J. needed a kidney why didn't he contact his son? This makes no sense. This isn't right. We need to fight this, Jack."

Again, Whitman knew he needed to tread carefully. "I knew about Elena when I was in law school at Cornell. She and your brother definitely had a relationship. She was a foreign student from Russia who wanted to be a model. P. J. told your father that she was pregnant and wanted to have the baby, so your dad drafted a letter in which he agreed to pay her a hundred grand to have an abortion and never to contact P. J. or anyone in your family again."

"So did she take the cash?" asked Amanda.

"She did. And a private detective hired by your father verified that she kept an appointment with a Planned Parenthood clinic near Boston to have the abortion. After that, she disappeared, and now this Mickey Kaye is claiming that she never had the abortion and that he's P. J.'s son."

"But what about the letter agreement? If she took the money, then her son should have no claim to P. J.'s estate, right?"

"Unfortunately, no. The so-called agreement was written by your dad, not a lawyer, and is more extortion threat than agreement. P. J. never agreed to give up his parental rights, and besides, an agreement to get an abortion, even if supported by a large cash payment, is definitely not enforceable. Paul Senior gave us a copy of the letter before he died. I've made a photocopy for you."

"This just sucks, Jack. So, what do we do? How do we stop this?"

Whitman knew how this conversation would go, so he'd already devised a strategy to respond to Fallon's petition and, more important, to deal with Amanda. "Ultimately, the court is going to order DNA testing to determine whether there is a genetic match between Kaye and P. J., but, before that's done I think we should retain a good private detective agency to prepare a complete background report on Mickey Kaye. There may be something in his past that precludes him from pursuing his claim."

"But are you telling me that if he is P. J.'s son and his claim is successful, then he gets everything, including control of Barton Industries?"

"That's definitely a possibility," Whitman reluctantly admitted.

"It can't happen," she said. "Do we know whether this Mickey Kaye has any children?"

"No. But that's certainly something we can find out. Why do you ask?" Whitman had an idea, but hoped he was wrong.

"If somehow this Mickey Kaye weren't in the picture, would anyone else have a claim?"

He wasn't wrong.

FORTY-THREE

Mickey Kaye finished his shift with the SPFD at 6:00 on Thursday evening and decided to drive over to his sister's place in Minneapolis. This time he wouldn't call first, since she hadn't returned any of his calls and was clearly trying to avoid him.

Today at work he'd responded to his first emergency call, a car fire on the shoulder of I-94 about a mile east of downtown. A twenty-something mom taking her two-year-old to a day care provider before heading to work at a credit union pulled over when black smoke started billowing from the hood of her 2009 Caravan. By the time Mickey arrived on the scene, the front end was engulfed in flames and mom was screaming as the heat intensified and smoke filled the interior. She leaned into the open passenger sliding door and tried to undo the straps on her daughter's car seat. She gave Mickey a helpless look as he gently moved her aside and, ignoring the smoke while two of his colleagues attended to the fire, cut the nylon belt securing the seat with a utility knife and lifted it and the toddler out of the minivan. Everyone was fine. It had been the first adrenaline rush he'd felt for a few weeks. Not the rush he'd wanted as an emergency room physician, but it would have to do for now.

He parked the Tacoma a couple of blocks from Donna's duplex on Fremont Avenue South. She was in Unit 2, which was the upper unit of an older brick building but had a separate entrance off the front porch. The outer door was locked, and Mickey decided that pressing the doorbell button wouldn't elicit the desired response from his sister even if she were home. Instead, he went around to the back of the property to see if her car were parked in the detached garage. Taking a circuitous route through a neighbor's yard to avoid detection if Donna were looking out a back window, he could see two cars in the three-car garage through a side window. He was fairly certain the black Honda Accord was hers.

The rear elevation of the duplex consisted of two large porches or decks, one on top of the other. There were no stairs leading to the upper porch, but Mickey saw a way to climb up one of the shared end posts, using an occupational skill he'd developed since prison.

Once on the upper deck, he could see into Donna's unit through two kitchen windows. Donna was sitting on a sofa in the living room watching something on a big screen TV hung above a fireplace mantel. He deftly pulled the handle of the outer screen door and wasn't surprised that it was unlocked. Carefully turning the knob on an ancient oak storm door, he was surprised that it, too, was unlocked. Now he had her. At least for an unpleasant conversation.

Hearing someone in her kitchen, Donna jumped off the couch and grabbed the container of pepper spray she kept in a front hall cabinet. Then she heard a familiar voice.

"It's me, Donna! You knew you couldn't avoid me forever." Mickey walked from the kitchen into the spacious main living area of Donna's two-bedroom apartment. She'd set up a home office on one side rather than using the space as a dining room. Mickey sat at an old oak office chair behind a used executive desk Donna had purchased from her landlord.

"What are you talking about?" Donna asked. "I'm in the process of changing jobs and have been crazy busy. I was about to call you and suggest that I make dinner for us over here."

Donna and Mickey had never been close. Mickey was quiet, serious and studious, a rule follower and loyal to a fault. Donna was outgoing, ambitious, and willing to do just about anything to get what she wanted. Each of their personalities had been shaped by a loving, protective mother who'd made countless sacrifices so they could succeed and an unscrupulous, often violent, and feckless father and stepfather, who'd abused everyone in the family in different, yet significant ways.

"Just like all the times you called me, wrote to me, and visited me when I was in Auburn. But I'm here now so let's forget about excuses. I need some honest answers from you for once."

Donna went into the kitchen and grabbed two bottles of Modelo Especial from the fridge. She popped off the caps under a Formica counter, set a beer on the desk in front of her brother and sat on a tan poly fiber sofa facing the desk. She knew the truth wasn't an option.

"Are you hungry?" she asked. "I could order a pizza or there's a good Thai place nearby for takeout."

"The beer will do. I tried to call you after Ray was killed. What was your involvement in that murder?"

"There's no conclusive evidence that it was anything but an accident." Donna took a sip of her beer and made a mental note that her half-brother was more muscular and ruggedly handsome since the last time she'd seen him before his conviction.

"You're so full of shit, Donna. When our mother told us about her family, she did it on condition that we never contact them and never have anything to do with them. I know you despised Ray and wanted to avenge mom's death, but that didn't give you license to contact her brother. Now look what he's done."

"I don't know what you're talking about," said Donna. "You know how upset I was when you decided not to hire a decent lawyer to defend yourself. There's no question in my mind that you would have been acquitted because you reacted like a normal, feeling human being to that violent maniac. But no, you had to be the martyr. You think that's what our mother would have wanted? Really?"

"I did what I thought was right at the time. Swinging the knife at Ray, I was no better than him. But that didn't give you the right . . ."

"Hey, wait a goddamn minute. I was in law school and knew what I was talking about, but you didn't listen to me. You did what you thought was right, even though it was totally fucked up. I never reached out to mom's family. But her murder was front page news in the *New York Times* and other places. I was shocked when her brother knocked on the door of my apartment in Alexandria. Sergei Krasikova is or was the scariest, most imposing human being I've ever met. Our Uncle Sergei was going to avenge mom's murder no matter what I told him. He was a professional assassin." Donna was confident her brother wouldn't be able to separate the truth of what she'd just told him from the lies.

"Yes, Mom told me all about her brother, the KGB killer, and also told me never to contact him. Her mother died of some kind of cancer twenty-five years ago. She would have been the only one I would have been interested in knowing. I'm not surprised that her brother was involved in killing Ray and, by the way, an innocent police officer, but what I don't understand is why these people were involved in the Barton murders. I think only you know the answer to that."

This was the subject that scared Donna the most, and Mickey may not be the only person she'd need to convince of alternative facts. "Sergei knew the identity of your father. I don't know how he knew, but he told me he would return to the States after handling some business in Europe to ensure that you and our family received our rightful inheritance from the man who'd abandoned his sister and forced her to marry a pig. That was his description."

Mickey wasn't buying it. "And so, you moved out to Minnesota months before this killing machine returns to the States with nerve gas and a machete. How did he know that Barton didn't have other children or a Will or Trust giving everything to them or to his wife or to charity? I think you came out here to learn everything you could about Paul Barton and then, when you knew I would get everything, you made some kind of deal with this killer to eliminate Barton and his wife and then to disappear. Just like he'd disappeared after killing many times before. But this time the crazy killer fucked up and now you could be implicated, or, even worse, your convicted felon brother, who's also a blood relative of the killer, could be implicated. That's much closer to the truth, isn't it Donna Rae Rossi?"

Donna cringed at the mention of her former name and a recitation of facts that was very close to the truth. A partial confession would be necessary. "It is closer to the truth. Just as the fact that neither Ray Rossi nor Paul Barton, the two men who used our mother, deserved to live. Barton was as bad as Ray in his own way. He manipulated a woman to get her son's kidney and then discarded her just as he discarded our mother. So, yes, I did my homework on the Bartons and then decided to use a family resource to turn the tables on those assholes. I knew in your heart you'd want to rectify the situation for the sake of our mother."

"I don't want anything enough to commit horrible crimes in order to get it. You're pathological, Donna, no different from your uncle, the Ghost. Were you expecting me to inherit millions and then share the wealth with the two of you?"

"That would have been totally up to you, but at least the wealth and power that goes with it would have been in our family." Of course, once Mickey had landed the Barton fortune, Donna had intended to let him know her involvement had altered the timing of events, creating more than a little leverage against a convicted felon.

"So why shouldn't I simply go to the authorities now and disclose what you've done?" Mickey asked. "I can withdraw my claim to the Barton fortune and continue my life as an EMT in St. Paul."

"Really? You'd do that to me? After everything that's happened to our family?"

"What choice have I got at this point, Donna? Someone's going to figure this out, and then you could be going to jail, and I will have a very difficult time separating my past and my story from yours."

Donna was having a very difficult time containing the rage she was feeling. If only Sergei had followed the plan. He'd be home, and no one would have a clue who'd committed the Barton murders. The murders of Oscar Fawcett, Larry Osgood and whoever the guy in Itasca County was would never have occurred, and she'd be spending her time helping Mickey inherit and spend the Barton fortune. Had she known that a professional assassin like Sergei, especially a greedy one, only knows one way to solve a problem, she'd never have told him about Mickey's father and Barton Industries. You hire a killer to kill. Now she knew.

"I'm begging you not to withdraw your claim, Mickey. That will arouse as much suspicion as pursuing it at this point. I don't see how anyone will be able to connect the dead Russian whose body is in a morgue in Duluth to you or me. Sergei was very good at keeping his identity a secret. That turned out to be his undoing. His irrational concern about someone identifying him. He didn't have a computer and destroyed his burner phones literally after each call. Other than my initial meeting with him at my apartment, all of my communications with him were via different burner numbers, and I guarantee you there does not exist a bank account, street address, credit card or billing of any kind in the name of Sergei Krasikova. Since the mid-1990s that man ceased to exist. He truly was a ghost."

"And if I do pursue the claim, what do you want, Donna? Because I want to use the money for something good—maybe to start a foundation for abused women in the name of Elena Krasikova, and I want to go to medical school. I have no interest in running Barton Industries or in becoming a billionaire. What do you want?"

"I'm not sure. I start a new job as an assistant U.S. attorney in Minneapolis next week. I went to law school because as the daughter of an abused foreign mother and the victim of abuse at hands of Ray Rossi, I didn't want to feel powerless ever again. I still want to convert the rage I feel every day into something positive. That might involve seeking some kind of political power to effect change. I've made mistakes, Mickey. I'd like a chance to do better."

Mickey did not trust his half-sister, but he also didn't have the internal makeup, the cold-heartedness perhaps, to turn her in to the authorities. He thought about confiding in Charlie Fallon, maybe the only person he trusted today, but for now he would continue with the new job and let Charlie handle legal matters.

"Okay, Donna," he said, getting up and setting the half-consumed beer on the kitchen counter. "I'll stay the course with the claim for now, but no more lies. You and I will never be close, but you're all the family I've got right now. I guess I'll use the front door to leave. Good luck with your new job."

Donna literally jumped off the sofa and grabbed Mickey's forearm as he reached for the front doorknob. When he turned to face her, she threw her arms around his neck and hugged him as tightly as she could.

"I'm so sorry for everything, Mickey. I promise to do better, so let's keep in touch, okay?"

"Sure," he said, wondering if the display was all for show but needing to give Donna the benefit of the doubt. As Mickey walked down the stairs to the front door of the duplex, Donna breathed a sigh of relief.

"That was easier than I thought it would be," she said to herself.

FORTY-FOUR

Jack Whitman had a standing 1:00 p.m. tee time on Fridays in September at Interlachen Country Club, so any legal work needed to be done in the morning. It was a few minutes after 10:00 when the firm's receptionist buzzed him on his office phone, a rare occurrence these days of cell phones, texts and emails.

"I've got a Charlie Fallon for you on line two," he said.

"I'll take it. Thanks," said Whitman.

"I haven't talked to you since you were on the bench, Judge Fallon. How are you doing?"

"It's just Charlie, now, and I'm great. Living the dream life for an old fart in Grand Marais. Thanks for asking. I assume you and your staff have reviewed our filing in the Barton estate."

"You assume correctly. As you might expect, my client is not very sanguine about the prospect of an outsider taking control of Barton Industries and her brother's fortune. She has instructed us to investigate and scrutinize the filing and your client very carefully, to put it mildly."

"I wouldn't expect anything less, but I was talking to Ed Higgins today about supervising DNA testing since he released Paul Barton's body to the family but has retained DNA and blood samples. Would you be willing to stipulate to paternity testing conducted by Dr. Higgins and any geneticist or other physician of your choosing so we can at least get that accomplished without a formal hearing?"

Whitman worried about Amanda's reaction to any agreement he would make with the opposition, but he knew the judge would order the testing in any event, and Higgins was the best in the business.

"Sure. You draw something up and email it to me, and I'll turn it around in a day or two."

"And I also assume your office already has a copy of that thirty-year-old letter agreement signed by Paul Barton's father."

"I'll pass on confirming that assumption, Charlie, but send me a proposed stipulation, and I'll be in touch."

"Great. Thank you, Jack."

FORTY-FIVE

Detective Lincoln Barnes picked up two large dark roasts and a couple of maple oat scones from Cedar Creek Coffee in Two Harbors before meeting the Lake County Attorney at the Law Enforcement Center. Sheriff MacDonald had suggested that the two women meet to review the Paul Barton estate file.

"Happy Friday morning, Counselor," said Barnes, handing Hallie Bell MacDonald a large cup of joe and then taking the bag of scones out of a side pocket of her navy windbreaker before sitting at the small conference table in the county attorney's office.

"Aren't you nice bringing coffee and breakfast," said Hallie, grabbing a couple of paper plates and napkins from a desk drawer and sitting across from her friend and colleague.

"How's the training going?" asked Barnes. Both women had entered the lottery to participate in the Twin Cities' ten-mile run as part of Twin Cities' Marathon weekend in early October, and both had been awarded spots in the race.

"Almost nonexistent," said Hallie. "A couple of slow five-mile runs this past week, but I need to pick up the pace to be ready, especially if I want to run with you."

"I got in a long one on Tuesday, thanks to the sheriff's mandate to stay home, but otherwise, three or four miles every other day. We've still got a few weeks, and it's only ten miles.

"Easy for you to say, Miss Triathlete."

"We're going to run together no matter what, and I'm still trying to convince Michele to run with us. I hate to change the subject, but I see you've already made photocopies of some of the Barton estate documents."

"As you know, this might be a dead end, but after I alerted Mac to the petition that's been filed by Charlie Fallon on behalf of the alleged son of Paul Barton, he told me to give you a copy of everything that's been filed and let you run with it. So, it's not much so far, but here it is." After handing Barnes a manila file folder with the copies, Hallie continued: "I would have emailed this to you, but, given everything that's happened in Lake County over the past several weeks, I thought it might be best to handle this the old fashioned way, face-to-face with paper. Mac and I agree that it might be beneficial for you to get a head start on the media and the feds once word gets out, but I think he's already given you the green light to share any of this information with your contact at the FBI.

"The petition and an affidavit signed by Mickey Kaye provide background and context. According to the documents, when Barton was attending graduate school at Harvard three decades ago, he had a relationship with a twenty-year-old Russian student named Elena Krasikova. She became pregnant and Barton's father, Paul Senior, pulled him out of school and threatened to send Elena back to Russia if she didn't have an abortion. There's an odd letter agreement drafted and signed by Paul Senior that outlines the basic terms. In exchange for a hundred thousand dollar payment, Elena terminates the pregnancy and never has any contact with anyone in the Barton family again. She accepted the money and kept her scheduled appointment at the clinic but then moved to upstate New York, got married and had the baby. There's not much more to it, but of course if DNA testing confirms paternity then, assuming Barton's parental rights were never formally terminated, this Mickey Kaye inherits everything, unless he was complicit in the murder of Paul Barton Jr. That's our only professional interest in the case."

"What about his mother, Elena?" asked Barnes. "She could certainly corroborate this story. Where is she?"

"The petition and affidavit state that Kaye's mother and stepfather are deceased. I'm sure you'll look a bit further into the circumstances. She'd only be in her early fifties."

"Mom also has connections to Russia," Barnes noted. "I'll follow up on that as well. The feds will also be interested in that aspect of this case."

"No doubt. Let's keep in touch on this. Maybe it'll be a good excuse to go on a few training runs in the next couple of weeks."

"Perfect. I'll keep our Super Sheriff apprised of any major findings as well. I have to say, Hallie, you'd think a man in his fifties with a toddler at home would stop picking fights with men half his age and twice his size." Barnes took the last bite of her scone, slid the manila file into a nylon portfolio and stood to leave.

"You're right of course," said Hallie. "But I believe the day he thinks about George and me before acting on instinct will be his last day on the job. You take care of yourself, and thanks again for breakfast."

With the exception of a couple of early morning runs along U.S. 61, Lincoln Barnes had spent the weekend conducting online research of Elena Kaye/Krasikova and Mickey Kaye with some surprising, if not alarming, results. Reviewing online newspaper accounts, public databases, and court and Auburn state prison records, she'd discovered a bankrupt construction company, a half-sister named Donna, a divorce, name changes, domestic assaults, and Elena's bloody murder at the hands of her former spouse, Raymond Rossi, followed on the same night by Mickey Kaye's attempted murder of his stepfather. But what grabbed her attention more than anything else was what had happened next—the killing of Ray Rossi and a police escort by an unidentified assailant who'd stolen a dump truck and used it as a murder weapon. The Ghost had used a stolen truck as a murder weapon in the death of Oscar Fawcett, so Barnes wondered whether anyone in law enforcement in Albany County, New York, had collected DNA samples from that stolen dump truck.

Before noon on Monday, Barnes had formulated a game plan from her cubicle in the sheriff's office to determine whether Mickey Kaye could be implicated in one or more of the capital crimes attributable to Ivan Serov, aka the Ghost. She'd persuaded Sheriff MacDonald to contact his counterpart in Albany County, New York, to ascertain whether DNA from the dump truck had been extracted and saved, and, if so, whether they could provide a sample to the forensic services division of the Minnesota Bureau of Criminal Apprehension for comparison with the Ghost's DNA.

She needed to know more about Mickey Kaye than she could glean from court and online records. He didn't appear to have a presence on Facebook, Instagram, LinkedIn or X and, though there were hundreds of Donna Morgans on various social media sites, Barnes hadn't been able to find the former Donna Rae Rossi anywhere. What she had discovered was a press release from the U.S. attorney's office in Minneapolis from only a week ago. It only appeared in a couple of fairly obscure publications, *Bench & Bar* and *Minnesota Lawyer*, not obscure for Minnesota lawyers but for everyone else. The office announced that Donna Morgan, a recent graduate of Georgetown Law School and associate in the largest law firm in the Capital Region of upstate New York, had accepted a position as an assistant U.S. attorney in the Civil Division of the Minneapolis office. Mickey's petition had provided a St. Paul address and employment as an EMT with the St. Paul Fire Department, not the typical occupation of a convicted felon. So, they were both living and working in the Twin Cities but couldn't have moved to Minnesota more than a few months ago.

And if Mickey were a convicted felon in New York, convicted of a crime of violence, how was he able to leave the state so soon? Barnes had spent a couple of hours tracking down Mickey's parole officer in Albany county. They'd traded voice messages and agreed to schedule a Zoom virtual meeting on Tuesday afternoon. Depending on what she learned at that meeting, Barnes thought interviews of Donna Morgan and Mickey Kaye would be next.

As she was about to leave her cubicle to grab some lunch at the Vanilla Bean, she answered a very important call on her office phone from the special agent who was her contact at the FBI on the Barton case.

"Agent Gilmore, are you still in Minnesota?" Barnes asked.

Bruce Gilmore, a short, wiry graybeard, was a former Green Beret and an expert on foreign and domestic terrorism. He'd been the most special of special agents since he'd left the army as a major in 2010 after multiple stints in Iraq and Afghanistan. Never married and without any children of which he was aware, he remained a valuable asset, notwithstanding he was well north of sixty.

"No. I flew out of Duluth on Friday and am calling you from my home in Virginia. We kind of hit a dead end on the Larry Osgood case. We're convinced the kidnapping and then assassination scheme were concocted by the Chileans at a very high level, but their now-dead security director will take the blame, at least for now. Homeland is still very interested in the true identity of Ivan Serov and whether he had help here in the States. I have two items of new information I thought you might want and hoped you might have some for me as well.

"Based on sightings of the stolen pickup truck, we believe Serov had been living in a cabin in Knife River between Duluth and Two Harbors. It's a very nice place on Lake Superior. The owner lives in Florida and was shocked to find out that someone had disabled his security system and cameras in such a way that they appeared to be working even though a bedroom window had been breached and the intruder left definite signs of using appliances and sleeping in the master bedroom. This guy was truly a ghost. He left no fingerprints, no garbage and no traces of the nerve agent used to kill the Bartons. However, as you know, he did leave one burner, and I just got off the phone with a technician at your BCA who had an update on their analysis. Serov made two calls on that phone. The last call he made was to a phone at the Russian embassy in Ottawa, Canada. That's not particularly helpful. But he made an earlier call to a cell phone with a 518 area code. It's a phone with a Verizon plan, so we're getting a federal subpoena to determine the identity of the owner and phone records over the past six months."

"Did you say 518?" asked Barnes.

"I did. It's upstate New York."

Barnes shared the news about the probate court filing made by Paul Barton's alleged biological son, Mickey Kaye, and about her investigation of his background and the existence of a half-sister named Donna Morgan. "They've both moved to Minnesota recently," she noted, "having lived most of their lives in upstate New York; either one could be tied to that cell phone number."

"That's good stuff, Detective. I'm very curious about their mother's

Russian heritage. Let's hope there's DNA from that dump truck that we can compare to both Serov and this Mickey Kaye."

"I'll get more background information on Kaye tomorrow afternoon. I've scheduled a Zoom meeting with his parole officer," said Barnes.

"That's great," Gilmore replied. "I'm sure your boss is communicating with Wilson, but I'd sure appreciate any further updates on Serov's identity or potential conspiracy crimes."

"I'll share whatever I find out," said Barnes.

FORTY-SIX

Though the summer had been one of the hottest on record on the North Shore, September was turning out to be unseasonably cool, wet and wild. Sheriff Sam MacDonald set the windshield wipers on the Tahoe on high as he strained to see the road through a torrential rain. He was driving south on 61 on his way to work at the Law Enforcement Center. It was half-past six. In his rear view mirror, he saw the muted light of a cloud-shielded sun creeping over the eastern edge of the lake. As he glanced to his left to catch a glimpse of the lake through pine, birch and poplar trees, he saw thrashing waves and whitecaps that were stirred up by thirty-to-forty-mile-per-hour winds that had prompted the National Weather Service to issue gale warnings on Superior until noon. Fortunately, traffic was light, so he decided to use hands-free Bluetooth to take the incoming call on his cell phone.

"Good morning, Woody. I was going to call you later today."

"I thought I'd be leaving you a message, Mac, but you were always an early riser."

"Early to rise and late to bed can only mean an old cop who's sick in the head," MacDonald rhymed with a whimsical chuckle.

"Wow. Did you just make that up?"

"No one else would want to own it," said MacDonald. "I assume you've heard about the claim being made by the young man who says he's Paul Barton's son."

"I have, and I'm confident that between your detective and our special agent all that's capable of being known will be uncovered. But that's not the reason for my call. I wanted to let you know that Tri-Metals is suspending their Minnesota operations for now. I think the Chilean family has been embarrassed by the hare-brained scheme that clearly backfired."

"It's truly pathetic," said MacDonald. "Using their security director as a scapegoat for a staged kidnapping and murder and then having him killed as well is third world at best. It reminds me of the Saudis. Too much wealth and no accountability. I'll tell you what, though, Woody, if the MAGA regime, and I think I'm using that word appropriately, gets back into power in the upcoming election, Tri-Metals will be back at it."

"You're probably right, but here's what I don't understand. The worldwide demand for copper and lithium is through the roof, and your state has some of the richest deposits on earth, so don't you think they're going to be tapped eventually?"

"Absolutely, but not where Tri-Metals has the bulk of their current mineral rights. There's another huge conglomerate headquartered in England that has a subsidiary involved in a joint venture called New Range that is much further along in the permitting and approval process, but they're not trying to mine under Birch Lake or on the border of a dedicated wilderness area. We need mining in northeastern Minnesota to sustain the economy. My dad spent time as a foreman for Reserve Mining in Silver Bay, and his brother, my uncle, worked in a copper mine in White Pine in the U.P. and was a longtime member of the United Mineworkers Union, but we can't continue with unsustainable mining and forestry practices that pollute the water and destroy other natural resources that make this part of the country so great. I think reasonable compromises need to be made, but with cheating mining companies on one side and zealous environmentalists on the other, it's tough to make progress."

"Hey, I hear you, Mac. I've got relatives who live in West Virginia on both sides of the coal-mining debate. It can get pretty ugly, even within families. Speaking of which, I understand that Tri-Metals has already paid Larry Osgood's family several million dollars in exchange for an

NDA."

"I'm not surprised. It's all about the money for them. It's frightening to think of the astronomical amount of short-term profit that could be made in non-ferrous mining around here, profit that motivates these people to murder their own employees and then spend huge sums to cover it up."

"I wonder who ended up with all the money in Ivan Serov's bank accounts that have conveniently disappeared. That man, whoever he turns out to be, was aptly named the Ghost. I need to run to a meeting, my friend. I hope we can wrap this matter up within the next few weeks."

MacDonald wondered what his long-dead father would have thought about the current state of mining and politics in Minnesota. His dad taught him to listen more than speak, to treat the vulnerable and the weak better than the gifted and the strong, and, more than anything else, to be self-reliant. He would surely be disgusted with both mining and politics in Minnesota as well as with the partisan divide in America. And so was his son.

Jack Whitman was preparing for a noon lunch meeting with Amanda Barton at Zelo in downtown Minneapolis. Sitting in his office at 10:00 on Tuesday morning, he was upset, very upset. About a week earlier, he'd contacted a private investigation firm in Albany, New York, based on a referral from a law school classmate who was a high-stakes white collar criminal defense lawyer for a boutique firm in Schenectady. He'd requested a complete background report, including all public records, available private information and family history, on Mickey Kaye. For a prepaid fee of twenty thousand dollars, plus expenses, E. H. Murray & Associates would provide a written report, plus copies of all associated records, within two weeks; for a fee of thirty-five thousand dollars, the report would be furnished within a week.

Whitman had received an encrypted email with the PDF report on Monday evening. With attached records, it was over three hundred pages. He'd reviewed it twice and taken notes. The report confirmed what he'd suspected. Elena Krasikova, the beautiful young Russian woman he'd met over thirty years ago, did not terminate her pregnancy, and her son, now known as Mickey Kaye, was very likely P. J. Barton's illegitimate biological child. But that's not what upset him. DNA testing would confirm or deny the biology, and there was nothing either he or Amanda could do about that. Mickey's Russian heritage and felony conviction needed to be vetted further to see whether he was part of a conspiracy to murder the Bartons. If so, he could be prosecuted and, more important, disqualified from inheriting a dime from Barton's estate. That vetting might be difficult, but that's not what upset him either.

What upset Whitman was the section on Mickey Kaye's family. According to the report, Mickey had a half-sister who was two years younger. Her birth name was Donna Rae Rossi. She claimed her father had been physically abusive to her and her mother on multiple occasions, and was completely estranged from him after her parents' divorce. She changed her name to Donna Morgan when she was in college. A graduate of Georgetown Law School and a member of the New York bar and, within the last few months, the Minnesota bar, she was recently hired as an assistant U.S. attorney in Minneapolis.

Whitman now knew he'd been played. Donna had infiltrated the law firm that represented Barton Industries and P. J. Barton to get inside information about P. J.'s estate plan, his lack of a Will, and his prenuptial agreement with Melanie. And he had given her access to everything. But was she capable of planning and helping to execute a double murder? The thought made him sick to his stomach. The other question rattling around his brain related to the night of the Barton Industries gala: If Donna wanted to hasten her brother's inheritance of Barton's estate, why did she tackle Becky Fawcett and probably save P. J.'s life? After he mulled that question over a bit more, he concluded that Donna might be the most diabolical person he had ever met.

The E. H. Murray report found no obvious connection between Mickey or his mother and the Russian "spy" who, according to *New York Times* reporting, had likely poisoned the Bartons and committed other capital crimes in Minnesota. However, the report included a disclaimer with respect to any information, records or identities related to Russian citizens or the Russian government and suggested contacting the Department of Homeland Security or Federal Bureau of Investigation for assistance on such matters.

Whitman was worried that if Amanda learned that his former paralegal was the half-sister of the man who was trying to rob her of control of her company, she would fire him and the firm. He needed to keep her from reading the report or alter some of the language so Amanda would never know that Donna Morgan was Donna Rae Rossi, Mickey Kaye's half-sister. In either case, something was becoming clear to Jack Whitman: He was screwed.

Donna Morgan sat at her kitchen table and ate her usual breakfast, an everything bagel with a smear of garden vegetable cream cheese and a bowl of fresh blueberries and raspberries drenched in half-and-half. Unlike her brother, she didn't drink coffee. She preferred a royal blend black tea with a shot of real cream.

Donna re-read the *Times* article about the Russian spy. Now there was a follow-up piece by the same reporters that had also been picked up by the *Star Tribune.* Unlike the first article, no federal officials were referenced as the source of the information, which was mostly conjecture based on the fact that the Kremlin had distanced itself from the former KGB and FSB agent and star assassin, and the only name that had surfaced for this man other than *Prizrak* or Ghost was the name on his passport and Russian bank accounts, Ivan Serov. Of course, Donna knew his real name, but she had counted on the fact that no one in the States other than Mickey would ever know he existed, much less his true identity.

Donna was supposed to start her new job with the U.S. attorney in less than a week. That had been part of the original plan. But according to the original plan, her Uncle Sergei would have been home in St. Petersburg and not rotting in a Duluth morgue. She could have, and probably should have, advised Mickey to abandon his claim against Barton's estate, but she was willing to risk everything, including her freedom, to stick it to the Bartons and to gain a share of their fortune. She knew Mickey wasn't interested in either money or power. He was a fucking boy scout who simply wanted to get his life back. He'd have happily given her control of Barton Industries and most of Barton's assets. That's why she'd enlisted Sergei Krasikova to do the dirty work, and if he'd simply followed her instructions, everyone but the Bartons would still be alive, including Sergei. But he was a single-minded, paranoid killing machine, and now she needed a Plan B. She knew Whitman would ultimately discover that she and Mickey were related. But if the Kremlin didn't disclose the Ghost's identity, and it appeared they wouldn't, and if Sergei had followed through on his promise to destroy his burner phones, then no one but Whitman could implicate her in a scheme to eliminate the Bartons. And if he turned against her, he'd be risking his marriage and his biggest client.

Always calculating, she gave herself a 50/50 chance of avoiding prison. She knew she would turn on Whitman in a heartbeat, but the question she kept asking herself was would she turn on Mickey, a convicted felon, to save herself? She didn't think it would come to that, but this experience had convinced her of the importance of contingency plans.

A dissonant chord from her phone signaled a text. It was from her boss at the U.S. attorney's office. He wanted to meet her for happy hour on Thursday at the lobby bar at the J. W. Marriott in Bloomington, ending his text with *last Saturday was so much fun.* She wondered whether that venue was chosen because it was forty miles from his home in Forest Lake or because of its proximity to a hotel room. Probably both. Once she started working for the feds, she'd have to remind her new boss of the rules against office romances with subordinates in a firm but friendly manner, unless it made sense to keep him dangling.

The walleye Milanese was Jack Whitman's favorite dish on Zelo's lunch menu, but he was having trouble enjoying it while being grilled by Amanda Barton, who was thoroughly enjoying her organic salmon salad and second glass of wine. Whitman had reviewed the highlights of the E. H. Murray report and the high probability that Mickey Kaye was P. J. Barton's son and heir. He also explained the process for DNA testing and the irrefutability of the results, information that Amanda already knew. Though she was clearly losing patience with the lack of positive news, she let Whitman drone on while she ate and pondered her next move. Her demeanor changed suddenly when her lawyer mentioned Mickey's conviction for assaulting his stepfather and three-year prison sentence.

"So, you're telling me that my brother's bastard son is a convicted felon?" she asserted more than asked. "Doesn't that mean he loses his inheritance rights?"

Whitman shook his head. "Only if his crime contributed to P. J.'s death. He definitely has Russian relatives on his mother's side, but none in the States. The report indicates Elena Krasikova, or Kaye after her name change, cut all ties with her family in Russia in the early 1990s.

"Both Lake County and the feds are still investigating whether the Russian assassin had a local accomplice. Our private detective firm didn't find any, but that kind of investigation is beyond their capabilities. We need to let the FBI take the lead on this."

"I want a copy of this report," Amanda insisted. Whitman thought about discouraging her, but decided the effort would be futile. He was glad he'd given his admin a redlined copy that deleted all references to Donna Morgan. She was in the process of creating a "revised" version of the report for Amanda.

"I'll email you a copy this afternoon," he said. "I'll also contact a friend of mine who's been a financial crimes prosecutor with the U.S. attorney's office and ask him to look into the Barton murder investigation. I have a call in to Sheriff MacDonald up in Lake County as well."

"Those hicks up there couldn't distinguish a dog's ass from a hole in the ground," Amanda scoffed. "I'll ask Billy if he has any connections in New York or D.C. with experience in this type of case. I don't care what it costs."

There was only so much ignorance and bullshit that Whitman could take, regardless of the consequences. "Sam MacDonald is no hick, Amanda. He's a former head of a branch of the Secret Service who probably has more relevant connections in D.C. than anyone else in the state. But you do whatever you and Billy think will keep control of Barton Industries. I'll do whatever I can to help. How is Billy doing, by the way?"

"Better," said Amanda. "He's walking with a boot and a cane, but he's still not happy about Rebecca Fawcett's plea deal."

Billy Slocum was the epitome of a sleazy P. I. lawyer, a man with a huge network of referral sources that included chiropractors, rehab consultants, nurses and mostly undocumented Russian hustlers. His ugly, bearded visage sticking out of a three-piece silk suit was seen on more billboards owned by Barton Media than anyone or anything else. What Whitman couldn't understand was how a woman as smart and sophisticated as Amanda could be taken in by such a worthless prick. "That's a done deal, Amanda. Fallon and the county attorney are tight."

"I know, Jack. I've got more important things to worry about right now than Billy's fragile ego. P. J.'s memorial service is on Saturday, and I still have some details to work out."

"I got an email yesterday that the service was going to be at Wayzata Country Club. I'm a bit surprised it won't be in Duluth. P. J. hated the Twin Cities."

"P. J.'s dead, Jack, and more of our employees, vendors, clients and VIP guests live down here or will travel here versus Duluth. The service will be short, no religious bullshit or family eulogies, but some short speeches by colleagues, competitors and at least one congressman. We'll also have a jazz band with a female vocalist playing a few of his favorite songs. I haven't asked yet, but I'd like you to say a few words, Jack. He didn't have a lot of friends, but he always considered you to be his best friend."

"Of course, Amanda. But what about Melanie? Will she have a separate service?"

"Her sister in California is her closest relative. She's already claimed the body and had it cremated in Duluth. I'm sure you know this, but Melanie spent most of her life in the L.A. area before she moved to Minnesota to marry P. J. She has a trust which designates her sister as trustee and her nieces and nephews as the main beneficiaries. Melanie owned a townhome in Santa Barbara and has a couple million between bank and retirement accounts. Her sister called me a few days ago, saying the trust's lawyer wouldn't make a claim against P. J.'s estate if we agreed to pay her five million."

Whitman knew that Melanie had a home in California and a net worth of three or four million based on disclosures that were made at the time of the prenup, but he didn't know any of the specifics of her trust or financial accounts. She didn't trust P. J.'s lawyer with her personal business. "What was your response?"

"I told her I might not have control over P. J.'s estate, but that I would personally pay her a million dollars to go away. Surprisingly, she accepted, but I want you to draft an ironclad release, so we never hear from her or anyone else on behalf of Melanie's family again."

"I can do that," said Whitman. Suddenly, his appetite returned and he scooped up a forkful of fish and mashed potatoes. I can do that, he thought, but I don't think I want to do this anymore.

FORTY-SEVEN

Detective Lincoln Barnes opened her laptop in a small conference room in the Law Enforcement Center to ensure that her virtual meeting with Mickey Kaye's parole officer would be private and undisturbed. She double-clicked the Zoom icon on her screen and typed in the password for a meeting hosted by the Lake County sheriff's office. It was five minutes to three, but Kathleen was already in the waiting room. Barnes let her in with a greeting and a smile.

"Good afternoon, Kathleen," she said. "Thank you so much for doing this."

Kathleen Morris was an African American woman in her early sixties. She'd been a parole officer with the New York State Department of Corrections and Community Supervision for twenty-two years and a probation officer with Albany County for ten before that. Married at twenty-three and a mother of three boys at twenty-seven, she'd started out as a part-time teacher's aide in a public elementary school in Latham, New York, even though she'd majored in criminal justice at SUNY-Albany. Her spouse had been an assistant professor in the history department of the same school when they'd met on a blind date. When he died of colon cancer at thirty-five, Kathleen's widowed mother moved in to help with the boys, and she embarked on a career in law enforcement. An attractive older woman with a short gray-and-black Afro and expressive brown eyes, she wore white hoop hearings and a white, loose-ribbed cotton sweater over black stretch pants as she sat at a desk in what appeared to be a small den or library in her townhome.

"I'm happy to help, especially in this case," she said. "I'm only working a couple days a week now. I take care of two of my grandbabies two days a week. Today is actually my free day. How'd you end up in the tundra up there in Minnesota, girlfriend?"

"It's a very long story," said Barnes. "I started out in Chicago, moved to Minneapolis to escape a bad relationship, and moved to the North Shore of Lake Superior because I fell in love with the area and needed to leave a toxic work environment." She decided not to mention the judge. That was a longer story. "Tell me what you know about Mickey Kaye, Kathleen."

"I know a lot," she said. "First and foremost, the young man got royally screwed. I didn't meet him until six months before his release from Auburn, but like a lot of folks in the Capital District, I read about his case. His stepfather was a serial abuser with a violent streak. This young man was an honors student in high school and a high achiever in college. He had just decided to attend medical school and had been accepted at Cornell. Over a winter holiday break about five years ago, he came home to his mom's house to find her savagely murdered. He was probably in shock and admits to being enraged. He slashed at his stepfather with the murder weapon and sliced his neck open. Then he called for help. His stepfather, a guy named Rossi, didn't die that day, but was killed, maybe murdered, by some crazy person driving a dump truck on the eve of his murder trial."

"And they never caught the person driving that truck, right?" asked Barnes.

"Right. They recovered the stolen truck but never made an arrest."

"Did Kaye have a lawyer?"

"He actually qualified for a public defender at the time because his mother's small estate was in limbo and he had virtually no assets or funds in his own name. At first he asked a college friend who was a corporate lawyer to help him, but ultimately he dealt directly with the prosecutor and told the judge he did it and would accept the consequences at his first appearance. If he'd retained a competent lawyer, I think two out of three juries would have acquitted him under the circumstances. His sister, I can't recall her name, but she was in law school and was livid that he wouldn't hire a decent lawyer or put up a defense. And Rossi was her birth father. She hated that man with a passion."

Barnes took notes on a legal pad. This interview was creating a different picture of Kaye than she'd anticipated. "How did he do in Auburn?" she asked.

"He survived. He was a model prisoner, but given his youth and good looks, he was attacked a few times. He was able to defend himself for the most part, but I think he was gang raped once, though it was broken up quickly by a guard. The guards and other staff liked him because of his good attitude and interest in improving himself. He served the minimum time and worked on getting an emergency med tech certificate. The demand for those skills is so great he had a job waiting for him when he was paroled eighteen months ago. He checked in with me on schedule for the duration of his sentence. I guess I don't know what else to tell you, Lincoln. He is a polite, thoughtful young man. He had incredible love and respect for his mama and felt strongly that she would have wanted him to atone for attacking Rossi. Unfortunately, his girlfriend dumped him right after he entered the guilty plea. She comes from a wealthy family in Elmira, and apparently her mom and dad influenced her to distance herself from Mickey. Within a year of his sentencing, she married someone else. That was a blow to him as was the fact that no one visited him in prison, not even his sister."

"This is very, very interesting," Barnes remarked. "Fascinating, really. Did Mickey say anything to you about his birth father or about why he moved to Minnesota?"

"I think the primary reason was to leave New York and the bad memories he experienced here. He said he had recurring nightmares about the night in December when he discovered his mom and attacked Rossi. The whole prison experience was another nightmare for such a good kid, and the girl he had dated for three years is from here as well. But the other reason he picked Minnesota was curiosity about his birth father. He wanted to meet him."

"What about his sister? She moved out here several months before him."

"He never talked about her. Remember, she was his half-sister who practically disowned him for pleading guilty. But I'm sure she figured into the equation as well. When you indicated on the phone that his birth father had been killed and that he's making a claim against his estate, I was a bit surprised. I know he wanted to return to medical school at some point, and he mentioned starting a nonprofit some day for victims of domestic violence to honor his mom, but you said this guy was a billionaire, right?"

"Let's just say, if Kaye's claim is valid and accepted, he'll inherit hundreds of millions at a minimum," said Barnes. "But part of it may be revenge against a family that forsook his mother and him and compelled her to marry Rossi to stay in the U.S."

"That makes some sense to me," said Morris. "He did mention to me once that his mother was forced to give the hundred grand she received from the father of her boyfriend to Rossi to save his construction business, only to go bankrupt a year or two later."

"This has been incredibly helpful, Kathleen. Thank you so much for talking to me, especially on your day off. Would it be okay for me to call or email you if I can think of any other questions?"

"You are most welcome, and you can certainly follow up at any time. In my line of work, it's not very often that I encounter a man as special as Mickey Kaye."

As she signed off, Barnes thought it was not very often she was this confused.

Barnes shut down her laptop and returned to her cubicle to make some calls and catch up on the daily emails. She and Sheriff MacDonald had been copied on an encrypted email from a crime lab analyst with the Office of Forensic Services in Albany, New York, to Dr. Higgins at Midwest Medical Examiners indicating that they had two DNA samples from the stolen dump truck used to murder Raymond Rossi and a police escort and that, given the nature of the potential match, someone from the U.S. marshal's office would be delivering it to Duluth within the next forty-eight hours. Although this was good news, after hearing Kathleen Morris describe Mickey Kaye, she was more skeptical than ever about his involvement in Barton's demise.

She called Charlie Fallon to schedule an interview with Kaye and was surprised when he answered after the first ring.

"Good afternoon, Fallon here."

"Hello Mr. Fallon. This is Detective Barnes with the Lake County sheriff's office. How are you today?"

"It's a beautiful day up here in Grand Marais, though we did have our first frost this morning, and it's not even September 15th. What can I do for you, detective?"

"I'm investigating the murders of Paul and Melanie Barton. We're looking into possible ties to the Russian national who likely poisoned them. You've no doubt heard about him in the news."

"Yes. Rather bizarre circumstances. Sounds like he went on a killing spree. One of Putin's henchmen no doubt."

"I can't disagree with that," said Barnes. "The county attorney informs me that you're representing a man who's making a claim against Paul Barton's estate alleging he's Barton's biological son. She also says that your client's mother was a Russian immigrant. You can understand why we think the timing of his first contact with his alleged father is a bit suspicious, especially considering the size of Barton's estate and the fact that your client is a convicted felon involving a violent crime."

"Are you aware of the circumstances surrounding that violent crime?" Fallon asked.

"I am now," said Barnes. "I had a long conversation with Mickey Kaye's parole officer in New York. But I'd still like to interview your client to close a few open items on my case and to make my own assessment of Mr. Kaye. You can certainly be present if you'd like, even though I wouldn't even call your client a person of interest at this point."

"I assume you'll want to do this interview in person," said Fallon. "My client has already provided a DNA sample to a testing firm approved by Jack Whitman, who's representing Barton's sister, so Mickey has no reason to travel up this way until there's a required in-person hearing in Two Harbors. Besides, he recently started a new job in St. Paul. His next day off is next Monday. If you're willing to travel to the Twin Cities, I'll check on his availability. I rent a small suite of offices in the old Gilbert Building in downtown St. Paul. We could meet in the conference room. Would that work for you, Detective Barnes?"

A quick trip to the Twin Cities was appealing to Barnes for a number of reasons. She could visit her mom and her sister's family in St. Paul and maybe have lunch with her old partner, Warren. "That works for me, Mr. Fallon, but I'd like to know whether your client can make it within the next day or two."

"That won't be a problem," said Fallon. "You'll know by tomorrow at noon. Have a good evening." And he was gone.

Her call to Donna Morgan didn't go as well. She'd hoped to interview her in the Twin Cities early next week, since she'd decided to spend a few days there. She was bothered by a couple of things in Donna's past. She tried to reach her at the U.S. attorney's office in Minneapolis but was told by a receptionist that she wouldn't be in until Monday, her first day on the job. That surprised Barnes because she knew Donna had moved to Minneapolis five months earlier. The receptionist wouldn't give her a personal number, so she told her it was an important police matter and asked that she have Ms. Morgan call her as soon as possible.

FORTY-EIGHT

Absent a serious conflict, Sheriff Sam MacDonald and his good friend Ed Higgins, M.D., had met every other Friday for the past five years to play tennis, even throughout the COVID pandemic. Once a month they'd play in Duluth and once a month in Two Harbors. Loser would buy lunch; winner would choose the restaurant. Fortunately, they were fairly evenly matched: MacDonald, the more skillful player; Higgins, the most competitive person the sheriff had ever met.

Both men were hovering around sixty, MacDonald a few years under and Higgins a few over, and both had various age-related degenerative conditions and occupational injuries that increasingly became the source of complaints and excuses. This summer MacDonald suggested that on one of their two monthly meetings, they play doubles pickleball in Duluth instead of tennis, arguing that within a few years, that's all they'd be able to do. Higgins reluctantly agreed.

Higgins brought his two sons-in-law to the Woodland Community Center for their mid-September meeting. In their late twenties, they were too quick and athletic to play on the same team, so Higgins chose the more experienced and skilled pickleball player to be on his side of the net. After ninety minutes of serving, swinging, sweating and swearing on a cloudy, cool fall day, Higgins would be buying lunch for the sheriff, who was quick to admit that luck had been on his side that day, though he always relished sticking it to his overbearing friend.

"Do your daughters play pickleball that well?" asked MacDonald, as the two men were seated at Tavern on the Hill, a popular spot for lunch near the UMD campus in Duluth. "No way," said Higgins. "They think it's a geriatric pastime. They're both still playing softball competitively, and they'd rather be kayaking on Lake Superior or hiking in the Boundary Waters. Fortunately, their husbands are racquet nuts."

Both men ordered ice teas and chicken chopped salads, and when their server left, Higgins looked around to see if anyone was eavesdropping on their conversation and then leaned in and spoke in a husky whisper. "I received the DNA samples from New York on Wednesday night and, of course, I needed to make the testing a high priority."

"We appreciate that, Ed. Are you going to keep me in suspense or tell me that the man who mowed down Ray Rossi is the man we're calling the Ghost?"

"My report won't be final until Monday afternoon, but I'm telling you there's a 99.9 percent chance that they are one and the same evil son of a bitch."

"Now we just need to figure out who this son of a bitch really is and whether the man claiming to be Paul Barton's son used him to accelerate his inheritance."

"Sounds like a logical explanation to me," said Higgins.

While her boss was playing pickleball in Duluth, Detective Lincoln Barnes was making final arrangements for her trip to the Twin Cities. Mickey Kaye had agreed to be interviewed on Monday morning at 10:00. Barnes would drive down to St. Paul early Saturday morning and have lunch with her mom. She'd spend Saturday and Sunday nights with her sister, Wanda, and her family in Highland Park and get a practice run on the TC-10 mile course on Sunday. She had a call in to Warren Lindquist, her old partner at the MPD, to see whether he could meet for coffee or lunch on Monday. She planned to return to Two Harbors on Monday afternoon, pending any response from Donna Morgan. So far there hadn't been one. A late morning call from a data analyst at the BCA was one of the biggest shockers so far in the bizarre Barton murder case. It also shed some light on Donna Morgan's lack of response.

"Hi Al," said Barnes. "Did you track down my Verizon customer?"

"More than that, Detective. I've got a name and six months of cell phone records for that number."

"Nice work, but don't keep me in suspense."

"The customer is a Donna Morgan. I've got her current address in Minneapolis and a former one in upstate New York. The burner phone you retrieved called her number only once; however, during the six months of records we obtained, she received calls from eight different untraceable phones. That's a huge red flag for anyone not an undercover cop."

"Agreed. Your timing on this call could not have been better, Al. I assume you're going to send me what you've got?"

"Both you and our friend at the FBI. Check your email for an encrypted message from us."

"Will do."

Barnes quickly called the area code 518 number that was the penultimate call made by the Ghost. She went right to voicemail and heard a message that was short and to the point:

"Hello, you've reached D. R. Morgan. Please leave a message."

Barnes left her name and number and indicated she wanted to interview Donna on Monday afternoon in connection with her brother's claims against Paul Barton's estate. She didn't mention anything about the Ghost or about Donna's phone, but she did say she'd meet with her after working hours if necessary. Barnes didn't expect a return call.

Packing her laptop and gathering the files and other items she'd need for her trip to the Cities, Barnes saw a familiar yet unexpected name on the display of her buzzing iPhone.

"Michele, I thought you were still in Tennessee?"

"We won't be back up north until tomorrow," said Deputy Michele Sams, "Our flight from Minneapolis to Duluth got canceled because of high winds, so we're going to stay in the Cities tonight and fly up tomorrow. We're going to see one of Craig's favorite jazz bands at the Dakota and spend the night at the Hewing Hotel. But I didn't call you to brag about the fun we're having. We had lunch with a college classmate of Craig's who works for the Minneapolis Park District. We met him in the skyway near the Hennepin County Government Center, and who did we see walking and talking with a couple of suits heading for the Courts Tower?"

"I have no idea," said Barnes, but she really did.

"Your Judge Gildemeister. I was pretty sure it was him, but I went online to look at his photo on the courts' website, and Craig agrees it was Gildemeister. He was wearing a dark suit with a white dress shirt and fancy tie."

"Have any idea who the other people were?" asked Barnes, thinking that the Hennepin County attorney may be close to charging the judge with a crime, though she was pretty sure if he were charged with murder in the county where he'd been a judge for fifteen years, the attorney general or a different county attorney would handle the prosecution.

"We both pegged them as lawyers. I just thought you'd be interested in knowing he's not still cloistered away up on Madeline Island."

"Thanks, Michele. I appreciate the call. I'm actually heading down to the Cities tomorrow morning to see my mom and Wanda and to interview a guy who's filed a petition claiming to be Paul Barton's illegitimate son."

"You are kidding me! You think he might have had something to do with Barton's murder?"

"I don't know what to think right now," said Barnes. "Any chance you'll still be in the Cities tomorrow afternoon? I was thinking of doing a practice run on the TC-10 course."

"I'd love that, Lincoln, but our flight leaves at ten in the morning. I'm in for a long training run early next week, though. I know I told Hallie I had shin splints and thought about backing out, but I feel totally rejuvenated now."

"Great," said Barnes. "I'll check in with you when I get back on Monday or Tuesday. This guy I'm interviewing has a half-sister who had a different father. Coincidentally, she moved to the Twin Cities from New York five months ago, and he moved here right after Barton died."

"Sounds mighty suspicious to me," said Sams. "I don't return to a regular shift until Thursday, so let me know if I can do anything to help. This whole deal with the Russian is the most interesting case I've worked on since I started working for Mac."

"Will do, Michele. I'll want to hear all about the big trip next week. You and Craig have a great time tonight."

"Thanks. I'm sure we will."

Now Barnes wouldn't be able to get the judge out of her mind. As usual, common sense dictated that she just forget about him. After all, more likely than not, he murdered Kate Patterson. Ditching his cell phone, cutting off all communication with her, and hiding out on Madeline Island—those actions were odd. But then transferring the title to his cottage to her, not to mention the Mercedes in the garage—that made it uniquely Gildemeister. When she was with him, she couldn't imagine that the brilliant, funny, thoughtful man could be a murderer, but she'd seen the impact of passion and rage on others and knew that anyone, everyone, was capable of murder.

FORTY-NINE

Saturday was a day of reckoning for Jack Whitman. He'd struggled trying to compose a eulogy for P. J. Barton. Even though he'd been his friend since college and his client for thirty years, Whitman hadn't really liked him much since he'd taken over his father's business empire and even less after he jettisoned Becky Fawcett and balked at giving Oscar a decent settlement for giving up a kidney. So rather than recounting anecdotes about their many business deals and golf outings—there were none that portrayed Barton as a funny or even sympathetic character—it was easier for Whitman to tell a few innocuous lies about the man and to throw in a few meaningless platitudes about his generosity and business acumen. It ended up being very lawyer-like—pure bullshit.

He finished his notes at about 10:00 in the morning, which gave him about two hours to shower and dress for the 1:00 p.m. memorial at Wayzata Country Club. He was about to leave his study to get ready when Nancy walked in and sat on the antique love seat adjacent to his desk. He was surprised to see her in tennis attire.

"I'm not going to P. J.'s service," she announced.

"Why not?" Whitman sensed there would be more to this discussion than P. J.'s memorial.

"Because I couldn't stand the man is the short answer. But the only reason I would even consider going is for you, though I really don't think you care whether I go." Before Whitman could respond to this statement, Nancy made a preemptive, nuclear strike.

"I want a divorce, Jack, and before you respond to that statement, I want you to know it's not about Donna Morgan. I never thought she was really interested in you, but I was hoping that you were having an affair with her, so I could use that as a pretext for what I want.

"Let's face it, our relationship has taken a back seat to our careers for over a decade. And that would have been fine in most respects. I mean we have the kids and grandkids that we love and share, and that won't change. But even our kids have confided in me that they're concerned about our relationship and wonder why we stay together. I mean we don't even have non-client couples that we go out with, and we don't vacation together anymore.

"I met a widower at the tennis club about a year ago. His wife died of an aneurysm out of the blue during the pandemic. She was fifty. We played mixed doubles tennis at first and then had drinks together and then dinner. I've been spending a few afternoons a week with him at his home in Eden Prairie, and now we both want more. P. J.'s death made me realize how foolish it is not to live for today. I'm sorry, Jack, especially if you're actually hurt by all of this, though I really didn't think you would be. I haven't tried very hard to hide what I've been doing, but you've never questioned any of it."

Jack couldn't argue that he'd essentially been ignoring Nancy's career and their social life for years. But the fact that she'd chosen someone else as a partner at this stage of their lives stung more than a little. He was very curious about the identity of her lover, but it really didn't make a difference, and he'd find out soon enough. On this day, he would not interpose a defense or argue with anything she'd said. He needed time to reflect on what he really wanted because it wasn't apparent to him today.

"I'm so sorry, Nance. You're right, of course, I wasn't paying attention, and I have neglected you and our relationship for years. I still love you and want you to be happy, so let's set aside some time to talk about what you want the next steps to be."

Nancy was a bit surprised that he didn't put up a small fight to save their marriage, though that's not what she wanted. Not knowing the truth about Donna put her at a disadvantage.

"I appreciate that, Jack. I'd like to have that discussion early next week. Money won't be an issue. I suggest we each keep our own retirement accounts. You can have the house and cabin with the big mortgages and we split everything else 50/50."

That proposal made Jack think of two things. First, Nancy had been contemplating this move for a long time. Second, this guy must be loaded.

"Sure," he replied. Then he got up from the desk. "I need to get ready for a service I'd like to skip as well," he admitted. He touched Nancy's shoulder as he leaned down and kissed her on the cheek. "I am truly sorry, Nancy."

While he shaved and showered, Whitman could only think of one thing, and it wasn't his relationship with Nancy; it was Donna Morgan. Nancy was right—Donna would never be interested in him. She'd used him to get information about P. J.'s assets, accounts, and estate plan and then conspired with her brother and some international assassin to murder the Bartons. He didn't understand why Oscar Fawcett was included in the carnage, but it didn't make much difference at this point. He needed to tell Donna they were through and then decide whether to share what he knew with the authorities. He knew he should, but he needed to ponder that for a while. Although he was irate at Donna for the way she'd used him, most of his anger was self-directed. He had been the dupe, the fool. Nevertheless, imagining Donna Morgan spending most if not the rest of her life in prison was not something he relished.

When he was dressed and ready to go, he sat in his Jaguar in the garage and composed a text message to Donna:

I know who you are, Donna Rae Rossi. You used me to gain access to Paul Barton's legal and financial files before you plotted with your brother and others to kill him and his wife. Needless to say, we are through. Feel free to tell my wife all about our relationship; just never contact me again. Jack Whitman

After hitting send, he backed out of the garage and started the drive to Wayzata, not sure he'd ever get there.

FIFTY

"I can't really talk now, Donna," said Mickey Kaye, "I'm working this weekend and could get called out any second."

"Mickey, I need your help. I'm totally fucked. A detective from Lake County wants to interview me. The FBI subpoenaed my cell phone records, and Verizon gave them six months of my phone calls and texts. Sergei must have had a burner on him when he was killed. He called me a couple of times to make threats about what would happen if we didn't pay him five million for taking care of the Bartons. I was too scared of him to do anything but hope that he'd finish whatever he was going to do and return to St. Petersburg. This could implicate me, Mickey, not to mention jeopardizing my new job with the U.S. attorney."

"I don't know what to tell you, Donna. Sergei Krasikova was a horrible, evil man. Mom told us to stay away from him. When I talk to the detective on Monday, I will try my best to protect you, but I won't lie. Honestly, most of what I know about Barton's murder I read online or heard from you."

"I know you'll protect me, Mickey. You know that's what Mom would have wanted. I appreciate anything you can do. Sorry to bother you at work." And then she ended the call.

Donna believed Mickey would do what he could to save her, even though nearly everything she'd told him had been a lie. She'd turn on

Mickey in a second if necessary to save herself, but then he'd forfeit his inheritance, and everything she'd worked for would be lost. What concerned her the most was not the call or calls from Sergei's burner. She could explain those away. What concerned her was the text message Jack Whitman had sent her today. The subpoena of her phone records would include the text if the assholes who served it were paying attention. And, even worse, if Whitman contacted the FBI or her bosses at the U.S. attorney's office and shared everything he knew, she would lose her job and likely be charged with conspiracy to commit murder. She couldn't let that happen, but how could she stop him?

After manipulating her brother, Donna decided to return the call from Detective Barnes. She was relieved when Barnes didn't answer. She left a brief message indicating she was starting a new job Monday and would definitely not be available for an interview until Friday after work or Saturday morning. She was glad she'd met her new boss at the J. W. Marriott on Thursday. He could be her savior of last resort.

On his way home after completing a four-to-midnight shift with the SPFD, Mickey Kaye couldn't get the phone call from Donna out of his head. He knew she was lying and likely had conspired with Uncle Sergei to murder her own father. He didn't know whether she was involved in the rest of it, but believed that his brilliant, cold, conniving half-sister had thought she could control the Ghost, a man his mother called the personification of evil. He would try to protect her, but only because she was right about one thing—their mother would want him to do whatever he could to save her.

FIFTY-ONE

As she entered the lobby of the Gilbert Building on Monday morning, Detective Lincoln Barnes felt good about her weekend trip even if the interview of Donna Morgan would be delayed. She always enjoyed Wanda's perfect family of four, and the past weekend had been no exception. She'd had lunch with her mom at her condo on Saturday and spent most of Saturday and Sunday watching movies and playing various sports and video games with her nephews, Henry and Theo, who at nine and seven still thought she was "cool." She'd also run the ten-mile course on Sunday afternoon, though the sweltering heat, a near record eighty-seven degrees for mid-September, had hampered her time.

Mac had called her on Saturday with DNA results that confirmed her hypothesis. The Ghost had been in the dump truck that had killed Ray Rossi, Donna Morgan's father. That was the kind of evidence they'd been looking for, and now with interviews of Mickey and Donna, Barnes needed to complete the connection, a connection that was solidified earlier this morning when her contact at the FBI had called to share a revealing text message they'd gotten from Verizon under the continuing subpoena of Donna Morgan's phone records. It was from an AT&T customer named Jack Whitman. Fortunately, he'd included his name on the text. It didn't take much research to learn that Whitman was a senior partner at Cooper Harding, and more important, the lead attorney for Barton Industries and Paul Barton, and the attorney representing Amanda Barton in the Barton estate filing.

Barnes checked the building directory and found Charles Fallon & Associates on the third floor. There was no receptionist in the small waiting area, but within seconds of her arrival Charlie Fallon appeared from a narrow hallway. He was dressed casually in a black short-sleeve mock tee and tan wool slacks, which made Barnes feel overdressed in a dark olive business suit over a white poplin dress shirt.

"Detective Barnes, good to see you. Can I get you a cup of coffee or tea or a bottle of water this morning?"

Normally, Barnes would pass on any beverages after she'd had her morning caffeine fix, but she'd been so dehydrated after yesterday's run, she accepted the offer of water.

Fallon grabbed a bottle from a mini refrigerator behind the reception desk and led Barnes through the hallway to a conference room where his client sat at a round oak table with four blue, leather-trimmed captain's chairs. Fallon handed Barnes the bottle of water after she declined a glass with ice and, before she could say thanks, the client stood and extended his right hand to her.

"Detective Barnes, Mickey Kaye," he said, applying a firm but respectful grip while looking her square in the eyes. "Very pleased to meet you," he added in a voice that was so deep and pure it made her flinch.

The combination of the handshake, voice and his appearance sent a surge of sexual energy up Barnes's arm, down her spine and into some other dormant parts. Kaye wore a short-sleeve navy polo over light gray khakis. Taller than Barnes by two or three inches, he had a slim but muscular build with Popeye forearms and hands nearly as large as MacDonald's. He was clean-shaven with thick black hair cut too short to comb and hazel eyes with glints of gold and green. There was a vague resemblance to Paul Barton, but this man was handsome in a dark, mysterious way that reminded Barnes of one of her father's favorite actors, whose name she couldn't recall. It made her wonder what Elena Krasikova looked like in her youth. She had scoured the internet to find photos of the woman, but could only come up with a couple of fairly recent black-and-white grainy reproductions, one from her realtor's license and one from her obituary. Even so, Barnes could imagine how beautiful she must have been.

To Barnes's great surprise, Fallon said there was no need for him to be present during the interview; that his client could respond to questions without counsel. He would be in his office down the hall if Mr. Kaye needed his assistance. He did inform Barnes that results of the DNA tests that he and Amanda Barton's counsel had ordered should be available in a day or two, and that he had no doubt about the outcome.

Barnes was developing a scenario in her mind involving Mickey, Donna, and the Ghost, though the criminal elements of the scenario only involved two of the three.

"I want to be upfront with you about what we know and what we don't know," said Barnes. "We have strong evidence that the Russian national who poisoned the Bartons and committed other crimes in this state is the same person who stole a dump truck and used it to murder your stepfather, Raymond Rossi, the man that you assaulted with a knife, several years ago." Mickey couldn't hide his wide-eyed reaction to Barnes's disclosure. But he didn't say anything.

"We also know that your half-sister, Donna Morgan, formerly known as Donna Rae Rossi, communicated with this Russian national via cell phone on at least one occasion near the date Paul Barton was murdered and probably at other times, but we're continuing to research that. Ms. Morgan also got a job at the law firm that represents Paul Barton and his companies about five months ago and has been accused by one of her bosses of using her position to gain access to Paul Barton's personal, legal and financial information. Given the size of Barton's estate and your potential claim to most of it, you can see how suspicious this looks."

Mickey was beginning to feel a knot in his stomach. He could sit back and keep listening to the barrage of evidence that made him look like a gold digger and a killer, or he could tell her the truth, maybe shaded a bit in Donna's favor. He had an immediate, visceral attraction to this smart, confident woman, especially her athletic physique, heart-shaped lips and flawless light brown skin, but at the same time couldn't imagine a woman in law enforcement wanting anything to do with a felon.

"Let me stop you right there, Detective. My mother, Elena Kaye, though I always think of her as Elena Krasikova, was the most important person in my life. She made tremendous sacrifices in order to stay in this country and for my sister and me to have a good life and get a good education, which we both did. My mom literally escaped her family in St. Petersburg, Russia, in the early 1990s. Her father had been a senior Russian army officer who was killed in Afghanistan in the late seventies. The family moved from Kazakhstan to St. Petersburg after his death. Her two uncles and older brother were KGB agents. Her brother had been a very close associate of Putin until he was the subject of some bad publicity and became a recluse and an assassin for hire who was used by the Kremlin for special projects.

"My mother never should have married Ray Rossi, but because she needed to stay in the States and would never give up her baby, she had few viable alternatives after Paul Barton abandoned her in her time of need. And then Barton's father threatened her and threw money at her. So, when she died prematurely, I set out to learn more about the only family I really had. My mother never talked about her family in Russia until Donna and I were in our teens and I was preparing to go to college. She gave us a brief family history, told us her mother was dead, and made it very clear that we were never, ever to contact any of the men in her family, especially and specifically, her brother Sergei Krasikova, the man you and the media are referring to as the Ghost, and a man who literally no longer exists in Russia. Ironically, now he truly is a ghost. I have never met him, seen him or spoken to him." This was pretty much everything Mickey knew firsthand, so he stopped there.

"Thanks for all the information," said Barnes, happy finally to have a name for the Russian Ghost. "Do you know whether Donna Morgan contacted your Uncle Sergei after your mother died?"

"You have to remember that Donna and I were kind of estranged at the time. She was in law school and disagreed with my decision to plead guilty and accept a prison sentence. She never told me she was going to contact Sergei. She has since told me that he read about his sister's murder in the *New York Times* or, more likely, someone else read it and told him about it. Donna claims Sergei contacted her at law school with questions about Ray Rossi and the Barton family. She said she was afraid of him and gave him information about our family and the Bartons but was never involved in any of his crimes. I've heard how resourceful and relentless he was from my mother. Donna referred to him as a runaway freight train. I believe he killed both Ray Rossi and Barton as acts of vengeance for how they treated his sister."

Barnes thought that might have been the motive for the Rossi killing but not Barton. This Sergei Krasikova was an assassin for hire with a documented lust for money. She sensed that Mickey was walking a tightrope, trying to protect his sister.

"Clearly, your Uncle Sergei kept in touch with Donna, though. And I don't understand why she would take a job with Barton's law firm if not to get information about him and his assets."

"If that's true, I don't know why. I suppose it could have been a coincidence, but you'll have to ask Donna about that."

Barnes sensed that Donna had told her brother only what she wanted him to know. She was guilty of multiple crimes; Barnes had no doubt about that, but proving any of it beyond a reasonable doubt would be a challenge. She'd need to record her interview of Donna Morgan, if she ever got one.

"I will," said Barnes. "I definitely will. I think that's all the questions I have for you today, Mr. Kaye. Thanks for agreeing to meet. If I think of other questions or matters to discuss, I will contact Mr. Fallon. Is that okay with you?"

"Certainly," Mickey replied. "Do you have anything set up with Donna?"

Barnes closed her portfolio and stood. "Not yet," she said.

Mickey also stood and moved closer to Barnes, once again offering his right hand. "I have to say I enjoyed meeting you even under these circumstances."

Barnes gently shook his hand and they lingered, holding hands and gazing at each other. Barnes worried that Mickey would try to kiss her and that she'd let him. But instead, he released his grip and stepped back.

"Goodbye, Mr. Kaye," Barnes said. She walked by Fallon's office and thanked him for facilitating the interview of his client, still bewildered that he wasn't present but sure there was a good reason for it.

Detective Barnes thought she'd be early for her lunch with Warren

Lindquist, her former partner and mentor, at the Red Rabbit in St. Paul, but he was already seated at a square wooden table in the back of the popular restaurant in the Crocus Hill neighborhood.

"It's been a while," she said. Warren stood up and gave her a bear hug and a kiss on the cheek, nearly losing his balance on the prosthetic leg he'd earned on his last day of active duty with the Minneapolis Police Department.

"Whoa," he said. He was fortunate that Barnes was strong enough to steady him and help him return to his tall wooden chair. "How's life on the North Shore? I read about the Russian spy who must be keeping you busy."

"I've got lots of help," she said. "But let's not talk about that. How are you doing? You look great, my friend."

"I've been pretty bored. The good news is that Diane and I are spending more time at the lake with the girls, and I've had time to learn how to navigate with this new limb, even got myself a recumbent bike to stay in some kind of shape for a sixty-two-year-old cripple. The great news is that I heard this morning that I have a new part-time job as the treasurer of a local nonprofit that helps disabled cops."

"That's wonderful, Warren, and right up your alley." Lindquist had a finance degree and had worked the white collar crime beat for years before switching to homicide.

"I hate to change the subject from me," Lindquist said, "but have you heard anything from former Judge Gildemeister lately?"

"Not a word from him in months, though a friend in the Lake County sheriff's office said she saw him at the Hennepin County Government Center last week. The last information I had he was hiding out on Madeline Island."

"You're probably going to get a call from your old boss in the next few days. I had coffee with him last week. He said a metro county attorney was going to move ahead with an announcement in the Patterson case in the next few weeks but was adamant that he couldn't tell me the name of the defendant. He said it would be huge news. I'm guessing that means it's Gildemeister, and Hennepin County won't be handling it because of the obvious conflict. He was probably here last week to discuss how and when he'll surrender to authorities. I'm so sorry."

"It's okay, Warren. I'm glad it should be over soon. Last week I decided I can't keep living in his house. Hallie Bell drafted a quit claim deed transferring ownership back to Robin. As soon as I find a decent place, I'll be gone. To be honest, I don't understand or appreciate how he's handled this whole thing. He's just not the person I thought he was." But still a person who dominated her thoughts.

"I'm sorry about that too," said Warren.

They both ordered Italian chopped salads with Arnie Palmers and reminisced for another hour.

FIFTY-TWO

After returning home from the Cities, Lincoln Barnes had mixed feelings about the trip. She'd enjoyed her time with family and seeing Warren, but the news about the judge's probable fate haunted her thoughts. That pain was in contrast with the physical attraction and strong positive feelings she had for Mickey Kaye, feelings that were wrong for many reasons, but that she couldn't suppress. She spent most of Tuesday working from home, preparing notes for a meeting with the sheriff and county attorney on Wednesday morning to discuss how to move forward with a case against Donna Morgan, as she was convinced there was no case against her brother. She sat at a patio table on the deck overlooking Lake Superior wearing Minnesota Lynx sweatshirt and shorts on a sunny but cool fall day on the North Shore. She'd been spoiled living on the lake, and would be looking to rent a place that at least had a view of her new favorite place.

"I wasn't expecting to hear from you so soon, Charlie," said Jack Whitman, who'd taken the call from Fallon even though it was 2:30 and he'd promised to meet Nancy at her lawyer's office at 3:00. All of a sudden she was in a rush to end their thirty-five-year marriage and to play house with some rich widower. Well, she could wait for him to finish more pressing business.

"I have both bad news and good news for your client," said Fallon. "The bad news will be delivered separately to you if it hasn't already. The DNA test results definitively prove that Paul J. Barton Jr. is the biological father of Mickey Kaye. I don't think you're terribly surprised by that, Jack."

"Not at all. So, what's the good news?"

"My client has authorized me to make a settlement proposal to Aunt Amanda. Sorry for that reference, but I couldn't resist." Whitman had to chuckle to himself over that one. He really liked Charlie Fallon.

"I'm all ears."

"By the way, Detective Lincoln Barnes from Lake County interviewed my client yesterday. I just want you to know that Mickey Kaye had absolutely nothing to do with the murders of Paul and Melanie Barton. You have my word on that, Jack, and any implication or inference that he did has nothing to do with this offer. In exchange for an order of the Lake County District Court acknowledging that Paul Barton is the biological father of my client and a cash payment from the Barton estate in the amount of fifty million dollars, he will dismiss his petition with prejudice and release all claims against the estate, including all claims to any interest in Barton Industries. That's less than five percent of what I estimate is the net value of Barton's estate. Finally, if your client doesn't accept this offer by the end of this week, it's off the table."

Whitman couldn't believe what he'd just heard. Even if Kaye had orchestrated the murder of P. J. Barton, this was a great deal for Amanda.

"I have two questions, Charlie. Why? And why fifty million?"

"This is a wonderful young man. Yes, he's a convicted felon, but if you've done your homework, and I'm sure you have, you know that most young men who'd have come home to see their mother slaughtered by a psychopath would have done exactly what he did. Based on my sordid history, you know that's what I would have done. And if he had even a mediocre defense lawyer, he never would have been convicted. But he has something that's sorely lacking today. He has character. He chose fifty million because he wants to set up a foundation in his mother's name to help women who are victims of domestic violence. I told him if he wants to make a difference he should fund it with at least twenty-five million dollars based on some boards that I used to sit on when I was a judge. He also wants to go back to school to be an emergency room physician. I'm not sure how he plans to use the rest, but I don't care, and you shouldn't either.

"So, please check in with your client and let me know if I can start drafting settlement documents. Because it's a formal probate, I think we might have to appear before the judge to get the agreement approved, but I assume that's going to be a virtual hearing."

"I'll get back to you by tomorrow at noon, but I'm confident we'll have a deal. One more thing, Charlie. I'm seriously thinking about quitting Cooper Harding and putting up my own shingle on a part-time basis. I'd like to get out of the Twin Cities and am considering the Duluth area. I love the North Shore, and I've been up there so much for Barton Industries, it's like a second home. But after this deal, I'm done with the Bartons. You have any interest in a loose association with the likes of Jack Whitman?"

"Jack, I'm turning away more business than two experienced lawyers could handle. I was hoping that Robin Gildemeister would be opening a practice in Two Harbors and would take some of it, but that probably won't happen. Let's play a round at Northland and talk about it."

"Great. I'll set it up."

FIFTY-THREE

“Good morning, Woody. I assume you’re calling about my email and Detective Barnes’s report.”

“It’s an excellent analysis, Mac, and our lead agent from the FBI and I agree with her conclusion that Donna Morgan had to be deeply involved in planning the Barton murders and likely the Fawcett killing. Taking the initiative to test the dump truck DNA from the Ray Rossi murder with the dead Russian’s DNA was top-notch investigative work by Detective Barnes. That, followed by her interview of Mickey Kaye that produced the identity of Sergei Krasikova, really impressed my staff. Our ancient CIA guys remember the name but haven’t heard it for over twenty-five years. But they all know about the Ghost. And they all agree that he was a total mercenary who wouldn’t cross the street unless he got paid.

“Mac, there’s no way he risked his life simply to avenge the death of a sister who forsook the family and Mother Russia. We also appreciate your willingness to defer to us the prosecution of Donna Morgan for conspiring with a foreign national to commit murder and fraud.”

Sheriff MacDonald sat in his office feeling relieved that the mystery of the Ghost had been solved and proud that his talented young detective had been instrumental in the investigation. He’d made an extra strong pot of Guatemalan roast from Duluth Coffee Roasters for the early morning meeting with Hallie and Lincoln Barnes and was the only one of the three of them to eat any of the glazed donuts he'd picked up at a local bakery.

"Detective Barnes and the county attorney agree with me that at this point it doesn't make sense to pursue state charges against someone who'll probably spend the rest of her life in a federal prison, not to mention the possibility that Albany County might be interested in charging her for multiple murders there now that we've identified her Russian uncle as the probable killer. The convenient irony is she's now a federal employee, so she should be easy to find."

"We've already alerted the U.S. attorney in Minneapolis. He wasn't involved in hiring her other than to sign off on it based on her credentials and a strong recommendation by the head of the civil division, but we've got probable cause to take her into custody, which will happen in the next day or two. That's not to say that proving the case against her will be easy because it won't, especially considering she saved Paul Barton's life just prior to his murder."

"A brilliant hedge if that's what it was," MacDonald remarked.

"No doubt. What do you know about Jack Whitman, the lawyer for the Barton family who sent her the incriminating text message?"

"Not a lot. I've met him a couple of times, the most recent when we interviewed Paul Barton in connection with the Oscar Fawcett killing. Hallie also mentioned his name as the lawyer representing Amanda Barton and the Barton estate. He seems like a decent guy who had client control issues and clearly was duped by Donna Morgan."

"I'm guessing more than duped," said Wilson. "But if we prosecute her, he'll be a key witness."

"Will you be providing any of these new revelations to your friend at the *Times*?" asked MacDonald.

"Not a chance, Mac, but how many times do I need to say I'm sorry? That was a one-time deal that was foisted on me by the Secretary. We'll circulate the Ghost's true identity to the media and our foreign contacts because the Kremlin tried so hard to keep it a secret. Once Donna Morgan is arrested, there'll be a feeding frenzy for information."

"That will likely create some negative press for Donna's half-brother, Barton's illegitimate son and heir," said MacDonald. "According to Detective Barnes, he and his mother are both sympathetic victims in all this."

"I don't disagree. It seems the Ghost created a slew of victims whenever he took on a new job."

"At least that will never happen again."

Jack Whitman's world had been turned upside down in a matter of weeks. He'd woken up before 5:00 on Wednesday morning in a state of confusion. He knew he'd had too much to drink the night before; the pounding headache and cotton mouth were evidence of that. He also knew he hadn't spent the night at his home in Edina. He'd taken a piss and gulped two glasses of water accompanied by four ibuprofen and fallen into a deep sleep until he was awakened by a vibrating cell phone that must have slipped out of his hand and lodged between his legs after he'd checked the time when returning to the king bed in his suite at Hotel Ivy, a few blocks from his office.

It was 9:30. Amanda Barton had left him about a dozen messages since he hadn't shown up for P. J.'s memorial service on Saturday. The first message had a hint of concern for his welfare. Subsequent messages had become nasty, threatening to take all the Barton business to a different firm and informing Whitman that she and Billy had retained the Covington law firm out of Washington, D.C., to investigate Mickey Kaye's Russian connections. He needed to get back to Charlie Fallon by noon today, so he girded his flabby loins and answered.

"Good morning, Amanda."

"Good morning?" she responded as sarcastically as humanly possible. "What the fuck, Jack? Where were you on Saturday? You don't show for your best friend's service and leave a huge hole in my program. Then you don't return my calls or texts for days. I assumed you were either hospitalized or dead. Then I call your office this morning and learn you're taking the day off, which the old Jack Whitman would never have authorized his office to disclose, even if it were true. So, what gives, Jack? I'm actually worried about you at a time when I need you at your best."

Surprised by Amanda's lack of venom and perhaps even concern for him, Whitman thought about apologizing for missing P. J.'s service, but Amanda wouldn't have accepted his true reason for spending that afternoon at the club, so instead he gave her the good news supplemented by the impending change in his marital status.

"I'm fine, Amanda, but I'm spending the rest of the week at a downtown hotel while Nancy and her boyfriend move most of her belongings and whatever else she wants out of the house in Edina and into his place."

"Holy shit, Jack, I'm so sorry. I had no idea you and Nancy were on the rocks. She has a boyfriend? How long has this been going on?"

"It's mostly my fault for letting work and golf take precedence over our marriage," Jack admitted. "Truthfully, I think it's for the best at this stage of our lives. We'll sell the big house and stay civil for the sake of the kids and grandkids. I do have some excellent news for you, though."

"I'm all ears," said Amanda, quickly shifting a hundred percent of her attention onto herself.

"The paternity tests confirm that Mickey Kaye is P. J.'s biological son, and I don't believe the young man had anything to do with P. J.'s death."

"Well, we'll see about that," Amanda interrupted.

"I don't think spending a boatload of money on that D.C. law firm will reveal anything significant, Amanda; however, Kaye has offered to settle all claims challenging your appointment as personal representative and seeking to inherit your brother's estate in exchange for a court order acknowledging his paternity and a single cash payment of fifty million dollars, less than five percent of the net value of the estate, most of which he plans to use to establish a foundation in the name of his deceased mother to assist victims of domestic abuse." That was a mouthful that made Whitman a little dizzy.

"What!!? You are fucking kidding me, Jack? This kid is willing to release all claims against the Barton Industry stock and everything else for fifty mil?"

"That's what I said."

"How quickly can we get this settlement signed and executed?"

"Because this is a formal probate with a contested hearing on the docket, I think the presiding judge needs to approve our settlement, but Fallon says we might be able to do that as early as next Monday if we alert the court today and sign the documents by tomorrow. Apparently, Kaye's days off as an EMT are Monday and Tuesday."

"I need to go to Duluth Friday to have meetings with the corporate staff up there. I'll be there for at least a week. I'm going to close all of the Duluth operations and move them down here. Do you think we could have an in-person hearing in Two Harbors? After all, this guy is my nephew, and if we're paying him fifty million, I'd like to see him in the flesh. And what about his half-sister? She was in that report you sent me. Donna something."

"She's not your blood relative, Amanda, and, for all I know, she might have been involved with that Russian criminal. Let me talk to Fallon today about an in-person hearing. It might be doable."

"Sounds good. Let me know ASAP."

"One more thing, Amanda. When we complete this settlement with Kaye, I'm done."

"Done? Done with what?"

"I'll be resigning my partnership at Cooper Harding and leaving the firm by the middle of October. I don't know what I'll be doing next, but I won't be representing Barton Industries in the future. I'll get Kevin Brophy up to speed on all corporate matters, but, as you know, you'll be free to retain other counsel if you and the board choose to move."

"You've been our family's lead lawyer for over twenty-five years, Jack. I'm worried that you're not emotionally stable right now. Please take more time to think about this before abandoning ship."

"I'll be in touch about the settlement, Amanda."

FIFTY-FOUR

Mickey Kaye had left several messages for Donna between Wednesday afternoon and Friday morning, at which point he'd given up trying to reach her. After his Friday shift at the SPFD, he made a couple of hamburgers, one for Roger, his golden lab, and one for himself, and then took Roger for a long walk along Summit Avenue in St. Paul. It was a beautiful fall evening with a light breeze out of the west and only a few stray cirrus clouds in the sky. The massive oak, maple and ash trees along the parkway, beginning to turn various shades of orange, red and yellow, reminded him of the foliage in some of the old neighborhoods in Schenectady. He was comfortable in a long-sleeve tee with nylon sweatpants and a Minnesota Vikings ballcap, a recent acquisition. When his new Samsung Android phone started playing "We are the Champions" by Queen, his mother's favorite song, he didn't recognize the number that popped up on his screen but, as was his practice these days, he answered it anyway.

"Mickey Kaye speaking," he announced.

"Mickey, it's Donna. I needed to trash my cell phone, so if you've been trying to reach me, I haven't been ignoring you. I'm leaving, Mickey. My boss let me know that the feds are going to arrest me when I come to work tomorrow."

"Where will you go?" asked Mickey, worried about his sister even though he now suspected she was more involved in the plot to kill Paul Barton than she had ever admitted.

"I'm driving up to Crooked Lake and the Canadian border tonight. Uncle Sergei gave me the names of some loyal contacts he had in Moscow and St. Petersburg, and there are still a few of his pals in the Russian embassy in Ottawa. Basically, I make it to Canada, and I'll get to St. Petersburg where Sergei has a son and substantial assets. Maybe someday I'll be able to come back, but besides you, there's nothing here for me anyway."

"But what kind of life will that be?" asked Mickey. "I'm settling my case against the Barton estate. I need to drive to Two Harbors on Monday and appear before a judge, but after that I can help you." Mickey could feel his heart begin to ache. He knew how this was going to end.

"I'm disappointed that you aren't pursuing those rich, narcissistic pricks for all of it, Mick. You could have had it all, and we could have created an empire but for the idiosyncrasies of that crazy, reckless fuck. If only he had followed the plan, none of this would have happened. These stupid hicks wouldn't have had a clue about who he was or where he came from, but in the end his paranoia destroyed him. I gotta' go, Mick."

"I love you, Donna," Mickey cried into the phone. But she was already gone.

Mickey stroked the fur on Roger's back as he started the return walk to his apartment. He felt alone in the world, but it wasn't the first time. He'd agreed to drive up to Two Harbors on Monday at the advice of his attorney, but also because he hoped to see Lincoln Barnes. He'd left her a voice message and even sent her a text:

Will be in Two Harbors for a hearing Monday. Would like to see you.
Mickey Kaye

It was uncharacteristic of him to be so aggressive, but he couldn't get her out of his mind, and at this point he had nothing to lose.

FIFTY-FIVE

Detective Lincoln Barnes had spent the weekend looking for a new place to live. She'd tentatively agreed to lease a two-bedroom condo on Burlington Bay in Two Harbors beginning October 1. It wasn't the judge's cottage, but it had been tastefully updated and had a balcony overlooking the lake.

Sam and Hallie Bell MacDonald had hosted Barnes, Michele Sams and Craig Darrow at an outdoor barbeque on Saturday afternoon to recognize their dedicated and courageous efforts on the recent murder cases. MacDonald had disclosed that federal marshals apprehended Donna Morgan in Ely on Friday night. Her arrest was noted in both the Duluth and Twin Cities' Sunday papers and would be included in a major story about Sergei Krasikova in the Sunday edition of the *New York Times*. After her lunch with Warren, Barnes had expected more news on the Kate Patterson murder and the impending indictment of Robin Gildemeister, but so far nothing.

Barnes sat at the bar at the Harbor Rail Pub in Two Harbors. Mickey's hearing was at 3:00, and she'd agreed to meet him at the pub at 4:30. That was fifteen minutes ago, but Barnes wasn't worried. Excited might be a better descriptor. Hoping to give him an unforgettable first exposure to the North Shore and Lake Superior, she'd stocked the cottage with snacks, beer and wine and prepared a tray of smoked whitefish, crackers and veggies just in case. Some might question a peace officer's attraction to a convicted felon. But the heart wants what the heart wants. Or perhaps it was a different organ. In any case, she was convinced that Mickey wasn't a killer, and that's more than she could say about the judge.

Mickey was bringing his golden lab on the trip north and planned to spend the night with Charlie Fallon in Grand Marais. Fallon had offered to take the dog up to his place so Mickey could meet her for dinner. Dressed in white jeans and a royal blue cotton sweater over a sports bra, Barnes nursed a Castle Danger Cream Ale with one eye on a replay of *SportsCenter* on the TV behind the bar and the other on the lookout for her date.

"Hi Detective, it's good to see you," Mickey said, as he climbed onto a low-back bar stool next to Barnes dressed in a black linen blazer over an oxford cloth white shirt and gray wool slacks. He'd already removed the tie that Fallon had lent him. "That was easier than I thought it would be." He leaned toward Barnes and briefly enveloped both her beer mug and the fingers holding it with his right hand. "What are you drinking?"

"It's a local cream ale," she said, wishing he'd left his hand in place. "Would you like to try mine or order something else?"

Mickey raised his hand meekly to get the bartender's attention. "I'll have what she's having," he said.

They'd had a long conversation on Sunday night about the settlement, Amanda's demand for an in-person hearing, and Fallon's offer to help get him into the U of M medical school. Barnes waited until Mickey had taken a long draw of his beer before asking any questions.

"How was Amanda?" she asked. "I've heard she can be intimidating."

"I think she was more curious than anything else," he said. "Her husband asked me what I thought about Donna's arrest and all of the criminals in my family. Then he said, 'But I guess you're a convicted felon too.' Amanda told me to ignore him."

"Did you?"

"I really like this beer," he said. "My mom loved a good French Bordeaux or Napa Valley cabernet, so I developed a taste for bold red wines over the years." Then he gave her an impish smile that made her want to kiss him and said, "I told Mr. Slocum that I love my sister and would do anything I could to help her. I didn't tell him and Amanda that I intend to give Rebecca Fawcett the five million dollars that my father should have paid her."

"I think that's great, Mickey, but why didn't you tell them?"

"If there's one thing I learned from my time in prison, it's the wisdom of restraint, especially around people who can hurt you."

"I get it. How about I order a pizza from the Green Door in Beaver Bay, and we take it to the place I'm renting in Castle Danger. I've stocked the fridge with snacks and we can build a fire down by the lake. What do you think about that plan?"

He guzzled the rest of his beer and stood. "I'll follow you," he said.

"This place is amazing," said Mickey. "Who owns it?" He'd changed into jeans and a Cornell University sweatshirt while Barnes was picking up a sausage and mushroom pizza at the Green Door.

"A former judge from the Twin Cities who grew up in Two Harbors and inherited this place from his grandmother. I think he's living on Madeline Island. It's across the lake on the Wisconsin side. Feel free to look around while I get all the food out."

"Can't I help you?" he asked.

"You can pick out a couple bottles of wine from the oak cabinet in the great room. I'll bring out some beer and water and meet you at the long table in front of the fireplace." Barnes noticed that her phone was nearly dead at three percent and plugged it into a charger on the kitchen counter while she retrieved the tray she'd prepared from the refrigerator and carried it and the pizza into the great room. She watched Mickey walking by the firepit in the backyard and continuing down to the lake. Not knowing her preference for wine, he'd set a Rombauer chardonnay and a Silverado cab on the table. When he opened the sliding glass door and came in from the deck, she handed him a plate.

"You go first," she said. "I hope you're hungry."

"Thanks. I've heard about Lake Superior and got glimpses of it when I drove through Duluth to Two Harbors, but I've never seen anything like it. I've been to Lake George and the finger lakes near Cornell, but they're nothing like this."

They filled their plates and spent a few minutes eating in silence.

They each had a beer and then opened the Silverado. Mickey started grilling Barnes about her family, her time as a softball star at Illinois State, and her career as a peace officer, things she rarely discussed but wanted to share with him. She even talked about her failed marriage in Chicago and her years with the dysfunctional Minneapolis PD. She briefly discussed the Kate Patterson case, but only to explain how Warren lost his leg and why she decided to move north. She didn't mention Robin Gildemeister or how he'd influenced that decision. It was weird for her to be in his house and have emerging feelings for someone else. It had also occurred to her that while she was fifteen years younger than the judge, Mickey had to be at least five years younger than she. Was that better, worse or irrelevant? Tonight, it felt irrelevant.

By 7:00 they had finished eating and consumed the bottle of Silverado. Barnes had stocked the firepit with logs and kindling earlier in the day, and she didn't want to waste the effort.

"It'll get pretty cold when the sun goes down in about ten minutes, but if you want to open another bottle of red, I'll light a fire out at the pit, and we can enjoy the night sky."

"Sounds perfect," he said. Before he picked out the wine, Mickey texted Fallon, indicating he would be very late if he made it at all tonight. The only response was a thumbs-up emoji.

It was dark by 7:30. They sat next to each other in Adirondack chairs and enjoyed a raging fire and a clear night over the lake.

"Looks like that big ship is anchored out there," said Mickey. "It doesn't seem to be moving."

"It's riding high in the water," said Barnes, proud of what she'd learned about Lake Superior and the port of Duluth. "It's probably empty and will get a load of grain or iron ore in Duluth or Superior."

"I'm impressed," said Mickey. "What can you tell me about the hundred billion stars I see up there?"

"All I can say is I've never seen as many stars anywhere as we can see over this lake. It's incredible."

Barnes extended a hand in Mickey's direction, and he gently took it in his and rested it on the arm of his chair. They sat in silence for the next five minutes, sipping wine and enjoying the night, the scenery and each other.

"Let's walk down to the lake," Barnes suggested. She emptied the remains of the bottle into their glasses, and Mickey followed her down the natural stone path to the rocky shore.

"The sound the waves make against these huge rocks is mesmerizing," said Mickey, looking out at the shimmering lake and then down at Lincoln Barnes. Without saying a word, she slipped her hands under his sweatshirt and felt the taut muscles of his upper back and shoulders. Without hesitation, she pulled him towards her and kissed him softly on the lips. Then they embraced as the wind picked up and exchanged another brief but passionate kiss that was cut short by Barnes taking his hand and leading him back to the house. All the lights were off both outside and in, but there was plenty of light from the moon, the stars and embers from the dying fire.

Once inside, she led him up the winding stairway to the bedroom in the loft where they both instinctively shed their clothes and enveloped each other in a sexual frenzy that lasted until after midnight when, exhausted in every way, they fell asleep in each other's arms.

Barnes didn't even think about her charging phone, but maybe she should have. There were two urgent messages, one from Warren and one from Lieutenant Sherm Moe, her former boss at the MPD.

Dehydrated and still exhausted, Lincoln Barnes struggled to wake up in total darkness. She was startled by the sound of gunshots, two, three or more. Was it a dream? No, not that sound. When her eyes finally opened she was disoriented. Sitting up, she was surprised to see that Mickey was gone. The clock on the nightstand read 2:35.

She heard someone on the stairs and saw the flickering light from a flashlight dancing on the walls of the great room.

"Mickey?"

But it wasn't Mickey. She recognized the man who entered the bedroom with a flashlight in one hand and a pistol in the other by the reflection of his unmistakable profile in the mirror over her dresser.

Robin Gildemeister had returned, and her life would never be the same.

Printed in the United States
by Baker & Taylor Publisher Services